"More fun than an exploding Whoopie Pie! When plus-sized and out-of-work news producer Kate Gallagher heads for Durham, North Carolina, the 'Diet Capital of the World,' to take up residence at a diet clinic, she finds more than low-cal meals and fellow dieters. Instead, the plucky heroine is introduced to a dead diet doctor with a love for S and M, dueling diet clinics, and more suspects than she can shake a carrot stick at, not to mention a charming detective who finds Kate delightfully delicious."

—Sue Ann Jaffarian, author of *Too Big to Miss* and *The Curse of the Holy Pail*

"A delightful debut. Plus-sized TV producer Kate Gallagher is as irresistible as a pint of mocha chip ice cream—without the guilt."

—Susan Kandel, author of *Shamus in the Green Room*

"Dishes out generous servings of humor and whodunit. . . . Fun and fast-paced, this quirky cozy truly puts the *die* into *diet*."

—Susan McBride, author of the Debutante Dropout Mysteries

"*Dying to Be Thin* made me laugh so hard, I choked on my M&M'S. They say comedy comes from pain, and anyone who has tried to lose that pesky last fifty pounds knows how painful that can be. When spunky, chunky Kate takes on a murder investigation while trying to take off weight, the result is sheer delight. Kate Gallagher is the funniest, most adorable heroine in recent memory. Bridget Jones, eat your heart out!"

—Pamela Eells, executive producer of *The Suite Life of Zack and Cody*

"Ms. Lilley has crafted a humorous story and blended in a delightful cast of characters."

—The Romance Readers Connection

"Kate Gallagher is quirky, witty, and tough when she needs to be. She can also ferret out information better than a homeland security interrogator." —Pop Syndicate

Also by Kathryn Lilley

Dying to Be Thin

A KILLER WORKOUT

A Fat City Mystery

Kathryn Lilley

AN OBSIDIAN MYSTERY

OBSIDIAN
Published by New American Library, a division of
Penguin Group (USA) Inc., 375 Hudson Street,
New York, New York 10014, USA
Penguin Group (Canada), 90 Eglinton Avenue East, Suite 700, Toronto,
Ontario M4P 2Y3, Canada (a division of Pearson Penguin Canada Inc.)
Penguin Books Ltd., 80 Strand, London WC2R 0RL, England
Penguin Ireland, 25 St. Stephen's Green, Dublin 2,
Ireland (a division of Penguin Books Ltd.)
Penguin Group (Australia), 250 Camberwell Road, Camberwell, Victoria 3124,
Australia (a division of Pearson Australia Group Pty. Ltd.)
Penguin Books India Pvt. Ltd., 11 Community Centre, Panchsheel Park,
New Delhi - 110 017, India
Penguin Group (NZ), 67 Apollo Drive, Rosedale, North Shore 0632,
New Zealand (a division of Pearson New Zealand Ltd.)
Penguin Books (South Africa) (Pty.) Ltd., 24 Sturdee Avenue,
Rosebank, Johannesburg 2196, South Africa

Penguin Books Ltd., Registered Offices:
80 Strand, London WC2R 0RL, England

First published by Obsidian, an imprint of New American Library,
a division of Penguin Group (USA) Inc.

First Printing, October 2008
10 9 8 7 6 5 4 3 2 1

Printed in the United States of America

To my parents, with love

Chapter 1

The Case of the Disappearing Double Digit

Look around any TV newsroom in America, and you'll see that female reporters in double-digit sizes are an endangered species. Broadcast News Land is crawling with Barbie Doll women who teeter around in stilettos and tiny suits (size zero to six, max).

As an on-air gal, how can you keep up with this crowd, cosmetically? How do you enter the queendom of single digits?

You must find the thin woman inside you, and set her free with exercise.

—From *The Little Book of Fat-busters* by Mimi Morgan

Exercise can really be murder.

I learned that lesson the hard way last spring, when I signed up for a fitness boot camp in the Great Smoky Mountains. I enlisted at the camp—called Body Blast—to do some emergency downsizing on my butt, only to wind up sugar-crashing it in the middle of a gruesome crime scene. That's when I discovered that a diva-sized *derriere* is a small thing compared to a broken neck. A full figure even has certain advantages, I ultimately realized; for example, a big ass can cushion your fall when somebody pushes you off a cliff.

But before I left for that camp, I was constantly

fretting about my body's proportions. See, I make my living in TV news, a job where porking up can put a pox on your career faster than you can suck down a pound of M&M'S. So when I picked up a few Christmas kilos over the holidays, it felt like the end of the world. My outlook turned even gloomier when my employer, the management at Channel Twelve Action! News, in Durham, North Carolina, distributed the March personality ratings. The report showed that my audience approval numbers had belly flopped in the category of "professional image" (read: "weight").

Then there were the e-mails that viewers sent in—bless their rotten little hearts—about my expanding girth. These missives contained *oh*-such-helpful advice:

> To: Kate Gallagher, Investigative reporter, Channel 12 News
> From: A concerned fan
> Subject: Have you tried Curves?
> Kate dear, love your work, but what's up with your weight? I noticed that your hips are getting wider these days. You don't want to end up looking like a Clydesdale in a field of TV Thoroughbreds.

Worse—egad!—were the phone calls that came in to the studio:

"Please tell Kate that she just needs to exercise twenty minutes a day, and those pounds will come right off. But wait—is she expecting? Oh, my God, is Kate *pregnant*?"

After a few of these calls, management posted a "cosmetic reminder" that warned the on-air talent to "maintain a healthy BMI, or risk having your on-air time reduced." They might as well have scrawled my name across the top of that memo in big, fat neon letters—no one else's dress size was in the double digits.

It all seemed so unfair, because it's not like I was

morbidly *obese*. But that's the pressure you get when you're five foot five, a hundred and seventy-five, and you earn your dollar on the boob tube. I tried shifting the focus to my assets—wavy auburn hair and blue eyes—by telling the cameraman to shoot me only from the shoulders up, avoiding full-body stand-ups like the plague. But nothing helped. No one gave a hoot that investigative reporting is a stress-eater's nightmare, long on stakeouts and short on healthy eating opportunities. Or how hard it was to order a salad while the cameraman grabbed his super-sized fries—sometimes I just *had* to have a Big Mac, you know? All the negative nattering was enough to drive a girl into a round of emo eating.

But instead of diving into comfort food, in desperation I sent an SOS to Riley Matthews, an old friend who'd grown up in my hometown of South Boston. I hadn't seen Riley in years, but I knew he'd undergone a dramatic body transformation since high school. Back then, Riley had been pale and skinny-looking, but later he'd pumped up his muscles and went on to a career as a bodybuilder—without using steroids, he claimed. From that point forward, Riley had developed an almost cultlike following as a Pied Piper of physique makeovers. Riley owned Body Blast, which was a sort of boot camp for weekend warriors. Fortunately for me, the camp was located in the Great Smokies, within driving distance of Durham.

Riley sounded delighted to hear from me when I called. He suggested that I spend a couple of consecutive long weekends at his workout camp. That would be enough time, he assured me, to reclaim—or at least locate—my AWOL waistline. The first weekend was to culminate in a triathlon to raise money for charity, so I arranged with my news director, Chuck Beatty, to cover the event as a feature story for Channel Twelve.

Even if he weren't getting a story out of the deal,

I know Beatty would have been only too happy to give me the days off and expense my stay at boot camp under the tax category of "ratings support." Ratings support, my ass. Literally.

To get to the Great Smokies from Durham, I headed my TR6 west on the interstate for a long while, combating Thursday morning commuter traffic. Eventually I turned south onto a winding two-lane highway that snaked through the foothills. The mountain air was noticeably nippier than in the flatlands of Durham, and grew colder with each foot of elevation. But I didn't mind the chill because it was such a sheer joy to wrap the vintage sports car's low center of gravity around the undulating turns. Just two weeks earlier, with the help of a friendly gearhead at my local Triumph car club, I'd souped up the engine's performance with triple Weber carburetors, a hot camshaft, and tighter shocks for suspension. The TR6 made a throaty, satisfying roar as I downshifted into the switchbacks and goosed the tachometer against the inclines of a section of road called the Dragon's Tail.

In the middle of one stretch, my cell phone rang. The LED display said DAD.

My father spoke before I had a chance to give a greeting. "Oops, sorry, Tiger. I can hear the engine—I didn't know you'd be driving right now," he said. "I just want to make sure you remember the recovery protocols for brake failure on mountain roads. Call me later."

"I do remember, Dad, thanks. I'll call you later. Love you. Bye." As soon as I hung up, I gunned the car around another hairpin turn.

My dad, Captain James Gallagher, commands South Boston's Sixth Police District. Ever since I was a teenager, he's been sending me "advisories" about how to survive every possible disaster in the universe, including mechanical meltdowns while driving.

But of course, my brakes were in splendid shape. I wound up having so much fun flying in the car that I forgot to watch for the turnoff. Just as I decided I'd overshot and was about to turn around, I spotted an arrow-shaped wooden sign with black lettering:

BODY BLAST, 2 mi.

I was expecting to find something primitive like teepees and Tarzan ropes when I pulled into camp after lunch (which was a "last hurrah" burger—and fries, natch—at Sonic), so I was pleasantly surprised to discover a collection of log-sided buildings with angled glass fronts, nestled into the slope of a rolling hill.

I unloaded my luggage and was making like a Sherpa bearer for the largest building when a tricked-out black Escalade with tinted windows careened into the parking lot. It slammed to a stop without bothering to pull into a space. A young guy with a buzz cut got out from behind the wheel. Flicking away a cigarette, he threw open the hatch and unloaded a pile of gear. The guy's movements were abrupt and jerky, seemingly fueled by barely suppressed fury.

A girl emerged from the passenger side. She appeared to be about nineteen years old, with a bulging figure and dark hair that hung limply about her shoulders. She stood quietly off to the side, fiddling with her purse.

Tossing a sleeping bag onto the pavement, the guy planted himself directly in front of the girl, arms crossed as if challenging her to speak. She continued to dig in her bag with studied indifference.

After a few more seconds of the Bag Treatment, the guy wilted. He turned away and dragged tail back to the car. Then, after revving his engine a couple of times to announce that he had rediscovered his inner alpha male, he tore out of the parking lot, screeching rubber on his way.

I was actually relieved that someone in worse shape than me had turned up for boot camp—I would have hated being the fattest one.

"Need some help?" I took a step toward her. "Somehow I still have a free hand."

The girl looked slightly startled, as if she hadn't noticed me before then. "Thanks," she said, angling an oversized backpack toward me. "I'm Marnie Taylor."

I lifted the bag by one of its straps and heaved it over my shoulder. "*Oof.* Kate Gallagher."

"Huh. You look . . ." Marnie squinted slightly, as if trying to place me.

It was a look I was familiar with from being on the news. People recognize me and think they've met me before, not making the TV connection.

"I work for Channel Twelve News in Durham," I explained.

Her eyes widened. "Oh, my God, yes! I'm from there, too. I've seen you," she exclaimed. "You do those investigative stories, right? I remember that one about a diet doctor who was murdered."

"That's right." Up close, I could see that Marnie's eyes were red. She looked as if she'd been crying. "Are you okay?" I asked.

Marnie shrugged. "I guess, yeah," she said. "My boyfriend, Antonio, was just having an anger management issue. My *ex*-boyfriend, I guess I should say," she added with a grimace. "We broke up last night. He insisted on driving me up here—claimed he had business to do in the area—but then he acted like a total A-hole the whole way."

"I know how that is," I said, although actually I didn't. I was pretty happy with my current boyfriend, an Atlanta-based lawyer named Lou Bettinger. But Lou had just thrown me a curveball the previous weekend, by unexpectedly proposing marriage (after offering me a diamond the size of a candy pumpkin). That was something I was planning to do during the next week—mull over his proposal.

Marnie and I staggered under our loads and made our way up a pathway to the main building, which was perched halfway up the hill. Inside the lobby, a floor-to-ceiling window overlooked a sports field below. Beyond the field rose a panoramic mountainscape, its overlapping ridgelines swathed in the signature bluish green mist of the Great Smokies.

I glanced around the lobby to see if I could spot my friend Riley anywhere, but he wasn't in sight. So Marnie and I joined a group of about eighteen men and women who were sitting on their gear piles. Their heads were bent over clipboards, pens going.

Overall, it was an ultra–body conscious group. Except for one or two average-looking joes, the men were all pumped up to a fare-thee-well, with an exorbitant amount of pec development going on. Several had stripped down to their wife-beaters and were horsing around, flexing to show off their biceps, which shone as if they'd just rolled off a buff-and-wax line. What did *they* need boot camp for? I wondered. Most of the women looked like the yoga bunnies who always claimed the front row of my weekly Vinyasa class. My usual spot in that class was in the far rear, where I cowered and hoped that the teacher wouldn't criticize my Awkward Chair Pose.

Oh, shit, I thought. I'd been hoping that a few more exercise novices would show up. But except for Marnie, this was looking like a very tough crowd.

A tall, bony Nordic-femme who introduced herself as Erica handed me a board and a stack of forms.

"Liability releases," she announced briskly.

I glanced down. Across the top sheet was a message: *Attention NOBIT (Novice Boot in Training): Press hard. You are making three copies.*

The forms were our promise not to sue Body Blast in the event we met injury or—yikes—even *death* during the boot camp, followed by an entire paragraph of all the ways you could eat the dirt, including falling, being crushed, drowning, and heatstroke. For the first time, I started to feel anxious. What exactly had I let myself *in* for?

Erica stepped to the center of the room and announced that our first activity at Body Blast would be the Evaluation course—an obstacle challenge—that would prepare us for the upcoming weekend.

"Our drill instructors will be observing you closely during the Eval course." She swiveled her head, sizing up the assembled recruits. Her radar sweep stopped on the pudgiest blips in the room—me and Marnie.

"As you know from your intake agreement, if you can't make it through the Eval course, you'll be reassigned to Remedial Fitness." Erica kept her eyes on the two of us.

"Reminds me of the army—I had to go through basic training twice," a guy to my left muttered to no one in particular.

When Erica approached to collect our paperwork, Marnie opened her purse and started fishing for her ID.

Erica's eyes snapped on something inside her bag. "What's that?" she said. "Is that *chocolate*?"

With her face turning crimson, Marnie extracted a Snickers bar.

Erica snatched up the candy. Dangling the bar from two fingers like a wad of slimy hair she'd plucked from a drain, she turned to face the other campers. "I'm sorry, but we have to ask you all to turn over anything with sugar or caffeine right now," she said in a loud voice. "Only *clean* foods are allowed at Body Blast. There should have been a sheet in your enrollment package explaining that," she added, lobbing a glance over her shoulder at Marnie. "Any of you NOBITs have anything else you need to turn over?"

A cowed silence gripped the room. Marnie turtled her neck into her shoulders, as if trying not to take up space.

Erica, you Viking bitch, I thought.

"I have some breath mints. You need those?" I piped up. Okay, it was a lame attempt at sarcasm, but I was gratified to hear a chuckle bounce around the room.

The skin around Erica's eyes tightened. "If they're sugar free, you can keep those," she snapped, then swiveled on her heel and left the lobby.

Some other drill instructors—aka DIs—wearing camouflage uniforms assumed control of the group at that point. Led by a gung ho young woman named Hillary, who looked like she'd leaped off the cover of *Shape* magazine, the DIs marched us in the direction of our rooms. The guest quarters were spread out in a series of bungalows clustered around the main building.

Marnie and I got assigned as roommates and "Body Buddies," which meant that we were supposed to look out for each other during the fitness trials ahead. Our ground-floor room was a spartan little rectangle that had twin beds covered by waffle-textured navy blankets. Through a small window I could see a couple of Carolina hemlocks—conifer trees that release a tangerine scent when you crush their needles underfoot—standing at attention, like sentries.

"Oh, goodie, I'm glad we'll be Body Buddies." Marnie gave me a shy smile as we dropped our loads on the floor. "I get the feeling I'm going to really *need* a buddy to make it through this thing alive."

"You mean to survive Evil Erica?"

"Yeah." Marnie grimaced. "She reminds me of my old PE teacher. God, that woman was mean."

"What made you decide to come here?" I asked her. "For me, it's all about the pressure to look like News Barbie—my airtime is on the line."

Marnie's lips pressed down at the corners. "I've got to get in shape before July," she said. "That's when the Tri-Kap sorority is having their pledge retreat, and I'm worried they won't take fat girls. So I've got four months to pull it together. I can do that, right?" She looked at me hopefully.

I nodded uncertainly, thinking of the Snickers bar.

"That chocolate was going to be my last cheat," Marnie said sheepishly, as if reading my thoughts.

"I totally understand. My last cheat before a diet is always a Whoopie Pie."

I turned toward the sound of a tap. A young, hip-looking Asian guy wearing desert camies stood framed in our open doorway.

"Kate? I'm Khan, Riley's business partner." His eyes were flat as slate, and the expression in them was just as cold. "After dinner tonight, can you stop by his office? He's tied up on a conference call right now, but he'd like to say hello to you later."

"Of course," I said to him.

Khan sniffed. His gaze slipped off me to Marnie, and he looked as if he were wondering why a member of the unfit brigade merited a special message from Riley. Then, wheeling about, he vanished from the doorway.

An air horn sounded. It was a signal to the NOBITs to assemble on the Eval course, where the weak were about to be winnowed.

Chapter 2

Thoughts about Thigh Spread

I once read that supermodel Cindy Crawford worries about thigh spread during photo shoots. If that's true for her, what the hell chance do the rest of us have?

Forget Donkey Kicks. The first step in eliminating thigh spread is to remove the excess fat that's covering your muscles. That takes diet and aerobic exercise. And while you're reducing fat, you should work the gym machines for each set of upper leg muscles:

- *The adduction/abductor machine, to tone your inner and outer thighs*
- *The hamstring machine, to harden the backs of the thighs*
- *The quadriceps machine, to strengthen the fronts*

One thing I don't recommend for thighs is overdoing the stair-climber. You want the lean, long legs of a dancer, not the bulked-up ham hocks of a firefighter.

—From *The Little Book of Fat-busters* by Mimi Morgan

I expected the Eval course to be difficult. I didn't expect to find a screaming DI in my face at every turn.

Laid out across the sports field I'd seen from the lobby, the obstacle course was divided into a series of "challenge stations." Each station had a little wooden sign next to it, giving it a name. The first few obstacles were easy enough—leapfrogging down a line of stumps, called Hop-a-longs; inching underneath some strings of barbed wire, called Barbie's Revenge—but from there, the challenges got progressively harder. Natural selection took hold, and the NOBITs quickly separated into four basic groups: the Freaks of Nature, the Workout Nuts, the Slow but Eager Beavers, and the Hopelessly Challenged. Meanwhile, DIs in camouflage uniforms roamed between the stations, braying at the laggards. The way they carried on, you'd have thought every DI had knocked back a double shot of *Hoo-ah!* before hitting the course.

Marnie and I formed the rear guard of the Hopelessly Challenged. Our laggardly pace soon drew the wrath of Erica.

"Move it, move it, *move* it!" she yelled in my ear, close enough to vibrate my eardrum.

To escape from her, I jetted ahead. Gasping and pushing myself to my absolute limit, I managed to catch up with a couple of thirty-something women who wore shorts despite the cold temperature. Their overdeveloped calves and thigh muscles suggested that they might be mountain bikers in the outside world.

The biker chicks and I approached the final and most dreaded challenge—The Beast. It was an eight-foot-high, redbrick wall with a couple of knotted ropes dangling to help us climb over it. We cheered each other on in our attempts to scale the wall. After a couple of embarrassing false starts, I finally made it over with the help of a squishy butt push from a guy who appeared to relish assisting the females.

I landed with an inelegant thud on the other side, twisting my ankle slightly on impact.

"Youch."

Amazed that I'd made it, I hobbled to the finish

line, then headed back to wait for Marnie. I figured she was going to need her Body Buddy to hurdle The Beast, big-time.

Marnie was lugging along several stations back, bringing up the far rear of the Hopelessly Challenged. Miraculously, Erica was no longer dogging her. Probably she'd already branded Marnie a Remedial Girl and had moved on to more promising targets.

"Hey-hey-hey *Marnie*," I called to her, summoning up the only high school cheer left in my memory archive.

As she approached the wall, Marnie looked bedraggled and soaked with sweat. Her cerulean T-shirt had damp navy stripes where her stomach rolls swelled against it, and there was a slight rip in the fabric near the center of her chest. Through the grommet of torn cloth, a patch of white bra showed through.

Marnie stopped dead. "I'll never make it over that thing." She stared up at the brick wall as if it were a woolly mammoth. Her lower lip quivered.

"You can do it," I said, a tad more optimistically than I felt. "I'll help you."

"Me, too," said Butt Pusher. He'd returned, evidently hoping to press more girl gluteus. From his expression as he stared at Marnie, however, it was clear that Butt Pusher thought he'd met his match.

Marnie grabbed one of the ropes and held on with a glazed expression.

"Okay, brace your feet against the wall," I said, "and start working your way up the knots. We'll push from behind."

Marnie set her feet against the brick and pulled while Butt Pusher and I went beet-faced, pushing. But it was no use, not even after another woman joined in the effort. All at once, Marnie lost her grip on the rope. The four of us collapsed into a human version of a freeway pileup.

It was clear the only way we'd get Marnie over the wall would be if I radioed in for air support. My co-pushers shrugged apologetically and took off, while I stayed behind to console Marnie.

Tears streamed down her face. "There's no way," she wailed. "This is totally insane. I'm just too *fat* for this."

I glanced around. Still no screaming DI in sight. "Look, this is not that important in the grand scheme of things," I said. "Just go around the stupid wall."

"Do you think it's okay if I do that?" Marnie asked, getting to her feet. She started to skirt The Beast.

From beyond the wall I heard a high-pitched cawing, like the sound a hawk makes when it's closing in on a rabbit.

Seconds later, Erica the DI descended on Marnie with her talons fully extended. "No going around! No going around!" she yelled. "You have to get over the wall."

Marnie set her jaw stubbornly. "I tried. I can't."

"Okay, then you'll need to go to the program director's office after dinner for a consult." Erica made a note on her clipboard. She shot me a baleful glance before turning away. Either she'd heard me tell Marnie to cheat, or she was still fuming over my crack about the breath mints.

I limped behind Marnie back to the finish line, where we both sprawled out on the cold grass.

"That Erica woman is so mean," Marnie muttered. "Why's she like that?"

"It's just Erica's job to be mean, but she really loves her work," a voice interjected.

Hillary, the DI who had shown us to our rooms, stood above us hugging a batch of bottled water. She squatted down. "Don't feel bad about not making it over the Beastie Wall," Hillary said to Marnie while handing each of us a bottle. "Remedial Fitness is much more fun, anyway—and I'll work closely with you. Darwin Innova will go over the details with you tonight. He's our program director."

"Darwin Innova?" Marnie blinked. "You mean the former pro tailback? *He* works here?"

Hillary rose to her feet. "Yeah, we were really lucky to get him," she said. With a distracted look on her face, she turned away and continued passing out her water bottles.

Marnie wiped the sweat off her forehead with the back of her hand. "I don't *believe* Darwin's here." She hunched over into a tight huddle.

"How do you know him?"

"Darwin played pro football on the Prowlers until he got a bad knee injury. My dad was his sports doctor, and Darwin, he . . ." Marnie fell silent. Chewing the inside of her lip, she plucked at a blade of grass.

It sounded like she had an interesting story to tell. But when I tried to prompt her with another question, Marnie only shook her head. Whatever juicy tidbit she had on this Darwin guy, she was keeping to herself.

Dinner at Body Blast—if you could call it that—featured a salmon-colored protein shake, a naked yam, and a tossed salad, heavy on the clover sprouts. The total absence of refined carbs—or tasty carbs of any kind at all—was enough to give me dark fantasies about calling Domino's. I would have loved to commiserate with Marnie about it, but she was AWOL.

I chewed my clover cud while simultaneously deflecting the enthusiasm of Butt Pusher, whose real name was Al. An accountant from Raleigh, Al had an owlish-looking face that seemed oddly mismatched with his muscular neck and shoulders. It was as if someone had stolen Superman's head and switched it with Ned the Nerd's.

"I'm always either crunching numbers or crunching weights," Al pronounced early in the discussion.

Al proved to be a bit of a pest. He recognized me from TV, and—evidently electrified by such a close encounter with celebrity—kept leaning into my face and tapping my wrist for emphasis as he quizzed me about the news business.

I was trying to think up an excuse to flee the table when Khan, Riley's business partner, materialized at my elbow.

"Are you through with your dinner, Kate?" he said. "Riley can see you now." Khan's expression hadn't defrosted one degree since I'd met him earlier that day, which made his query sound more like a summons. However, I nodded and got to my feet, grateful for an excuse to escape from Al.

Khan ushered me into an office, where Riley glanced up from a stack of papers on his desk.

"Kate! God, it's been—what—forever?" He rose from his chair and stepped around the desk to wrap me in a giant bear hug. "It's wonderful to see you. Sorry I wasn't around earlier—I've been totally crazed, trying to coordinate this triathlon we're having on Sunday."

"Wow, you look *great*," was all I could say as I emerged from the hug.

It was hard not to gape at Riley. I'd seen pictures of him since high school, but two-dimensional images didn't convey the full impact of his presence. Vanished was the bookish-looking beanpole of a guy I knew back then. What stood in his place was a tanned and bulked-up Terminator. Everything about Riley—down to his perfectly straight, ultrawhite teeth—seemed utterly transformed.

I felt a rush of affection for my friend. I'd never forgotten the cameo role that Riley had played in my life during senior year of high school. Senior year had been a particularly bleak era for me. Already socially out of step because of being younger than my classmates, I'd found myself struggling with a bout of depression in the wake of my mother's death. By the time Senior Prom rolled around, I'd fallen into a complete funk.

The evening of the prom found me holed up on the couch, proclaiming truculently to anyone who would listen that I didn't *believe* in proms (whatever that meant). But in reality, I was so withdrawn and depressed that I didn't have anyone to go with.

That night at eight p.m. sharp, Riley had appeared on my doorstep, corsage in hand. Like a knight in pale, skinny armor, he'd materialized out of the dark night. Unknown to me, my father had conspired with my aunt Myra to purchase the perfect prom dress for me.

Almost in a daze, I put on the dress and the dancing shoes, swept up my hair, and spent the rest of the evening feeling like Cinderella at the ball. Riley's gift of friendship that night had helped me turn the corner on what might otherwise have become a major depression. Ten years later, I still looked up to him. And—truth be told—I still harbored a bit of a crush on him.

"So, what did you think of your first day?" Riley smiled down at me. "How'd you do on our obstacle course?"

"Well, I thought it was going to kill me, but somehow I survived," I said.

Riley's expression changed. He shot a shrouded look at Khan, who crossed his arms and leaned against the wall. "And it was great fun, of course," I added hastily, thinking I'd sounded too flip. Now was definitely not the time to announce that my ankle had fallen victim to The Beast.

Riley's smile returned. "That-a-girl! I've assigned Hillary as your DI," he said. "She's great with women. She really goes the extra mile to help them reshape their bodies. Our other DIs—well, they're more like platoon sergeants. But hey, that's why the macho-macho men pay big bucks to come here."

In a sudden breach of silence, Khan blurted, "Body Blast is like spending a weekend with the Marines."

"Well, as long as they don't start calling me Maggot, I'll be okay," I replied.

Riley grimaced at the phone on his desk. "I'm afraid I have to finish making some calls—we're trying to line up a few more big names for the triathlon. We'll be doing a couple of events for the celebs, then a 5K run. You're still planning to do a story on it, right?"

"Yep. My crew will get here early Sunday morning."

After receiving a second hug from Riley and a stiff-necked nod from Khan, I headed back to my room. I'd turned right down a long corridor and was trying to find a route that would bypass Al and the dining room when a sound stopped me cold.

A raised voice came from the other side of a closed office door. It was muffled, but I recognized Marnie's voice. She was crying.

I kept my feet rooted in place while angling my torso and head toward the door to pick up the sound.

A second voice—tense-sounding and male—overlaid Marnie's sobs. Following that was a stretch of silence. Then, without warning, the door swung open.

A man emerged with his face turned away, looking back at the office. He practically fell over me as he stepped into the hallway.

"Oh, sorry." He grabbed me by the shoulders to steady both of us. Deeply tanned and even more deeply ripped, the guy could have been one of those discus-throwing Greek bronzes come to life. "Hi, I'm Darwin Innova, the program director."

"Kate Gallagher," I said, trying to look like I hadn't just had my ear plastered to the door.

Through the doorway, I saw Marnie's back. She was huddled in a chair facing the other way.

"Hey, right. Kate Gallagher. Channel Twelve in Durham—Riley told me you were coming. I hope you'll do a feature on our Wilderness Challenge sometime. That's our big adventure program." Darwin gave me a salesman's smile edged with flirtatiousness. *I'm a sexy beast,* the smile telegraphed.

"Kate?"

Marnie had rotated in her chair. Her eyes were wet, and she was staring at me as if I were the last ship pulling out of port. "Wait up," she said. "I'll walk with you."

Scuttling out of the office, Marnie practically Velcroed herself to my side.

Darwin's smile leveled off as he looked at Marnie. "We'll talk later," he said to her in a taut tone. After shooting a final stretch of his lips at me, he headed toward the dining room.

When we got back to our room, Marnie flopped on her bed and stared up at the ceiling with a fixed gaze. Still staring, she reached for her purse, dug deep, and pulled out a familiar dark brown bag. It was a package of M&M'S—the king-sized version. After ripping off one corner, she tilted up the bag and poured a stream of candies into her mouth. It was a sudden, dramatic flow, like the reopening of Niagara Falls.

I perched on my bed and stared at her. "That bad, huh?"

"Yeah." She extended the bag toward me. "Want some?"

I recoiled as if she were brandishing a sprig of poison oak. "Ooh, no, thank you, I'm allergic to M&M'S," I said. That was actually a true statement. I break out in fat.

There was something compelling about watching

someone—someone other than me, that is—plunge into an emo-eating binge. It was like watching an Olympic diving event. And if I were a judge, I would have given Marnie a solid ten for speed of entry.

But I knew it wasn't right to stand by as a looky-loo; I was Marnie's Body Buddy, so intervention was required. "Want to talk about it?"

Marnie lifted her free hand in a little half wave, then reached for her cell phone. "Thanks, but I'm really okay," she said. "I just need to call someone. Would you mind, possibly . . . ?"

"Oh, absolutely, I'll give you some privacy," I said, backpedaling out of the room. Well, they couldn't say I hadn't tried to help.

I spent the next couple of hours chatting with my fellow campers in the lobby's "bar," a table that was set up with a pot of lemongrass tea and some kind of fibery biscuits that tasted like you'd shoved a fistful of hay into your mouth. Beyond the lobby window, the deserted sports field spread in the distance below, patchily illuminated by a scattering of light poles.

The rest of the evening didn't turn out to be much fun. The only hot topics with this crowd were body-building events and Iron Man competitions. Both subjects left me so far out in the cold, my ass was getting frostbite. All the focus on musculature made me long for a stiff hot chocolate. With a minaret of whipped cream on top, thank you very much.

When I finally hit overflow on the tea and body babble, I returned to our room. Marnie's bedclothes were turned back, but she wasn't there. And her jacket was gone.

I washed up in the tiny bathroom and changed into an oversized T-shirt. My body was strongly protesting the day's activities. I could feel bumps and bruises from the obstacle course rising on my elbows and shins, and my ankle was throbbing from the rough landing at the brick wall. Thank goodness, I'd remembered to toss a bottle of Tylenol PM into my travel bag. After downing a couple of the painkillers, I eased back into the room and stretched out on the bed. It was a soothing release to get horizontal at last.

I cracked open my eyes Friday morning with the sensation that Munchkins were doing a little jig in my upper GI. It was probably an aftershock from last night's hayseed snack. Still groggy from the painkiller, I pressed my fingers into my stomach to settle it down, then blinked through the semidarkness at the clock on the dresser. It was six fifteen a.m. Breakfast was scheduled for the ungodly hour of six thirty. I'd have to dress superfast to make it.

Marnie's bed was rumpled but empty, which meant she'd slept in it at some point. She must have opened the window sometime during the night, too, because a steady draft of arctic air was freezing my exposed toes. I buried them underneath the blanket for a few precious seconds of warmth before heaving myself out of bed.

When Marnie hadn't turned up an hour later at the end of breakfast (which consisted of egg whites scrambled with Unidentified Fiber Objects), I started to really wonder where she was. I asked the biker chicks I'd met the day before whether they'd seen her. Then I asked Al—who snapped to attention like a meerkat—the same question. But no one had.

Near the end of breakfast, Erica did a flyby through the dining room, holding a sheaf of papers. She scanned the tables with impatient eyes.

I caught up with Erica in the lobby. "Are you looking for Marnie?"

"Yeah." Erica slowed down just long enough to respond. "I've found everyone who's starting Remedial Fitness today except her."

"I haven't seen her all morning," I said. "She wasn't in her bed when I woke up, either."

Erica rolled her eyes. "Where could she have gone?"

"That's what I'm wondering."

Hillary, the kinder, gentler DI, came in through the front door of the lobby with the air of someone just arriving for work. I asked her if she'd seen Marnie anywhere outside.

Hillary glanced from me to Erica with an uneasy look on her face. "No," she said. "Should I have?"

I shook my head, then glanced out the window that overlooked the sports field and Eval course below. It took a second for my eyes to adjust to an unexpectedly white vista—a dusting of late spring snow had powdered all the surfaces; the only splotch of color was the dull brick red of The Beast at the far end. Some activity there caught my eye. A man in a dark workman's uniform was standing next to the wall, frantically waving his arms. He was trying to get someone's attention.

"What's going on down there?" I said to Erica. "Does that guy need help?"

"What? I don't know, just—" Erica followed my gaze through the window to the field. A little frown appeared between her eyebrows. "I'd better go check that out," she said. After telling Hillary to go find Darwin and send him outside, she headed out the door.

Something about the way the man appeared to be desperately seeking help by The Beast made me feel uneasy. So as soon as Hillary took off to find Darwin, I trailed Erica outside and down the hill toward the obstacle course, making sure to stay far enough back so she didn't notice me.

The workman I'd seen by the wall came hurrying up the hill toward Erica. I couldn't hear what he said to her, but whatever it was caused her to break into a run.

The man continued his way up the path to the main building with a distressed look on his face. He didn't seem to register me as we passed each other.

Far ahead of me, Erica crossed the field to the brick wall. Then she stopped and dropped to her knees. A blast of staccato notes—it sounded like "*Eee*-yah-h-h"—carried across the grass toward me. It was the same hawk impression that Erica had done yesterday—only this time, she was channeling a panicky hawk. Erica was screaming.

I sprinted the rest of the way down the hill, which wasn't easy considering how sore I was from yesterday's workout. A thin frosting of snow crunched underfoot as I chugged across the grass toward the wall, pumping my aching legs and puffing out pale streamers of breath. Finally I pulled up next to Erica. She was huddled over a large, unmoving figure that was resting on the ground.

The figure was Marnie. She was lying on her right side at the foot of The Beast with her legs splayed out behind her. Her arms were stretched across the ground, hands curled.

And then I saw her neck. It was gruesome to behold. Distended and circled with a band of dark purple, shot through by crimson threads, her neck was bent back at a severe angle. It looked as if a giant hand had reached down from the sky and tried to wrench her head from her body. A dried rivulet of blood ran from one corner of her mouth toward the ground.

"Marnie?" I whispered, as if by some miracle she would answer me.

No answer came. Marnie was dead.

Chapter 3

Let's *Don't* Have a Cigarette on It

Some women start smoking while dieting because it fulfills that oral gratification urge and speeds up your metabolism.

Well, don't! In addition to all the known health risks, cigarette smoking makes you look like an old bag. You get little cracks around your mouth, which no amount of spackling with collagen will fix. And your skin gets thin and crepelike.

If that's not enough to scare you, just consider the "C" word.

Plus, do you really want to go around smelling like an ashtray?

—From *The Little Book of Fat-busters* by Mimi Morgan

Clutching my sides and panting from the footrace across the field, I stared down at Marnie's body. It took another full second for my synapses to fire the word "dead" all the way across my brain. In my peripheral vision, I saw Erica race toward a low, cabinet-type box that stood next to a light pole. The cabinet had a red cross painted on its side.

I squatted down, reached forward, and pressed my fingers against Marnie's neck. Her skin felt horrible to the touch. It was taut and cold, like a plum that had been left out on the freezing ground. Two oblong patches of snow had collected over her eyes; without thinking, I reached forward and used my fingertips to brush the snow away. Then I reeled back.

Underneath the snow, Marnie's hazel eyes were wide open. They stared up at me, glassy and unseeing—there was no life in them at all.

Her North Face jacket was unzipped and folded back from her chest in an oddly precise way; underneath the jacket, she had on the same sky blue T-shirt she'd worn the day before.

I gently shook Marnie's shoulder and hovered with my ear over her mouth, listening for any sound of breathing. Nothing.

Before I could do anything else, Erica ran back. She had a portable defibrillator slung over her shoulder on a strap.

"Did that workman go to call nine-one-one?" I asked her. "What about a cell phone?"

"He went to use a landline. This field is a dead spot for cells—our nearest help is a park ranger station." Erica unloaded the defibrillator from its case.

The device walked us through the resuscitation process with talking commands. The machine spoke in a chipper electronic voice that sounded completely bizarre under the circumstances. The chatty tone of the instructions reminded me of those airplane videos showing eerily calm passengers attaching life vests and blowing them up through tubes—when you know that in a real emergency, all kinds of screaming hell would be breaking loose.

"Announce 'clear,' " the machine ordered, after Erica placed the paddles on Marnie's chest.

"Clear," Erica echoed in a shaky voice. Despite the cold, a bead of sweat had popped out on her forehead.

I felt a surge of hope when, in response to a jolt from the paddles, Marnie's body twitched. But the hope was short-lived. After several more tries, there was no trace of a pulse.

Even the mechanical voice seemed to lose hope. "Contact nine-one-one for further advice," it announced bleakly.

My ears picked up a zapping sound. At first I thought it came from the defibrillator; then I realized that the light poles around us had just clicked off. They must have been set on an automatic timer.

What could have *happened* to Marnie? From my squatting position I studied the wall. Only one rope dangled from it. Yesterday there'd been two. The second rope was half-coiled on the ground near Marnie. Her outreached arms and curved fingers made it look as if she were grabbing for it, even in death.

The rope represented a giant question mark. Had Marnie gotten up before dawn to try the wall by herself, then somehow fallen and broken her neck? That explanation made zero sense to me. Marnie hadn't made it over The Beast yesterday, even with three people helping her. And she hadn't seemed the least bit worried about the failure last night, when she was lying on her bed popping M&M'S. Why in the world would she try the wall again? And by *herself*?

I cast back to our last conversation, trying to recall any sound of her leaving our room during the night or early morning. I couldn't, but then, I'd been knocked out from exhaustion and that painkiller. A battle of the bands probably wouldn't have roused me.

Led by Darwin, a stampede of camp employees came surging down the hill from the main building and surrounded us. Darwin hunched with Erica over Marnie's body.

"Dear God, what's this? God *dammit*." Darwin pumped his fist into the air, like someone lamenting to the gods onstage.

His reaction seemed forced and false. I instantly

flashed on how Marnie had emerged from his office—in tears—the night before. Now I regretted not having pressed her harder at the time about what had gone on between them. But one thing was certain: Darwin gave me a rotten feeling in the pit of my stomach. I glanced up the hill toward the main building, looking for any sign of Riley, or even Khan. Where the hell *were* they?

Through the trees, I saw the flashing amber light of a Park Services Jeep. It was winding its way up the twisting road. The driver bypassed the parking lot and steered the vehicle directly onto the field. It bumped its way across the frozen grass toward the brick wall.

I had no idea what to expect. I'm used to working with cops, but my knowledge of park rangers was based mostly on childhood cartoons with picnic basket–stealing bears.

The man who climbed down from the Jeep had on a green jacket and the familiar Smokey Bear hat, but that's where any cartoon resemblance ended. He was in his late thirties, tall and spare, with flinty eyes surrounded by lines that suggested years spent squinting into the sun.

Gripping an emergency medical kit, the ranger approached Marnie's body. Without saying a word to anyone, he knelt down and checked her over, looking for any sign of life. After a few moments, he shook his head and got back to his feet.

"What the hell happened here, Darwin?" he said.

From the ranger's tone, I sensed that he knew Darwin well. And not in a friendly way.

"A regrettable accident, clearly," said Darwin, who now seemed to be playing a PR rep doing damage control. "This girl evidently came out here on her own. She must have fallen and broken her neck."

"The SBI will determine exactly what happened here," the ranger snapped.

SBI was the State Bureau of Investigation. It seemed odd that state investigators would get pulled right away; usually a preliminary investigation is handled by local cops or the sheriff, and the higher-ups get called later if necessary. Maybe it was something to do with jurisdiction in this area.

For the first time, I thought about the impact this horrible event would have on my friend Riley. Beyond the tragic aspects of Marnie's death, this incident spelled trouble for him.

The ranger, who introduced himself as Senior Ranger Daniel Pike, quickly took charge of everyone at the scene. When he learned that I was Marnie's roommate, he asked me to return to our room and wait for an interview.

"Don't disturb anything of hers in the room," he warned me.

My legs felt wobbly and numb as I struggled back up the hill. I started to shiver, too. I'd made the mad dash outside without grabbing a jacket. Now, every inch of exposed skin felt as if it were covered with permafrost.

I let myself into the room. After dropping onto my bed, I sat with my chin cupped in my hand for several minutes and stared at Marnie's empty cot. A corner of neon pink paper poked out from the rumpled covers on her bed. I reached forward and extracted the sheet—it was a flyer, some kind of rah-rah discussion about the benefits of body sculpting for women.

Out of habit from my job, I opened my laptop, which had been leaning against my duffel bag, and opened a file. Then I tapped in everything I could remember starting from the first moment I'd met Marnie the day before, including each conversation and what was happening at the time. It's a process I call brain barf, because I always write down the tiniest details of a conversation, even inserting ellipses for the pauses.

Then I pulled a spiral notebook from my purse and, drawing from the detailed notes on the computer, jotted down a rough time line that I could carry around with me.

But when I looked over my time line, the only thing that seemed noteworthy about the day before was that crying scene between Marnie and Darwin. Sighing, I closed the notebook and shoved it into the pocket of my sweatpants.

My anxiety soon morphed into a case of restless leg syndrome. After pacing the room a couple of times, my eye fell on the little wooden table between our two beds. Marnie's leftover bag of M&M'S was sitting on top of it.

The sight of her candy finally uncorked my tears. A sob ripped from my chest, and I surrendered to a mini–crying jag. As soon as the weeping spell passed, my stomach let out a growl. The grinding went on and on, varying in pitch like an old-fashioned car horn. I was hungry—or maybe it was stress—to the point of feeling faint. All of which confronted me with the following sticky question: How evil would it be to eat a dead girl's candy? Then I remembered: Pike had warned me not to touch anything of hers.

A draft of frigid air lashed my face, reminding me that I'd never shut the window, which had been cracked open since this morning.

I lifted my hands to shut it, then glanced down. In a bare patch of ground directly under the eaves, I spotted a scattering of small white objects. I squinted through the glass and saw a handful of cigarette butts lying in a disorganized mound. Someone had evidently been chain-smoking just outside our room. Had Marnie spoken to the smoker through the cracked-open window?

I grabbed a fleece jacket from my duffel bag and headed outside. Then I skirted the building until I located the area underneath our window. Keeping my feet carefully on a stone to avoid leaving prints, I stooped to examine the pile of cigarette stubs. A mint green cigarette package lay at the edge of the bare patch. I could just make out the label: KOOL MENTHOLS.

"That's illegal, you know."

I wheeled around. Ranger Pike stood just behind me on the stone path.

"Littering," he said with a disapproving look on his face. "Get yourself an ashtray next time."

"These aren't mine." I nodded at the cigarettes. "I just noticed them here when I went to shut our window. Someone else was smoking out here."

"Maybe it was your roommate, Marnie. When was the last time you saw her?"

"Last night around eight p.m. in our room. She needed to make a call, so I went to the bar to give her some privacy. She wasn't in the room when I came back a couple of hours later, and I think I must have fallen asleep before she returned. When I woke up at six twenty this morning, she wasn't there, but her bed looked like it had been slept in." My inner broadcaster's ear warned me that I'd sounded breathless delivering all that information in rat-a-tat bursts.

Pike extracted a pad and pen from his jacket's pocket. "Maybe she went out for a smoke," he said. "She a smoker?"

"I don't think so."

"The SBI is on the way. They'll collect these and follow up." Pike nodded at the pile of butts while jotting something down.

"Why the SBI?" I asked, but got no reply. I glanced surreptitiously at Pike's notes as he wrote, trying to see if there was anything revealing there. But the ranger's chicken scratchings were about as decipherable as some ancient graffiti you'd find on the wall of a men's room in the Great Pyramid of Giza.

"Do you happen to know what time it snowed last night?" I prodded him again, hoping to get a feel for when Marnie had died. The fact that her eyes were covered with snow suggested that she'd been lying on the sports field for some time.

Pike glanced up from his notes. "You mean that little spring duster we had this morning? It would have been about six a.m. at this elevation."

He followed that up with some questions—my address and occupation, among other things. When I said I worked at Channel Twelve in Durham, his eyebrows rose.

"You a reporter there?"

"Yeah."

"I've talked to reporters before," he said, grunting in a way that showed how unimpressed he'd been by the experience. He snapped shut his notebook. "Let's go take a look at the room."

I led the way back and swiped the card key.

Before entering the room, Pike removed his wide-brimmed hat. His gesture struck me as old-fashioned and respectful. Almost quaint.

"This is Marnie's bed," I said, pointing. "I mean it *was* hers, I guess."

Pike stared at the bed, then swung his head left and right, surveying the room. "Did Ms. Taylor—Marnie—give you any indication that she was planning to go to the sports field for any reason during the night or morning?"

"No, she didn't say anything at all about that. And I can't imagine that she was even *thinking* about it. She seemed to have other things on her mind."

"Like?"

I told Pike about the tearful scene I'd observed between Marnie and Darwin the night before.

Pike looked surprised. "She was upset with Darwin *Innova*, you say?"

When I nodded, he added, "What was she crying about?"

"I asked, but she wouldn't tell me. Do you think she died accidentally? Or was it . . . something else?" The word "murder" was eager to spring from my lips, but I held it in.

In a tone that said *Back off*, the ranger said, "That's yet to be determined."

Perhaps in retaliation for my having had the audacity to ask him a question, Pike gave me quite the grilling. He pumped me for every detail about my interactions with Marnie, so much so that I finally pulled my notebook from my sweatpants to give him a rundown.

That move proved to be a stupid mistake; Pike's eyes widened at the sight of my notebook.

"Mind?" He snatched the pad from my hands.

"Hey," I snapped. "I'm trying to cooperate with you, but that's my work there."

Pike scanned a few pages. "These notes will be helpful," he said. "Besides, you don't need it anyway, do you? You're not one of those turkey vulture reporters who splashes stories about dead girls all over the evening news, are you?"

That's exactly what I was, although I much preferred the term "newshound" to "turkey vulture."

"Not really, but—"

With a triumphant expression, Pike pocketed the notebook. "I'll get this back to you later," he said.

"Thanks ever so much," I retorted, not bothering to hide my sarcasm. My real notes were on the laptop, however, so I didn't need to get on my journalistic high horse by refusing to turn over the pad. If Pike had tried to take the laptop, he'd have had a Bengal tiger on his hands.

Pike pulled on his hat. "Well, I have to go finish up the rest of the interviews," he said. "Make sure you don't disturb anything that belonged to your roommate until we get the all clear from the SBI." He gave me a terse nod, then left.

Thank goodness I hadn't scarfed down Marnie's M&M'S. Pike would probably have accused me of swallowing some evidence.

Moments later, Hillary knocked. The drill instructor who had been so friendly and outgoing at the obstacle course yesterday looked haggard now. Even haunted.

"Body Blast is shutting down temporarily due to the emergency," she told me. "We're offering full refunds, plus a free weekend to compensate for the inconvenience." Stepping through the door, she added, "Can you tell that to your roommate?"

Hillary glanced at the empty bed where I'd tossed the pink flyer. All at once it seemed to dawn on her that this had been Marnie's room. Her face collapsed. "Oh, my God," she blurted. "How awful. I didn't mean to—"

"That's okay," I said. "Do you know if Riley is here yet?"

"I heard he's on his way right now from his place in town."

I opened my mouth to say something else, but Hillary was already in full retreat.

I unzipped my duffel bag and loaded in the few things I'd unpacked yesterday. Meanwhile, I kept glancing at Marnie's gear, which was piled at the foot of her bed. A dingy bra was draped over the top of her backpack. I wondered whether her parents or the staff would pack her things.

I folded up my sleep shirt and stuffed it into my

bag. Touching the shirt was enough to set off a chorus of "if onlys" in my brain.

If only I hadn't been so wiped out last night, I would have heard Marnie get up. If only I'd started looking for her when I first woke up this morning, perhaps we'd have found her in time. But the biggest "if only" was tinctured with guilt: If only I had *been* there more for Marnie yesterday when she was upset, maybe I could have altered her course enough so that she'd still be alive. But I didn't try hard enough to help her. I hadn't been a good Body Buddy.

Outside the room, the corridor filled with the excited buzz of people leaving in the middle of a crisis. I heard doors slamming, heavy items being dragged. I stepped into the hallway.

Al the accountant, aka Butt Pusher, stood one door down, lugging an enormous backpack over his shoulders. His narrow face lit up when he spotted me.

"Hey, I didn't know we were neighbors." His eyes shone with excitement. "We're all being interviewed by a ranger or somebody before we leave. Wasn't that your roommate who got killed?"

When I nodded, he continued, "Her name was Marnie, right? I remember you looking for her this morning—and to think that she was lying out there dead the whole time. Horrible, huh?"

"Yeah, it's bad." I shifted sideways to move around him, then stopped. "You didn't hear any noise during the night, did you?" I asked him. "Anything unusual?"

Al's face flushed with excitement at being asked a question by a real live reporter. "Let me think," he said. "Wait a second—will you want my answer on camera? Is this for a story?"

I hesitated to announce that I would be covering the story—we were out of my viewing area, and there was my friendship with Riley to consider. On the other hand, Marnie was from Durham, so it really was local news for us. In fact, I was fairly positive that my news director would want me to write something about it for the broadcast that night.

"Well, I don't have a crew with me right now," I said to Al. "But maybe later—give me your card."

He fished for his card, then handed it to me. "You know, I *did* hear something—or rather saw something, around two a.m.," he said. "You know how sometimes you'll just half wake up from a deep sleep? Well, last night I was lying there and thought there was a firefly outside my window. Turned out the 'firefly' was the burning end of a cigarette. There was a guy outside, smoking. I nearly jumped out of my skin."

"Did you get a look at him?"

Al shook his head. "Nah, I figured it was just some insomniac taking a ciggie break. There was some murmuring like someone was talking. I rolled over and went back to sleep. Strange, huh?"

"Did you happen to hear a woman's voice?" I asked, thinking of Marnie.

Al shrugged. "I really wasn't listening, to tell you the truth. What do you think—"

"Okay, well, thanks for the information. I'll be in touch." I brushed past him to avoid being peppered with more questions.

As I headed outside on my way to find Riley, I wondered if Marnie had spoken to the mysterious smoker during the night. The open window certainly suggested that she could have. If so, had something about their conversation lured her to that wall?

It occurred to me that I hadn't seen anyone smoking at the camp. Body Blast attracted health nuts, not smokers. I'd seen only one person smoking yesterday, and that was Marnie's boyfriend. He'd flicked away a cigarette when he dropped her off in the parking lot. Her *ex*-boyfriend, she had kept repeating. Her ex-boyfriend who had acted "like a total A-hole" the day before.

The parking lot seemed worth checking out. I followed one of the walkways that led down the hill to the lot. The snow had melted away from the dark asphalt, so it was easy to spot things. Keeping my eyes fastened on the pavement, I baby-stepped around the area where Marnie had been dropped off the day before.

After a couple more minutes of searching, I got down on my hands and knees to peer under the cars. Underneath a Subaru SUV's bumper, I spotted a soggy, solitary butt. Out of a burst of caution—the police hadn't cordoned off the area, but you never know what might happen—I looked around for something to pick it up with. I finally found a large leaf, then scooped up the cigarette stub and took a sniff. Menthol. A band above the filter identified it as a Kool. It was the same brand of cigarette I'd found underneath our window.

A courtroom judge probably would have rolled his eyes at my evidence, but my gut told me I'd discovered something important: In the dead of night, and just before she died of a broken-looking neck on the obstacle course, Marnie's ex-boyfriend had paid her a visit.

Chapter 4

It's All in the Packaging

We gals spend a lot of time on our faces, trying to make ourselves look beautiful to men. But here's a dirty little secret about the opposite sex: Men are all about packaging. If you have a fantastic, toned body, it won't matter a hoot in hell if you weren't born with the world's most gorgeous face. Trust me—with a killer bod, a bit of makeup, and a little help from a push-up bra, you'll knock 'em dead. So if that's your goal, it's worth every second you spend in the gym.

—From *The Little Book of Fat-busters* by Mimi Morgan

If Marnie's boyfriend—Antonio was his name, I recalled—had come by our window to see her the night before, what had happened between them? And where was he now?

The "M" word that I'd suppressed earlier rose in my throat again like an upsurge of nasty bile. Did Antonio and Marnie have another fight last night, like the one that I witnessed when he dropped her off at the camp? Could Antonio have *killed* her?

Slow the heck down, Kate, I cautioned myself. *You're putting the crime way before the victim.* The way my brain kept casting around for suspects made me think I'd been covering too many murder trials of late. My investigative reporting job at Channel Twelve was obviously beginning to warp my thinking.

The truth was I didn't even know how Marnie had died. Like Pike said, that was for the coroner to determine. Her death could very well have been a freak accident.

With a sigh, I dropped the stub back to the pavement.

"If you're jonesing that bad for a cigarette, I've got a pack in my office."

The sudden intrusion of a voice startled me into dropping my leaf scoop.

Khan, Riley's business partner, was leaning against one of the parked cars. His dark eyes smoldered in his face.

I shifted uneasily. How long had Khan been standing there, watching me? "No, but I guess I shouldn't litter," I said, keeping my tone casual. "I just got a lecture about it from Ranger Pike."

Khan swore something under his breath. "Pike," he said. "He's as useless as they come. Riley wants to see you in his office.

"Chop-chop," he added with a sardonic edge, when I apparently didn't respond quickly enough.

I followed Khan across the parking lot and through the crowded lobby. The reception area was filled with campers being corralled by a few glum-faced drill instructors. I wanted to ask Khan a thousand questions about the morning's events, but the rigid angle of his back discouraged me from uttering a word.

Riley was talking into a phone when Khan dropped me off at his office, closing the door behind me. I was grateful he didn't linger—I wanted a chance to speak privately with Riley.

Riley nodded at me while continuing his phone conversation. "No, we're closing down today, but we still plan to do the triathlon on Sunday. *If* we can still do the triathlon, that is," he said to the person on the line. "Yes, the girl died, unfortunately. Yup, I know. Bye."

Riley clicked off. Heaving a sigh, he looked at me across the desk. His face looked as if it had aged five years since the previous night. "Thanks for coming, Kate." He spread his fingers and rubbed his eyebrows. "This whole thing is so awful. I was at my place in Ashland—that's the nearest big town to here—when I got the call about Marnie. She was your roommate and your Body Buddy, I heard. Have the rangers . . . ?"

"Ranger Pike already interviewed me," I said, nodding.

"Oh, okay. Are *you* okay?"

"Still kind of shook up, I guess. Have they figured out exactly what happened to her yet?"

Riley expelled a second, deeper sigh. "Well, Pike seems pretty sure this one was an accident. But—"

"*This* one? What do you mean? Something else happened?"

Riley drew his lips into a flat line. "Last October," he said. "Same sort of thing, actually—a girl broke her neck in a fall. Her name was Libby Fowler. The SBI is still investigating that one."

I felt a wave of dread break over my head. "Did the other girl—Libby—fall at the obstacle course wall, like Marnie?"

"No, not at all," he replied. "Libby was on our Wilderness Challenge. She left her tent before dawn for some reason and fell down a ravine. I was on that trip—it seemed totally like a freak accident—but the investigators gave us all the third degree, like they thought it was a . . . a *murder* or something. And of course we've got a major lawsuit on our hands from the girl's family." He shrugged, shifting gears abruptly. "But I have to put that worry in a different box."

I flashed on an image of the Grim Reaper liability forms we'd signed the day before. "The other girl who died—Libby—where was she from?"

"She was from Durham, too. Why?"

"I'm sorry, but my station will want to run something about this. The fact that both girls who died are from Durham makes it a local story for us. And it won't be just my channel—I'm sure you'll be getting some calls from other reporters, too."

"God, just what I need. Right before the triathlon, too—although that's not important right now." Riley kept rubbing his eyebrows so hard I was afraid he was going to draw blood.

"I know. This is one time I really wish I wasn't a reporter."

"Don't worry about it." He attempted a smile that tugged at one corner of his lips. "You're a reporter. This is news. But maybe there's something you can do for me."

"Shoot."

Instead of replying, Riley stood up. He crossed the floor of the office to stand by the window, which overlooked a breathtaking view of the Smokies.

He began slowly, "Back when that other girl—Libby—died, I got the feeling the cops thought someone on that trip was . . . was *involved*, somehow." He kept his gaze on the white-crested peaks in the distance, which glistened under the noonday sun. "But I just can't believe that. She left her tent by herself before dawn and fell down that ravine. That's how it *must* have happened."

"That might well be true, Riley. But I still don't understand how I can help."

He faced me again. "I know we haven't seen each other in a long time, Kate, but I hear from the guys back home that you really take after your dad, the Chief."

When I shrugged, Riley continued, "People say you've got great detective bones. Like the way you figured out that diet doctor's murder last year. They say you shoulda been a cop like your old man."

"People say that, yeah, but I'm *not* a detective, Riley. I only got caught up in that murder case last year because I was doing my job as an investigative journalist."

"So you'll be doing your job *this* time, too, right? Maybe while you're at it you could give me a heads-up if you learn what the SBI is doing, or if you think anyone around here is up to anything."

"If anyone is *up* to anything?" It seemed like a strange request. "Riley, what the heck is going on here, beyond the deaths of these two women? Are you in some kind of trouble?"

"Yes. No. Maybe—I don't know."

Riley returned to his chair. When he looked at me again, his shoulders had slumped. "There have been a couple of . . . of *incidents*, I guess you'd call them, since last October, when Libby died," he said. "Last month, someone broke into a storage shed where we had parked some brand-new equipment. They took the high-end stuff. Then a few days later, we had a shed fire that broke out in the middle of the night. No one was hurt, thank God. Then—just last week—someone jimmied open a drawer in my desk and swiped some cash. And now this girl Marnie is dead."

"And you think the two deaths, the thefts, and the fire might be connected somehow?"

Riley shrugged. "Right now, I just don't know *what* to think. It just feels like I'm under assault right now. Even if the SBI decides that both girls' deaths were accidents, we still look bad, like we're running a dangerous operation. But whatever's really going on, I need to know the truth."

"Well, that's my job—reporting the truth."

He searched my eyes. "Good. You said you'd be able to cover the triathlon on Sunday, right? So just keep your ears open for me. That's all I ask."

I hesitated long enough to consider whether my friendship with Riley would compromise doing my job as a reporter. To be honest, it might. But I'd simply have to make it work. "Okay," I said. "I'll keep my ear close to the ground and let you know what I find."

He looked relieved. "Thanks," he said. "So how do we start?"

"I'm curious about your program director, Darwin. I'd like to find out more about him."

"Darwin?" Riley hesitated. "What's he got to do with this?"

I described the crying scene I'd heard the night before between Marnie and Darwin, then said, "Yesterday, Marnie told me that her father is a sports doctor, and that he treated Darwin in the past for a knee injury. It sounded like she was holding back something sketchy about him, but she wouldn't tell me what it was. Next thing I know, I see her coming out of his office in tears. And the next morning, she winds up dead. Maybe it's just a coincidence, but . . ."

Riley's eyebrows beetled together. "Darwin quit the pros seven years ago because of a big knee injury," he said. "I didn't know him back then. All I know is that nowadays he really brings in the business for us. The weekend jocks think he walks on water."

"The whole thing just seems suspicious. Have you ever had any problems with him before?"

When Riley didn't answer, I pressed, "You *have* had problems?"

Riley shifted in his chair. "Well, Darwin likes beautiful women," he finally said. "Maybe he likes them a bit *too* much, sometimes."

"How much is 'too much'?"

"He's been known to hit on them occasionally. Most of the women don't seem to mind, but a couple of them have. One time, I had to give him a written reprimand."

I made a reaching motion for my notepad, then remembered that Pike had commandeered it. "Can you give me the names of the women who complained about Darwin?"

"There've only been two, but . . ." Beneath the surface of his golden tan, Riley blanched. "The second one was Libby Fowler. She complained about him the day before she fell down that ravine—the day before she died."

Chapter 5

Girls Love a Game, as Long as It's Live

A study of undergraduate students has shown that women love live sports just as much as men—but men rule when it comes to watching sports on television. Men reported watching eight hours of sports per week, while women watched less than three.

IMHO, this difference is because we women have much better things to do than watch a bunch of athletes grunting around on the boob tube. I mean, really—who cares?

—From *The Little Book of Fat-busters* by Mimi Morgan

I leaned forward in my chair to make sure I'd heard Riley correctly.

"You're saying that Darwin harassed the *first* girl who died—Libby—right before her death?" My heart knocked against my chest. "Are you talking about sexual harassment?"

"Well, not *legally*—it's only sexual harassment if the person works for you, right? At least, that's what my HR consultants tell me," Riley said. "Libby was a camper. I can show you Darwin's reprimand in his file, if you like."

"I *would* like. And I wouldn't be surprised if the

SBI considers Darwin a suspect. I'll make a few calls, see what I can find out. And now, with what I saw happen between him and Marnie, and now *she's* dead . . ."

Riley shrank against the back of his chair as my implication sank in. "The cops never indicated to me in any way that he's a suspect. I'd have fired him immediately if they had," he said in a bewildered tone.

I tried to wrap my mind around the new information. "Was Darwin on the camping trip when Libby died?"

"Yes, he and I both were. Neither of us were supposed to be. But a couple of my guys got hit by that stomach flu that was going around last October, so we both stepped in at the last minute. I just remember giving him this little lecture about not asking the female campers out on dates. Looking back, the whole thing *does* seem sketchy. But at the time, I'll admit I thought Libby was being a bit of a drama queen. It seemed like she was making a mountain out of a molehill."

"Yeah, well, it's easy to feel that harassment is a molehill unless you're on the receiving end," I said, hoping that response didn't sound priggish.

Riley's head drooped a bit from his neck. "Touché."

"I'm sure that the SBI will be taking another look at Darwin, because I told the ranger what I saw happen between him and Marnie. In the meantime, I could use any information you can spare about what's going on here at the camp. Your computer records, e-mails, employee files—whatever you have."

After pausing to think some more, I added, "And also a list of all the people who were on-site last night—guests and staff. *And* a list of everyone who was on that camping trip when Libby died." Even though there was no obvious link between the two women's deaths, I thought it made sense to compare the lists, to see who had been present during both incidents.

"I'll get Khan to put everything together for you," Riley promised, laying his tanned right hand on top of a stack of papers on his desk.

"Speaking of Khan, what's his story?"

Riley's expression turned guarded. "What do you mean, 'his story'?"

"I just get kind of a weird vibe from him."

Riley kept his hand resting on top of the paper stack, as if he were taking an oath on a Bible. "I'll level with you, Kate," he said. "In our business, I'm the brawn and Khan's the brains. I bring in the customers and he balances the books." He hesitated. "And I should probably also tell you that Khan and I, we . . . we live together. Do you know what I mean?" His eyes held mine.

"Ah. Yes, I see." Riley and Khan were a couple, he meant. My gaydar must have been on the fritz all these years, because that bit of news came as a total surprise—I'd never known that Riley was gay. It was something he had in common with our mutual childhood friend Brian Sullivan. Brian was a gay *cop*, truly a rare bird in South Boston. He must have known the truth about Riley's sexual identity all along, but he'd never said a word about it.

Riley held himself at taut attention, as if he were bracing for a negative reaction.

Finally, I said, "Darn, I guess this means I'm going to have to give up my Prom Night fantasy about you, which always ends with you ravishing me."

When he broke into a grin, I added, "I'll have to smack Brian for not telling me the truth about you. But I guess I should have known you were gay when my aunt Myra told me you helped her coordinate the shoes with my prom dress."

"Don't blame our buddy Brian," he said, barking out a laugh. "I made him swear not to tell anyone back home. I wanted to pick my own place and time. Southie doesn't exactly fly the rainbow colors, if you know what I mean."

"True. I should have thought of that. Where do you and Khan live?"

Riley's smile faded again. "We have a town house in Ashland, about twenty miles from here. So what were you going to ask about him?"

"I'm not in any way implying anything against Khan," I said, trying to pick my words carefully, "but I'd like you to assemble the records for me to look at, not him. By the way—was he with you last night?"

Riley opened his mouth to say something, then closed it again.

His silence made my antennae go up. "He wasn't with you?"

Riley shrugged. "No, he was. It's just—I was thinking that he's been moody as hell lately," he said, shifting his gaze to the ceiling. "I mean, Khan's never exactly been the Queen of Chat, but it's really hard for me to get a word out of him these days. I get the feeling he's got something heavy on his mind."

"Khan smokes, doesn't he?" I asked, remembering his offer of the pack of cigarettes.

Riley offered up a wan smile. "Khan's a smoker, a toker, and he likes to play the midnight jokers, I guess you could say. It's our Sunday morning ritual—I have to go find him at two a.m. at whatever poker party he's holed up at, drape him over my shoulder, and carry him home. He always loses, but he keeps on playing. *And* drinking."

"Has his gambling affected your bottom line?"

"Meaning?"

"Meaning, how well is your business doing?"

"I don't know every detail, but according to Khan

we're fine. Numbers and financial statements are like Greek to me, so he's always taken care of our books."

When I didn't respond, he added defensively, "I struggle a bit with ADHD. It's why I never went to college after high school."

Attention Deficit Hyperactivity Disorder or no, not knowing your own bottom line seemed like a risky way to do business. I wanted to be frank with my friend, because he had so much at stake. "I think you should consider getting an outside auditor to go over your books," I said to him. "And do you really think it's wise to trust Khan with the finances if he has a gambling problem?"

Riley's cheeks flamed. "I trust him," he said. "Besides, it doesn't have anything to do with the deaths of those two girls."

He ran his fingertips back and forth across the desktop and then rubbed his fingers together, as if checking for dust. "Look," he finally added. "When I first met Khan, I was a greenhorn trainer who didn't have two dimes to rub together. He took care of the money all that time, and he's been handling it ever since. He's never given me anything to complain about. And anyway, I love the guy."

It seemed pointless to argue with Riley. He obviously had an emotional blind spot when it came to Khan the Ice Man, who was a substance abuser with a serious gambling habit—*and* who controlled the finances. That could be the "problem" that was preoccupying Riley's partner—perhaps he'd gambled beyond his means, and the bill collector had arrived to demand his due.

But Riley was right about one thing—whatever Khan was up to, it probably didn't have anything to do with Marnie or Libby. Darwin, on the other hand, was another story. I needed to get more information about him. And for that, I'd need my laptop and Riley's records.

After getting the names of Marnie's parents from Riley—I had to find out whether they'd been notified about her death before reporting anything—and verifying that the facilities had wireless, I returned to my room. Someone had already removed Marnie's things and cleaned up. My bed was neatly made, but Marnie's was stripped down to the quilted mattress.

The sight of the bare ticking sent a wave of nausea through my gut. It underscored the void where Marnie had once existed.

The prospect of working in the room next to that empty bed was dismal in the extreme, but I thought it was better to stay put. It might be best for me to keep a low profile with the Body Blast staff for now.

To put together a game plan to cover the day's events I called the Channel Twelve assignment desk. To my dismay, my least favorite person in the world answered—a reporter named Timothy Thompson. Even in the ego-driven world of TV news, Timothy Thompson was the biggest ass I'd ever met.

"Beatty put me in charge of the newsroom today," he said, when I asked for our boss, the news director. He made this announcement with the gravitas of someone announcing that they'd been put in control of the White House. "Do you have something for tonight?"

Nothing I'm giving to you, I thought. Thompson was notorious for maneuvering stories away from other reporters, only to claim them for himself. Once when I was out of town, he piggybacked onto one of my stories to create an update that he constructed by simply folding in a bit of updated news. He later had the gall to submit the piece for an AP award—but didn't win, to my delight.

"I might have something about an accident," I said. "It'll be a voice-over. I'll call you back in a couple of hours with details." I hung up before he could pepper me with questions. No way was I going to tell Thompson that I had something big—not until I had Beatty backing me on the assignment.

After grabbing my laptop, I sat on the bed and popped open the screen. A search on Darwin Innova turned up the major highlights of his past. After spending four years as a star football player for the University of Tennessee, he'd been hired by the Prowlers pro team as a promising young tailback. A devastating knee injury a few years later had ended his career. Since that time, Darwin had been trying various ventures, none of them too successful, apparently. My search brought up references to a short-lived supplements company he'd started, and to an autobiography he'd written that was already out of print. Darwin's current job as program director at Body Blast seemed like a comedown for the former football star.

Staring at a picture of Darwin in his gold helmet and uniform, I remembered that I had a contact at the Prowlers team. At a network affiliate's party months earlier, I'd met the team's thirty-year-old manager, Fergus McPherson. Irish by birth, Fergus had a killer brogue—just thinking about the sound of his voice was enough to bring a smile to my face.

After consulting my address book, I picked up my cell phone and punched in Fergus's number. When the manager came on the line, I could hear the sound of men yelling and grunting in the background. It sounded as if he were standing on the sidelines of a practice field.

"Kate, darlin'! You've made my day by calling," Fergus said. "But please tell me this is a social call and not for one of your news stories. Otherwise, my manly ego will be crushed."

"It's a little of both, actually," I told him. Without

revealing anything about Marnie's death or the events at Body Blast, I told him that I was doing some research on Darwin Innova.

"*Darwin?* What kind of trouble has that dumb bastard gone and gotten himself into now?"

"What do you mean, 'now'? What kind of trouble did he get into *before* now?"

Silence fell on the other end of the line. It was broken by the shrill blast of a referee's whistle.

"Son of a bitch!" Fergus's shout was muffled, as if he were covering the phone with his hand. Then he spoke directly into the phone, "Sorry, darlin', I meant my dumb-ass lineman, not you. I can't go into the details about Darwin right this second, but I'm talking about how he quit the team."

"Then I guess I'm the last to know. I thought Darwin quit because of a knee injury."

"Well, that's what our press release said, and we paid our PR guys handsomely to stick to that story," he said. "But hey, darlin'—everything I'm telling you is on deep background, okay? You didn't get nothin' from me. I'm only telling you this because I have a major case of the hots for you, in case you didn't know it, young lady. I was telling my mum just the other day, I *needs* me a good woman, the kind with some flesh on her bones."

"Sure you do, Fergus, sure you do."

"How about this," he said. "I'll regale you with the whole scandalous story about Darwin if you'll let me buy you dinner tomorrow night. I'm leaving town for a game the next morning."

"Tomorrow?" That would be Saturday. His invitation forced me to concoct a forty-eight-hour game plan in my head. I hated to leave the camp so soon, but it was important for me to find out what he knew about Darwin. "Sounds great," I told him. "What if I pick you up around seven tomorrow night?"

"Ooh—I can't wait to tell my players that I'm gonna be tooling around with the hottest redhead in town."

It occurred to me that Fergus might know Marnie's father, the sports doctor who had treated Darwin's knee injury years ago.

When I asked him about it, he said, "You mean Dr. Hal? Yeah, sure, he works for the team on contract with some of my players. Dr. Hal's a great guy. How do you know him?"

I broke the news to Fergus about Marnie's death, describing it simply as an accident.

"Ah, Mary Mother, bless us. Dr. Hal's daughter has died?" Fergus's tone turned somber. "I met the dear girl a couple of times. This is terrible, terrible news. I'll spread the word to everyone who knows the family around here. Thanks for letting me know."

"Sure thing."

After getting Fergus's address, I clicked off and sat on the bed for a while, thinking everything over. It was probably just as well that I go home to do what research I could, and then return to cover the triathlon on Sunday. I'd stick out like a sore thumb as long as there weren't any other campers around.

After parking my gear in the lobby, I stopped by Riley's office.

"I need to follow up on a hot lead about Darwin," I told him. "And I need to get back to Durham to do it."

Riley gave me a worried look across his desk, which was piled high with file folders and scattered CDs. "What did you find out about him?"

"I'm not sure yet—I'll let you know. I'll be back early Sunday morning for the triathlon—if it's still on, that is."

"It's too late to cancel it, or I would." Riley handed me a short stack of folders and CDs, plus a schedule for the upcoming triathlon. "I've put you on Darwin's team for the event. Is that okay?"

"That's perfect, because it will give me a good opportunity to observe him up close. And this other stuff is . . . ?"

"The other files you requested. But I'll have to get the financial records to you later. Right now I can't locate them. Ever since that break-in we had, everything has been kind of a mess."

"Well, don't forget that idea we discussed, about getting your books audited by a professional," I said. "I know a good forensic accountant in Raleigh. I can give you his name."

"A *forensic* accountant? What's he do, look for fingerprints on the bank statements?" Riley's attempt at a grin fell flat.

"Something like that." I was concerned about my friend. It seemed as if he was in way over his head, on many levels. After saying good-bye, I returned to the lobby to pick up my gear.

As I passed by the long window that overlooked the sports field below, I glanced outside. The snow had melted away, leaving behind a grassy expanse that glistened in the sun. Near the brick wall in the distance, a couple of Park Services cruisers were parked at odd angles, their amber lights still flashing. Next to them was a hulking green truck with blue police lights and a logo I couldn't make out from this distance. I wondered if it was from the SBI.

Hillary the Drill Instructor came hard-charging through the lobby with her head down. She'd changed her hairstyle since this morning; now it was braided and looped over her ears, making her look like a Star Wars princess.

Hillary pulled up short when she recognized me. "Oh, you're still here, Kate?" she said. "Everyone else except for the staff is long gone."

"I had to stay behind to chat with Riley for a while," I said, adjusting the strap of my duffel bag over my shoulder. "He and I know each other from Boston."

Hillary blinked. "Really? He told me you guys were friends, but I had no idea that you went back that far."

"We do. And right now I'm trying to help him figure out exactly what happened this morning." I pointed through the window to the sports field beyond. "Can you think of any reason that Marnie would have gone out to the obstacle course before dawn? I can't figure that out. She didn't say anything about it last night."

Hillary rocked on her heels, as if my question had physically shoved her back. "No, I can't think of any reason at all," she said, without looking at the window. "Marnie's Remedial group wasn't scheduled to start working out until eight this morning. But I guess the rangers will let us know exactly what happened, right?"

"Well, hopefully. Does *anyone* ever go onto the field before dawn?"

"Actually, I think the lights come on automatically at five a.m., in case people want an early workout." She retreated another step. "But I have absolutely no idea what happened to Marnie."

"Okay, thanks. Before you go, can you tell me—"

Hillary shook her head. "Sorry, but I'm about to miss our staff's lunch meeting," she said. "And I'm afraid I just can't handle talking about Marnie anymore. It's been a really rough day."

Lifting her hands in the air as if to ward off more questions, she hurried off in the direction of the dining room.

A pang of protest emanated from my stomach region, informing me that it was lunchtime and I should follow her in the direction of food. But that didn't seem like a good idea. My quandary underscored how awkward it was going to be to cover this story. Everyone at the camp already knew I was a reporter—no secret there. But there was an added wrinkle in that I'd been enrolled at the program, and that I was Riley's friend. On the other hand, my job often subjected me to far worse tensions, like being manhandled off the premises by the irate target of one of my stories. At least there'd be nothing violent this time.

After loading my gear into the TR6, I hit the return road to Durham. I'd made it a few miles and was curling the car around the Dragon's Tail again when my cell phone rang.

It was Riley. I took the call even though talking required a precarious balancing of the phone in the crook of my neck while shifting and steering around the hairpin bends. One degree's mis-turn with the wheel and I would have been Great Smoky Mountain roadkill.

"You were *so* right, Kate," Riley blurted over a connection that crackled in and out. "I'm gonna get that audit of our books, like you said. What's that accountant's name in Raleigh?"

Before I could respond, he rushed ahead, "I think Khan was lying to me about the financial records. He's disappeared, and tons of our records are missing, including all of the accounts receivable."

In the background, I heard the sound of a metal drawer being slammed shut.

"Everything's gone," he said. "Absolutely everything."

Chapter 6

Move to the Groove, Even When You're Cooling Off

When you finish a workout, you should engage in active recovery (aka low intensity exercise) rather than passive recovery (aka flopping on the couch). Staying active is better for you, both physically and psychologically, when you are recovering from intense exercise.

I recommend shopping. It's a low-intensity exercise, and so rewarding.

—From *The Little Book of Fat-busters* by Mimi Morgan

"Gone?" I echoed. "You mean like *swiped*?"

"I have to assume that," Riley replied. "I found all these hanging folders that are completely empty. It's way too much stuff to have just been misplaced. He must have taken it."

"Did you check with Khan? Maybe he had some reason to take the files with him?"

"I can't find him right now. He took off for our place this morning after the whole thing with Marnie, and now he's not answering his cell phone."

"Well, why don't you talk to him before assuming that anything is wrong," I said, trying to make my voice sound reassuring. "Maybe there's a perfectly logical reason that the files aren't there. Maybe he's off making copies for you right now."

"Thanks, Kate." The tension in Riley's voice eased. "It's good to have you to talk to."

"Anytime. Keep me posted, and I'll do the same with you," I said. Before we hung up, I gave him the name of my accountant friend in Raleigh.

Throughout the rest of the long drive back to Durham, I felt sad. Worse than sad—spooked and jumpy. Every time a bug spattered against the windshield I saw Marnie's blank death-stare again, and the horrible way her neck had been twisted and bulging out, like Frankenstein's. It had looked so freakish. How could a simple fall have caused that kind of injury?

Both my mood and energy level were so low by the time I reached town that afternoon that I stopped off for a forbidden sugar fix at Francine's Dessert Café.

The moment I walked through the double glass doors into the bakery parlor, I was hit by the familiar warm, chocolaty aroma of Black Forest cake, my personal drug of choice. Its dense, melting taste of cocoa brought back a host of childhood memories, both happy, sad, and that middling ground called bittersweet. But even Francine's wondrous layer cake failed to boost my depressed state, which persisted long after I settled back into my apartment.

My unit was on the second floor of a sprawling complex on West Trinity Avenue. I loved the exterior landscaping with its lush plantings and a man-made stream bubbling through the middle of it. I'd originally moved in on a short-term lease, but something about all those meandering walkways and the flick-of-a-switch gas fireplace in my bedroom had lulled me into staying longer. I'd softened the sterile L-shaped living room with heirloom drapes and a Victorian-era sofa set that had been passed down to me through my mother's family. The net effect was lace-curtain Irish, a style that was retro enough to be considered chic.

As soon as I walked through the door, I felt a soft impact around my ankle, accompanied by the sound of a chittering mewl. Elfie the cat rubbed around my ankles in a furry circle eight.

"Hey there, gorgeous thing," I said, picking her up for a cuddle.

Elfie was my adopted Ragdoll cat. I'd inherited her from my boyfriend Lou, who, after adopting her, discovered that he was severely allergic to long-haired cats. How we'd work out the allergy thing if we got married, I had no clue. All I knew was one thing—Elfie was in my life to stay.

The pet sitter, Charlene, had left a note with her daily update on the dining room table: *Elfie was in good spirits on Day Two. Left food, then spent twenty minutes playing Crazy Mouse with her.*

I loved Charlene, who was a fierce protector and advocate for all things furry. I left a message for her to let her know that I'd returned home earlier than expected.

Already ruing my collapse into the chocolaty arms of the Black Forest cake, I headed for the bathroom to check in with my scale, trailed by Elfie. It's a trait of Ragdolls to dog their peoples' heels, and one of the reasons they're often called puppy cats.

I stepped on the scale—and this wasn't just any scale. Over the holidays, in a fit of thinking that if I knew more *about* my fat I'd carry less *of* it, I'd blown nearly a grand to purchase a state-of-the-art Dietary and Body Composition Analyzer. This digital baby featured a pie chart that showed every body statistic imaginable. It even talked.

But when I pushed ANALYZE, all it delivered was bad news.

"Your weight is . . . one hundred and seventy-five

point two pounds," the machine announced in a slightly snippy voice. "Your weight change since last weigh-in is . . . an *increase* of point two pounds."

Aargh. "Okay, you Digitized Dietary Dumb Cluck, those will be your last words for the week." I hit the MUTE button. "I'm busting you back to Display-only Mode."

When I returned to the living room, I realized I should call Lou, to let him know about my unexpected return to town. We might even be able to squeeze in a romantic rendezvous in Atlanta sometime during the week. Knowing Lou, he'd send his private helicopter to fetch me.

Lou was a corporate lawyer who had dropped from the skies into my life—literally—the previous summer. I'd met him while reporting about the death of a murdered diet doctor. Lou was my magic man, a human tornado of energy who swept me off my feet whenever we were together. I'm no shrinking violet in the personality department, but next to Lou, sometimes I felt in danger of becoming one.

But fifteen minutes later, I still hadn't reached for the phone. I realized the reason was that the next time I saw Lou, I wanted to have the Answer to his marriage proposal. Seeing him before I made my decision would seem *wrong*, somehow.

I glanced at a picture of Lou on the mantel over the fireplace. It showed him on top of the flying bridge of his Magnum Marine, a sleek racing boat that had a bow shaped like the front end of a shark. Framed by a backdrop of ocean, he had one hand on the helm, looking over his shoulder at me and smiling.

The day that photo had been taken was the first time he'd hinted about wanting a long-term relationship (although he hadn't yet mentioned the "M" word).

"So when are you going to save me and Kurt helicopter miles by moving to Atlanta?" he'd said that evening, as we grilled freshly caught yellowtail in the ship's burled-wood galley. "You could work at CNN, couldn't you?"

"I don't think I'm ready for network yet."

And it was true. Per my recent "cosmetic reminder" from the management of Channel Twelve, being less than rail thin—or in my case, more than—was a real obstacle to climbing the career ladder in broadcast news. Body-wise, I was barely hanging on to my local gig.

Now I kept a nervous eye on the clock. It was almost three. If the news director didn't call me back, Thompson or no, I was going to have to work up something for the six o'clock news.

I put in a call to the SBI's press office and left a message that I wanted to talk with someone in connection with the deaths of two Durham women at Body Blast. Then I set my laptop on the dining room table and popped it open. To start, I'd search for any mention in the local news about Libby Fowler's death the previous October. Riley had mentioned that a small weekly paper had written it up, but I had no idea which one.

A Google search on Libby's name didn't turn up anything useful, so I started looking around for small, regional newspapers. After a few minutes, I located an online edition of the *Maggie Hollow News*. Maggie Hollow was the town nearest to Body Blast, so I hoped its paper would have covered the incident. I did another unfruitful search for Libby's name, then scrolled through the paper's archives.

Most of the top news stories in Maggie Hollow involved small town incidents: an eighty-two-year-old woman who'd clobbered someone over the head with her breathing device; another woman who'd shot a pair of dogs that attacked her goats.

It's probably best not to cross mountain women, I decided as I continued reading. Then I found what I was looking for:

HIKER FALLS TO HER DEATH DURING WILDERNESS JAUNT

The front-page story described how Libby Fouler (her last name was misspelled, which explained why it hadn't turned up in my searches), a twenty-seven-year-old camper at Body Blast, had wandered out of her tent in the middle of the night during a wilderness trip, and fallen into a ravine. Libby's camping party had discovered her body the next morning, dead with a broken neck. The paper stated that her fall had been accidental, although I knew from Riley that the SBI was still investigating it.

Reading the story's details, I felt the hairs stand up on my neck. Libby's death sounded eerily like Marnie's—an unexplained, predawn solo excursion, with no witnesses. Death by a broken neck. The article quoted Darwin calling her death a "regrettable accident," precisely the same words he'd used to describe Marnie's fall.

I clicked forward, looking for any other mention of Libby's death. There was only one; the day after she died, a distraught family member—Libby's brother—had stormed into Body Blast and caused a scene. He was escorted off the premises by the park rangers. The brother's name was Theo Fowler.

The name rang a bell. After doing a bit of checking, I confirmed that Theo Fowler was the eponymous name of a used-car dealership in the city of Raleigh, Durham's urban neighbor to the southeast.

I'd have to drop in on Theo the next day, to ask him about his sister's "regrettable accident."

That's when my cell phone finally rang.

"Gallagher!" Beatty, the news director, put an extra

rasp into his usual greeting. "Thompson said you tried to call something in—what's up?"

"The boot camp I was at—Body Blast—has shut down for a couple of days. A girl from Durham died in a fall. Apparently, it was an accident," I said. "But here's the lead—this is actually the *second* death at the same camp. Both women were from Durham. And I still have to confirm this next part, but I have a source who says that the first woman's death is being investigated as a murder."

"Two Durham women dead at the same mountain camp, one of them possibly murdered? Hell, Gallagher, that's a *huge* story for us. This is your cell phone I'm calling, right? Are you still at the camp?"

"No, I'm back in Durham right now. I'm working on a lead for a follow-up story."

"Screw the follow-up; I'm thinking about tonight's show. I could have called our sister station in Ashland to send over a crew for you. You should have told Thompson about it when you called in."

"You're right, of course." I didn't want to say that I'd rather tell a snake about one of my scoops than Thompson. It didn't pay to complain openly about a colleague to management—you just might step on a political land mine.

So all I added was, "I just didn't want to haul in a camera right then—the girl who died was my roommate. And the camp is owned by a friend of mine."

"Ah." Beatty paused. "Sorry to hear that. That must be tough."

After a pause, he continued, "Look, if you think you're too close to this story, I can assign it to someone else. Like Thompson, maybe."

"*Hell* no," I blurted. "I've got it under control. This one's mine, okay?"

Beatty chuckled, then said, "Okay. You put something together for a voice-over. And gimme the address of that camp—I'll get the Ashland station to send over a crew to get some exterior shots and uplink them for us for the six o'clock. We'll really have to haul ass to make it in time, though."

After pausing to formulate a strategy in my head, I said, "I can do a live shot outside the SBI headquarters in Raleigh. My source says they'll be running the investigation. But we can't use Marnie's name unless we confirm that her family knows she's dead."

"I'll get someone on the horn here to call the girl's family to confirm—you just get your butt over to the SBI for the live shot. I'm slugging the story 'Dead Camper Girls.' "

"One other thing," I said. "Body Blast is closed now, but they're reopening for that triathlon event on Sunday. So that'll give me a good launch point for the follow-up piece on Marnie. We'll get two birds with one stone. Sound good?"

"Sounds fantabulous." From the other end of the line came the squawking sound of a two-way radio, which the assignment desk uses to communicate with crews in the field.

"You're in the newsroom right now?" I asked, feeling confused. "Thompson said *he* was running the assignment desk today."

"He ran it for an hour while I went to grab some lunch."

Typical Thompson, I thought.

I heard a squeaking of springs, which meant that Beatty was leaning back in his news director's chair to scan the assignment board.

Then he said, "Hey, I know you need to get cracking on this story, but I'm short a talent for the friggin' Earth festival tomorrow. Everyone around this place is sick all of a sudden. Can you do it?"

I tried not to groan too audibly. A festival story was one of those fluff-piece assignments I normally try to avoid. But teamwork called for pitching in when needed.

"Sure thing," I said.

"Fantabulous. And, Gallagher, remember—this is for the kicker piece at the end of the show. We need something light and happy. I'm talking kids, balloons, and ice cream, not how one of the sponsors is secretly promoting global warming. Don't give me anything depressing."

"Understood. I'll make it light and happy as hell."

"Attagirl."

When I clicked off the phone with Beatty, I put a call in to the SBI's communications office to see if anyone could confirm my information about Marnie's and Libby's deaths. Again, my call went straight to voice mail. I left another message, just so that I could legitimately report that "repeated phone calls to the SBI for confirmation were not returned."

Writing up a story with insufficient time to confirm the facts required me to do some major journalistic tap-dancing. I wanted to avoid looking like I was throwing a half-baked story on the air—which is exactly what I *was* doing. But being forced to deliver a story on the fly that way is simply a hazard of the job in deadline news.

When I was finished writing the voice-over, I e-mailed it to Beatty, who in turn would hand it off to a producer. Then the piece would go into the TelePrompTer for an anchor to read.

That done, I gave Elfie a final scratch behind her ears. Then I headed out the door to meet a crew for the live shot in front of the SBI headquarters.

At two minutes past six p.m., I stood with microphone in hand under the glaring floodlights of a broadcast news van, trying not to shiver in the cooling-down evening air. We were positioned in front of the main sign of the SBI building, with sixty seconds left before the live shot.

On the van's monitor, I watched my finished story about Marnie's death—and the information about the previously unreported death of Libby Fowler—come across the air. My story was the lead.

Miraculously, the piece looked solid. When it was all put together, you'd never know that the whole thing had been strung together with the broadcast equivalent of string and sealing wax.

Through my earpiece, a producer told me that they'd confirmed that Marnie's family knew about her death. That update came just in time, because through my other ear, I heard the anchorman, Perry Jones, complete the voice-over. Then his voice took on an urgent and-here's-the-latest-news quality.

"We have Channel Twelve's Kate Gallagher standing outside the SBI headquarters in Raleigh," the newscaster announced. "Kate's bringing us the latest available information on the deaths of the two Durham women in the North Carolina mountains. Kate?"

When the red light on the camera blinked to indicate I was live, I raised the mike and said:

"Perry, a source has told me that the State Bureau of Investigation is investigating this morning's death of nineteen-year-old Marnie Taylor at a fitness camp named Body Blast. I've also learned that they're investigating the death of a twenty-seven-year-old Durham woman—Libby Fowler—who fell to her death during a hiking trip with the same camp last October. Repeated phone calls to the SBI headquarters for confirmation were not returned. But as more information develops in this story, we'll keep you updated. This is Kate Gallagher, Channel Twelve News. Now back to you in the newsroom."

And *out.*

Chapter 7

The Vigorous Vegetarian

Oh, don't roll your eyes—it's simply true *that vegetarians have a healthier diet than us carnivores. A vegetarian is less likely to be obese (because she consumes more bulk and fiber on a daily basis). Eating nature's kinder, gentler way also does the following to enhance you and the world:*

- *Lowers high blood pressure*
- *Lowers levels of saturated fats, which promotes heart health*
- *Improves digestive functioning due to fiber intake*
- *Reduces cancer risk, because less fat and protein are consumed*
- *Reduces stress on the environment due to changed farming systems*
- *Spares the animal population, which is the humane thing to do*

If you want to become a vegetarian, it's best to go for a phased deployment. Give up one type of meat, then another, as you work vegetarian meals into your diet.

—From *The Little Book of Fat-busters* by Mimi Morgan

At the stroke of ten the next morning, I pulled into the lot of Theo Fowler's Quality Pre-owned Vehicles in downtown Raleigh. There were only a few Saturday-morning early birds browsing the cars in the lot.

After parking my TR6, I pretended to study a row of cast-off SUVs. Evidently other people shared my dislike of the vehicles, judging by the glut of inventory at Theo's.

It took less than sixty seconds for a salesman to draw a bead on me.

"That's a real cutie-pie you've got there."

The salesman, who wore a tie that was bright enough to have guided an airplane into its gate, glanced appreciatively at my green TR6. "We don't see too many of these anymore. You looking to trade her in?" he asked.

"Possibly," I lied, then launched into a discussion about a black Navigator that was for sale. When I asked to see Theo, the salesman was only too happy to show me into the manager's office, evidently thinking he was closing the deal.

Theo Fowler rose from his chair behind the desk when I was ushered into his office, offering me his hand and a bland business smile. The smile drained away when I explained that I was a reporter, and that I wanted to talk about his sister, Libby.

"I heard there was something on the news about her last night. That was you?" he said. "Why? What the hell is this?" Theo bounced a glare off his salesman, as if demanding to know why a cockroach had been escorted into his office.

Waggling his hands and shrugging to indicate *No clue*, the salesman fled.

I looked at Theo. "I'm so sorry for your loss, and I really didn't mean to upset you," I said, then gave him a brief recap of Marnie's death the day before. I told him that I was looking into Libby's death as a related incident.

"I'm looking into both their deaths," I continued.

"Libby's accident is part of the story I'm researching. Believe me, that's my only reason for coming."

Theo's hands, which had frozen midair in a gesture of outrage, slowly drifted down. He plunged them into his pockets. A gap of silence stretched between us, which broke when he dropped abruptly into his chair. A moment later he withdrew his hands from his pockets, placing them carefully on the desk in front of him.

"Do you want to write the real story about Libby?" he said, holding my eyes with his.

"Of course."

"My sister's death was no accident."

"No accident?" I gazed back at Theo Fowler. "What can you tell me about it?"

Theo's knuckles turned white where he'd knitted them together in front of him. His index fingers were pointed upward and leaning against each other, forming a peaked roof.

"Libby was much younger than me, and such a spirited little thing—always teasing everyone mercilessly, *especially* me," he said, half-smiling at the memory. "And so beautiful. Here, let me show you."

Unknitting his fingers, he turned around a picture frame on his desk so that it faced me. It was an eight-by-ten portrait of a young woman.

The picture showed a girl in a shimmering gold gown, seated in front of a fireplace. It looked like a photo from one of those mall studios where you pay an extra fifty bucks for the "glamour touch." But Libby probably hadn't needed the touch. With curving cheekbones and a sweep of chestnut hair pulled back into an updo, she'd obviously been a very pretty girl. Her froufrou style seemed totally unlike the yoga bunnies and Birkenstock types I'd seen at Body Blast.

"Did Libby enjoy hiking?" I asked him.

"No, and that's the irony. Libby *hated* exercise," Theo said. "Her idea of hiking was not valet parking at the Northgate Mall. But I guess she read an article in a stupid women's magazine. About pushing your physical envelope, or something asinine like that."

"What happened then?"

Libby had enrolled in the final Wilderness Challenge at Body Blast, Theo told me. "I only heard about that part *after* she died, of course. And then, she . . ." His eyes welled.

"I read about it," I said in a gentle voice. "She left her tent during the night and fell?"

Theo shook his head violently. "It just *couldn't* have happened the way they said," he insisted. "Libby never would have gone wandering around a mountain by herself at night. Someone must have been with her when she died. That person is responsible for her death."

"Did Riley—the camp's owner—ever speak to you about her?"

"That bastard?" Theo almost came out of his seat. "Yeah. I went up there after her funeral to demand an explanation. But he just called the cops—or rangers, whatever they were—and had me hauled away." He folded back down. "I guess her death is still being investigated—officially, anyway—but this is, what, six months later? Seems like a whole lot of nothing is happening, if you ask me."

"Well, sometimes these things take time," I said, feeling like I was parroting a useless bromide.

Theo slumped in his chair. "I feel completely defeated at this point," he said, his voice hollow. "Our family's suing the camp, of course. But what good does that do? It doesn't bring her back."

Theo's cheeks had sagged so much, it seemed as if they might slide off his face. Our discussion had clearly taken a toll on him.

I tried to think of something sympathetic to say that would help staunch his grief.

"Well, again, I'm so sorry." And again, the words felt manufactured and rote.

Theo nodded. Then, abruptly, he reached across the desk and grabbed my hand with both of his. "If you find out anything about Libby—anything at all—would you call me?" he said. "I don't want to learn about it from the news."

"I promise, I will."

Theo's eyes wrung my heart in a sympathetic twist. They reminded me of my father's eyes in the months after my mother died. During that time, I felt as if a giant hole had been punched in the atmosphere, sucking out all the happiness I'd ever known.

It was a hole that could never be completely refilled, not even with all the Black Forest cake in the world.

Later that afternoon, I turned up for Beatty's dreaded kicker assignment: the Celebrate Earth! festival. And at first glance, this particular assignment presented me with everything I feared most about fluff stories: moon bouncers, balloons, and baby buggies.

"It's funny to have *you* working with me on this one, Kate. Festivals aren't your usual bag, eh?" Frank the cameraman joked while he taped a game of I.Q. Chicken, where a girl was playing tic-tac-toe against a bird. The girl proceeded to lose the game and cried fowl.

"Yeah, there won't be any murders in this story, except for maybe the chicken," I said.

Frank (nee Franklin Stein, which of course gifted him with the after-hours nickname of Frankenstein), was the best videographer at Channel Twelve. Short, muscular, and feisty, Frank pursued his video quarry like a Chihuahua on steroids. I'd bet on Frank to get the shot every time over the biggest dog in the camera pool.

Leaving him behind to do some more taping, I wandered around the booths for a bit, looking for anything interesting we could use in the story Beatty wanted. It's not that I consider myself above writing puff pieces—I'm simply not any *good* at writing them. Turning light fare into entertainment is much more difficult than it looks; it's the one area where my reporting instincts always let me down.

I bought a veggie dog that the cart vendor's menu billed, somewhat off-puttingly, as a "tofu-furter." After loading it up with relish and mustard in a wild hope of adding some flavor, I took a big chomp.

"Ugh." I tossed it into a nearby trash can.

At the far end of a row of tents, my eye was drawn to one that had a green sign on it: NATIONAL FOREST SERVICE. I perked up. At least I might be able to get some background information about crime in the national forests that I could use somewhere down the line.

The Forest Service booth was almost deserted. The only person inside was a young and amazingly cute ranger, who was sitting on a stool next to the counter with a stack of brochures on it.

After checking in with my compact to make sure I didn't have mustard face, I introduced myself to the Amazingly Cute Ranger Guy, whose name was Russell.

Russell recognized me from the air. I was beginning to count on that reaction, because it made it easier to approach people for information. On the other hand, sometimes it *did* feel odd to talk to total strangers who acted as if we already knew each other. But the real downside was when I'd go to a store to buy tampons, and I'd just *know* that the smirking clerk would go home that night and regale his bar buddies with the news that the Channel Twelve TV chick was on the rag.

When I told Russell that I was doing some research

into crime trends in the national forests, he agreed to let me tape a brief interview.

"It's good the media is paying some attention to this topic," he said. "Lots of crime in the forests goes unreported."

"What kind of crime?"

"Oh, you name it. Most of the violence is centered around hidden narcotics farms—mostly marijuana, and . . . hold on." Russell paused to hand a sticker to a tiny girl whose eyes were barely visible underneath a green baseball cap that said EARTH CHILD on it. "There you go, sweetheart. That's from Smokey Bear."

When Russell's attention returned to me, I signaled to Frank, who was hovering nearby with the camera resting on his shoulder. That's one of the reasons I love working with him—Frank has a gift for knowing exactly when a reporter needs to get a quickie sound bite.

After Frank positioned himself and handed me a microphone, I picked up my questions with the ranger as though there'd been no interruption.

"You were saying there are violent potheads in the national forests? That almost sounds like an oxymoron, doesn't it?"

"Well, it's the pot *growers* who are dangerous, not the smokers," Russell replied. "The big narcotics farms are all run by major drug cartels. They mostly hire illegal aliens to guard them. Some of them are really vicious—one of our rangers in Oregon got himself blown up when he stumbled across a trip wire."

"Yikes. How do you locate the farms?"

"Mostly by helicopter. One time they hired a guy who had this incredible eyesight. He could differentiate more shades of green than a normal person—they took him up in the air and he was able to spot the marijuana, just by the color."

Thinking about Libby, I asked, "Are the forests dangerous for hikers?"

"Depends on the area. You just have to know where you're going. It's mostly safe if you stick to the well-known trails."

"What about the area around Pittman's Bluff? A woman from Durham was killed there."

"Pittman's Bluff? That's near Ashland, isn't it?"

When I nodded, he continued, "Seems like I've heard something about a big narcotics investigation going on in that general area. But that's off the record, okay? You'll have to go to someone higher up on the food chain to get anything official."

I continued talking with Russell, but made a surreptitious "cut" sign to Frank by drawing a line across the back of my neck with my finger. That was my signal that I had all the audio I needed.

Frank went into phase two of the taping, which was to get a two-shot of me talking to Russell, then a cut shot that showed me reacting to his answers. That's the shot where you see the reporter nod thoughtfully as the person being interviewed talks. Later on, we'd assemble all the pieces in the editing room.

When the interview wound down, Frank raised his eyebrows at me.

"Do you want to get a reporter question, Kate?"

"I guess so." I always hate taping the reporter question. When you're working with one camera during an interview, the camera focuses exclusively on the person who is being interviewed. If you want to get a shot of the reporter asking a question, you have to tape yourself asking the same question all over again, after the actual interview is over.

While Russell looked on with a bemused expression, Frank taped me repeating my question, "Violent potheads? Isn't that an oxymoron?" Then I held the mike out into empty space in front of me and pretended to listen to Russell answering the question. The whole thing always felt goofy.

Once we had all our interview shots, Frank lowered the camera. "What about the kicker for tonight, Kate?"

"I know," I sighed. We still had to do Beatty's confounded festival feature, and I didn't have a clue what to get for it. "A few tents down, I saw someone demonstrating solar-powered bikes," I told him. "Let's go check it out."

I thanked Ranger Russell. Then, with Frank in tow, I dragged hopelessly down the row of tents.

"Kickers," I muttered through gritted teeth.

With any luck, we'd be able to get some shots of a kid on a solar bike doing wheelies in a moon bouncer, holding a biodegradable balloon.

At the end of that night's six o'clock broadcast, I sat in the newsroom and watched my finished Earth festival story come across the air. It turned out okay for fluff stuff, but trust me, we're not talking *Entertainment Tonight.*

I only half paid attention to it, because I was already brainstorming a story based on my interview earlier that day with Ranger Russell. According to him, the authorities were investigating criminal drug activity in the vicinity where Libby had died. As soon as I could confirm his information on the record, and determine whether Libby had in fact been murdered, I could write up a story with that as a hook to open the piece. I already knew what the anchor's lead-in would be:

> The murder of a young Durham woman in the national forest has focused attention on a danger that often goes unreported: hidden narco farms, and the criminals who guard them.

I knew that I'd be the only reporter "focusing attention" on the dangers of drug farms, but that's a prerogative of reporting for TV news—the medium's roving spotlight creates a focus and intensity all by itself. Just ask Rodney King.

I didn't have enough material yet to put together the whole piece. Because Russell's information was off the record, I'd need to confirm whether there was any legitimate suspicion that drug criminals had anything to do with Libby's death at Pittman's Bluff. And, most importantly, I needed to get some visuals of a narco farm. Those wouldn't be easy to come by. I'd have to request a ride-along with whatever cop organization searches for those types of operations; getting that kind of access can take weeks to set up.

To speed things up, I put in a call to an agent I'd once met from the Drug Enforcement Agency, Phil Garcia. I left a message requesting a ride-along on the next search for pot farms in the North Carolina mountains.

There was one other requirement for a solid story, I realized; I needed to get some footage of the place where Libby Fowler had fallen down the ravine. I envisioned doing one of those CNN-type outdoor stories, showing me clambering around the ravine, describing how she died, and the possibility that drug operators were involved. That angle, too, would take some time to set up.

But right then, I had to hurry to make my dinner appointment with Fergus McPherson, the manager of the Prowlers football team. He'd promised to give me some hot information about his former pro player, Darwin.

Just before seven p.m., I pulled up in front of the Prowlers' stadium. It was practice–quitting time, evidently, judging by the quantity of primo athletic-looking men who were exiting from the players' tunnel.

As he emerged from the tunnel, Fergus looked more like a young quarterback than the team's manager. His light hair was coiled into damp curls, as if he'd just emerged from a steam bath. After greeting me with a kiss to the top of my head, it took him a second to shoehorn his long frame into the passenger side of my narrow car. Even though the early evening air was cool, he looked so wedged in that finally I put the convertible top down, just to give him more breathing space.

"Maybe I should just hang me legs over the roll bar for a quick drip-dry," he suggested in his Irish brogue.

We drove to Pico's, a new restaurant in Five Points that served fabulous Southwestern cuisine. When the waitress set down our drinks—a wine spritzer for me instead of the pricey margarita (pricey in terms of calories, that is), and a shot of whiskey for Fergus—I asked him to tell me what he knew about Darwin.

Fergus reached for his shot glass. "I will, darlin', but first—tell me, why are you interested in hearing about Darwin?" he asked, then took a swallow. "Ah, God bless America for inventing Gentleman Jack."

Without going into specifics about Marnie's or Libby's deaths, I told him that I was looking into some questions that had been raised about Darwin's behavior with women.

"Well, that's just Darwin—he's probably up to his old tricks again." He nodded.

"What tricks are those?"

"He got dumped by the Prowlers after getting himself into a bit of a jam with a young lady." Fergus paused. "Well, it wasn't the *jam* so much as the fact that the girl was so young. Turns out she was fourteen years old, although to me she looked about twenty. The way the parents let their daughters dress these days, I guess us lads should card them at the door."

When I didn't smile, Fergus gave me a nervous look. "Of course I don't know whether Darwin *knew* she was underage," he added quickly. "He claimed he didn't. Her parents made an incredible stink, threatened to press charges. Darwin was still recovering from that knee injury, so it was good cover for him to leave quietly. Since then he seems to have dropped off the radar. He's working as a camp counselor these days, you say?"

"Program director, actually. Do you know what happened with the girl he got involved with?"

Fergus shrugged. "I heard she got shipped off to a boarding school in Idaho. The kind with a ring of barbed wire around it," he said. "We finally settled with the family. It cost the team a pretty penny, but worth it to avoid the bad publicity."

The waitress returned with our meals. Because I'd tossed away my tofu-furter earlier that day, I rationalized that I deserved a good dinner. And so it was—a sizzling platter of fajitas, with guacamole and sour cream on the side.

Fergus marveled at the way I dug into the fajitas. "I love a woman who eats," he said, smiling. "Most American girls can't take a bite without crossing themselves and saying three Hail Marys first. But I have to tell you, darlin', that I have a wee bone to pick with you."

"Wumf-*ee* bone?" I asked, through a mouthful of flour tortilla.

"You told me that was partly a social call yesterday, but I think you were pulling this Irishman's leg," he said, carving into his lamb shank. "I got another call right after yours from one of your newspaper colleagues, Lainey Lanston. My players call her Pain-in-the-Asston. She was asking me all kinds of questions about Darwin, too."

"Lainey's not my colleague—she's my competition. She called you to ask about Darwin? Crap."

Lane E. Lanston, known as Lainey in her byline, was a sports reporter for the local newspaper, the *Durham Ledger*. I wondered if she'd gotten wind of anything about Darwin somehow, or whether she was working up a story about Marnie's death. It wouldn't be her normal beat to report hard news, but you never knew with Lainey. She was ambitious as hell, always on the lookout to break out of the Sports ghetto. Getting scooped by her on a story would be very, very bad.

"Did you tell her anything about why Darwin left the team?" I asked him in alarm. "That it was because he had an affair with an underage girl?"

Fergus slid a finger across his mouth as if he were zipping it shut. "Nope. I coulda been a secret agent man, I'm so discreet. I only told *you* about Darwin because, as you know, I'm also a horny bastard. But now, I feel so . . . so *used.*" Raising his napkin to his eyes, he pretended to dab at them. "I may have to take another shower when I get home."

Taking careful aim at a stray grain of rice that had fallen next to my plate, I shot it across the table at him.

"You'll be fine, Fergus," I said. "But look. If Lainey calls you again, do me a favor, would you—"

"No worries, darlin'. Mum's the word. Lainey would have to put on stilettos and torture me with a whip. Not that I'd *mind* that."

"Can you get me any information about the settlement the Prowlers made with the family that sued the team? Anything I can use? I won't attribute it to you, of course."

"Now you really *are* using me." Fergus finished his scotch and signaled the waitress for another in one fluid motion. "But I'll dig up something for you, simply because I'm such a horrible roundheel for redheads."

I turned our conversation to Marnie's family.

Fergus had some new information about that, because Marnie's father, Dr. Hal Taylor, was the Prowlers' team doctor. The Taylors would be having a service for Marnie Monday night at their home, he told me.

"I'm so sorry that the team will be out of town so that we can't attend. Her parents are completely torn up—poor Dr. Hal," he said, turning solemn for a moment. "This has been a terrible, terrible blow for them. I wonder if Darwin will show up for the service."

My fork paused in midair. "Darwin? Why would he go to Marnie's memorial service? Was he close to her?"

"I don't know about *that*, but Darwin and her father were close. They were at one point, anyway. Dr. Hal seemed to take a real liking to him—they both graduated from University of Tennessee, and the doc is a big booster on the UT alumni committee. They were quite chummy one summer, I recall. But that seemed to fade after a while."

"Do you have any idea why things cooled off between them?"

"No, none."

I wondered what had happened to the friendship between Darwin and Marnie's father. I'd have to stop by Marnie's memorial service to see what I could find out, even though I dreaded the prospect of visiting the Taylors' home. It would probably feel like walking into the eye of an emotional hurricane.

After dropping off Fergus, I called Riley from my car to coordinate my coverage of the triathlon the next day.

Riley sounded depressed when he came on the line. "Well, Kate, you're going to have lots of company at the triathlon tomorrow," he said. "All of a sudden, the whole friggin' world wants to cover it. A week ago, I was begging celebrities to attend. Now every channel in North Carolina has called, wanting to come. But all they want to talk about is Marnie and Libby. The timing of this thing tomorrow could *not* be worse."

"The best thing you can do right now is to get all the information out as it develops as fast as possible, and then move on," I told him. "Believe me, the media's focus will move on quickly, as long as it doesn't look like you're hiding anything. It's not easy, though, I know."

In response, Riley groaned.

After we hung up, I drove the rest of the way home thinking about the sudden burst of media interest in the triathlon. Fueled by the public's curiosity about Marnie's tragic death, the event was likely to generate major news. And that could spell trouble for me. I'd broken the original story, but going forward there'd be fierce competition for any new information. I needed that like I needed a pack of hyenas nipping at my heels.

Chapter 8

Our Gift from the Rain Forest: The Acai Berry, Nature's Perfect Food

Health experts tell us that the tiny acal berry (pronounced ah-sah-hee) may be nature's most perfect food. Acai pulp is said to have more antioxidants than any other food, and many more disease- and cancer-fighting properties. It's not cheap, and you may have to make a trip to a health food store or gourmet grocer to track it down, but acai is worth It!

—From *The Little Book of Fat-busters* by Mimi Morgan

The sun was peeking over the ridgeline the next morning when Frank and I reached the Great Smoky Mountains in a news van. I rode in the passenger seat, enjoying the way the slanting morning light transformed the mountainscape into a bas-relief of pale greens over deep navy, shot through with occasional waterfalls that appeared as glittering streaks.

When we pulled in to Body Blast just before eight a.m., the small parking lot was already jammed with vehicles.

I pointed through the side window toward the obstacle course, where a sizable crowd had already gathered. "Let's park down there on the field. That looks like it's going to be the center of the action."

"Okay. There's no sign of anyone yet," Frank said,

meaning other media. Then he glanced in the side mirror. "Shit. There's a van from a Raleigh station coming up right behind us. Let's go grab a spot." Without bothering to say *Hold on,* he swerved the van onto the grassy slope that led down to the field.

I clutched the armrest to avoid getting jostled around by the bumpy ride. "Head for that brick wall—they call it The Beast," I said. "That's where they discovered Marnie's body on Friday. So, just to review the game plan: The triathlon coverage today will be the backdrop for my follow-up story on Marnie's death."

"Gotcha."

Off to one side of The Beast, Darwin stood in the middle of a gaggle of women who were dressed in pink T-shirts and matching fatigues.

I tapped on the windshield to point him out to Frank. "While you're taping, I want you to focus on that guy, Darwin Innova. He may play a role in the Marnie angle of my story. I don't think he'll question the attention—he seems like a real show horse."

Frank squinted. "I remember Darwin when he played with the Prowlers," he said. "There was lots of hype when he signed with the team, but then his stats were really crummy. He isn't missed."

I smiled at him. "That's good character background, sports fan," I said. "Is it okay with you if I include that quote from 'an observer'?"

"Be my guest."

I needn't have worried about Darwin shying away from the camera. As we unloaded the equipment, he broke away from the pink-clad women.

"Kate!" Darwin approached me with an extended hand and a show of teeth. "It's great to see you again."

"Under much better circumstances this time," I said, meaning Marnie.

"Oh, of course." Darwin's smile faltered, then

glowed bright again. "You're going to be in my Pink Brigade today—our team is all women." He handed me some folded clothing and pointed to a tent that was set up across the field. "You can change over there. We're going to be competing against Erica's Evil Men and Hillary's Huffers."

"Sounds like fun." I looked around for Riley, but didn't spot him. Erica and her team were chanting a military-sounding marching ditty while jogging around a track that circled the field. In the distance on the far side of the field, I saw Hillary giving a pep talk to her Huffers team, who were dressed in blue and appeared to be made up of relative slackers, including a roly-poly weatherman I recognized from the town of Lumberton.

I headed toward the tent to change into my uniform. After dropping my clothing into a plastic bin that had my name on it, I discovered to my horror that the pink T-shirt Darwin had given me was a size medium. My double-D breasts are a medium the way a pair of cantaloupes are a medium-sized serving of fruit. At least the fatigues were roomy enough.

I tugged the T-shirt over my head, then studied the snug results in a narrow mirror that was propped against a supporting pole of the tent.

"Yikes." I was horrified by the fact that Frank was going to tape me exercising in this getup, which had obviously been designed for hiding out in a basket of pink Easter Peeps.

In the mirror, I saw the tent flap behind me open. A square of light spilled onto the ground.

"Kate?" I turned at the sound of a familiar voice.

Durham Ledger reporter Lainey Lanston stood in the opening to the tent. She was holding back the fabric flap with one hand.

"Hi, Lainey," I said. "Are you competing in the triathlon today?"

"No way." She dropped the flap behind her, then stepped farther into the tent. The reporter's dark hair was sleeked severely off her face, and as usual, she had a pen tucked behind her ear. I suspected that the pen was meant to remind people that every conversation with Lainey Lanston was on the record.

She did a double take at my outfit, then added, "Print reporters don't like to compromise their journalistic integrity by becoming part of something ridiculous like a celebrity triathlon."

"Oh, I thought print reporters didn't participate because they're not celebrities. It's good to know that it's all about ethics."

One corner of her mouth twisted up. "You're always quick with a comeback, Kate. I like that about you." She plucked the pen from behind her ear. "And by the way, that was an interesting story you broke the other night about those women's deaths here at the camp. It was a little light on details, but I guess that's par for the course for TV news."

When I responded with a shrug, she said, "I've been doing a little digging, and I've turned up an interesting new angle on that story. It'll be on the front page tomorrow."

I wasn't going to rise to the bait by asking her what she'd learned. "Well, now that I broke the original story, bully for you for doing a follow-up." I brushed past her, then threw aside the flap on my way out of the tent.

I stalked back across the field, steaming most of the way. But I couldn't help feeling a niggling worry about what Lainey was going to report the next day.

By the time I made it back to my team, more TV vans and trucks had arrived. Each crew had staked out a spot along the perimeter of the sports field.

Darwin was deep in conversation with a tiny blond

woman I recognized. It was my good friend, Mimi Morgan.

Mimi broke into a wide smile when she spotted me. "Kate!" She eased away from Darwin, then bounded in my direction. "I didn't know you were going to be here," she said, wrapping me in an enthusiastic hug. "But then, I didn't know *I* was going to be here until yesterday. I can't believe my producers roped me into doing this gig. But hey, it's all for charity. Aren't these pink fatigues insane?"

I hugged her back and said, "On me, yes, but they actually look cute on you."

Of course, *everything* looked cute on size-two Mimi. We'd known each other since working together at a station in Boston. Back in our Boston days, I was an investigative producer and Mimi was the noonday anchor. Now she'd hit the big time as the host of a morning talk show in Atlanta.

In addition to being a dynamo and a close friend, Mimi was my personal Yoda of dieting wisdom. She'd once lost a ton of weight to get her first job in television, and she was always updating me with her latest tips and tricks for staying fit, which we jokingly called *The Little Book of Fat-busters*.

Mimi rolled her eyes at Darwin, who'd already surrounded himself with another female gather-thon. "That guy really thinks he's God's gift to women, doesn't he?"

"Yep, he's definitely a hound dog."

I wanted to catch Mimi up with everything that was going on, but we were interrupted by the shriek of a whistle. Darwin, Erica, and Hillary were lining up their teams for the first event.

Mimi looked at me. "Are you ready for the Jack-off Challenge?"

"Sounds dirty. What is it?"

"We do jumping jacks until we drop. The last person standing wins." She made a birdlike flapping motion with her arms. "I'm supercharged for it—I drank a bunch of acai berry juice this morning."

I glanced down at my T-shirt. "Uh-oh. My chest isn't exactly built for jumping jacks. On me, they should be called flapping stacks."

Mimi giggled. "I'm sure you're exaggerating, Kate."

I'm sure I wasn't.

I was an early casualty of the Jack-off Challenge, barely making it through fifty jumping jacks before collapsing to the ground in a heap. Mimi went strong into the final rounds, until it was just her squared off in a duel against one of Erica's Evil Men, an anchorman from Charlotte who had the muscular neck and shoulders of a Marine. Most people would have put their money on Anchorman to win, but Mimi kept going like a pink Energizer Bunny. After another hundred jumping jacks, Anchorman began to look winded—he was obviously a sprinter, not a marathoner. Mimi was the last one standing.

My best event was the Yoga Challenge, which put us through a series of poses at a breakneck pace. Most of the men on Erica's team were clueless and bendless, so they were quickly eliminated for bad form. Hillary's Huffers also went down in short order. Mimi was immune from the challenge because she'd won the Jack-off, so I actually had a fighting chance. I wasn't the most in-shape person by any means, but my yoga form was decent.

Eventually, everyone was eliminated except for me and a fellow team member, a woman who seemed to have limbs made out of elastic.

I met my Waterloo with a death-defying pose called the Scorpion Handstand. If you can pull off that move, which requires you to do a handstand and then arch backward until you're essentially standing on top of your own head, congratulations—you can join Cirque du Soleil. Elastic Woman couldn't master the move, either, but at least she managed to get into a decent handstand before pancaking to earth.

Erica let out a shrill blast with her whistle to indicate that I'd been eliminated.

By the time the triathlon teams lined up for the Trail Run, my strained ankle had started acting up. So when Darwin fired the starter's pistol, I faked a jog for a while, then gave up and slowed down to a shameless walk. The running pack soon zoomed past me. By the time the last dregs of Hillary's Huffers had left me in their wake, I was hobbling alone on the deserted trail.

To my right, a row of evergreens flanked the path. Beyond the trees lay a sunny, open area with guest bungalows. I recognized a distinctive pair of Carolina hemlocks behind one of the buildings—they marked the window of the room that I'd shared with Marnie.

I stared at the trees and wondered whether the smoker who had visited Marnie on the night she died might have used this trail to access our window.

Pivoting right, I plunged through the trees. The air was quiet except for the squish of my feet pressing into a spongy carpet of dried pine needles.

I looked on the ground for tracks, or for any other sign that someone had cut through these woods recently. It was difficult to see clearly, because the overhead canopy of branches blocked most of the light.

I was still searching when I heard a soft footfall behind me. Someone was moving quietly through the woods.

I ducked behind a loblolly pine, then realized how stupid that was—the tree's narrow trunk was only half my width.

The footsteps came closer. I was debating whether to scream or run when I heard a voice.

"Kate? Kate, are you here?" Hillary emerged into a nearby clearing. She had a medical kit slung over her shoulder.

"I'm over here," I called to her.

"Oh, thank goodness." Hillary approached me with a worried expression. "I was following behind the runners and saw you limping, then stepping off the trail. Are you okay?"

"I'm fine, thanks—I was just checking something out."

There was no point in telling Hillary what I was up to, so I quickly added, "Have you seen Riley, by any chance?"

"Riley?" Hillary looked confused. "I saw him head for his office a little while back. Are you sure you're—"

"I'm really fine, but thanks for checking up on me." I beat a hasty retreat, cutting the rest of the way through the woods. Then I headed in the direction of Riley's office.

When I knocked on Riley's door, there was no response. It was only after I called out his name a couple of times that the door slowly opened.

Riley grabbed me by the hand and pulled me inside his office. "You're the only reporter I'm letting within a hundred yards of me today, Kate," he said with a wan expression on his face. "I'm hiding out from everyone else."

"I'm so sorry. What's going on?"

Riley grimaced. "I just heard this morning that I'm being sued by Marnie Taylor's family. When you add that to the lawsuit by Libby's family, I'm on the string for more than three million dollars in liability right now."

"You've hired a lawyer, right?"

"*Oh,* yeah. And that'll cost another 100K, whether I win or lose the lawsuits."

Behind us, there was a thump on Riley's door.

"Kate? Are you in there?" It was Frank.

When I opened the door, the cameraman stood silhouetted in the doorway.

"Where the heck have you been, girl?" Frank sounded out of breath. "Beatty called. He says there's a lot of hot stuff breaking today. He needs us to bring the van back to Durham, pronto. We'll have to scrap your live shot—he told me we should tape a quick stand-up and then head back. You got everything you need?"

I *didn't* have everything I needed, in fact. I was sure I was missing something important. For one thing, I was worried about what Lainey was going to report in the *Durham Ledger* the next day.

I looked at Riley. "Have you talked to a reporter named Lainey Lanston today, by any chance?"

Riley's eyes widened. "No, but she's one of the reasons I'm hiding out. She left a message on my machine this morning asking me to call her back—said it was urgent, but didn't say what it was. My staff keeps running in here to tell me that she's looking for me. I don't plan to be found."

"What do you think she might want to talk about?"

Riley glanced away. "I have no idea."

I would have pressed him some more, except that Frank was making strangling signs at his neck, to indicate what the news director would do to us if we didn't hustle back to the studio.

So I let the matter drop.

Chapter 9

Two Hours a Week—That's All We Ask

Women who exercise more than two hours per week can drastically reduce their risk of sudden cardiac arrest, according to studies.

Now you know *that we'll spend 120 minutes a week on completely stupid stuff, like watching reality shows. All you have to do is redirect those minutes into aerobic activity, and odds are you'll live longer.*

—From *The Little Book of Fat-busters* by Mimi Morgan

"Gallagher! In my office—*now*!"

I hadn't had time to set down my latte the next morning when Beatty's summons reverberated across the newsroom with enough force to rattle the ceiling tiles. It was the news director's famous bellow, the one he used when his summonee was in deep, deep doo-doo. The Beatty Bellow could strike fear into even the most street-hardened reporter's heart.

A couple of my coworkers prairie-dogged from their cubicles to watch me tramp across the floor of the newsroom to Beatty's office. Others, I knew, were cowering deep in the recesses of their spaces, sending up a prayer of thanks that they weren't Monday morning's victim.

Even though I had no idea what kind of bug Beatty

had up his ass that morning, my heart was beating triple-fast like a hummingbird's by the time I arrived at his door.

"You wanted to see me?" I said, plastering a sick-feeling smile on my face.

"Take a seat." Beatty had that morning's copy of the *Durham Ledger* spread on the desk in front of him. "Imagine my surprise when I read *this.*" He shoved the paper across the desk toward me.

I picked up the newspaper and looked at it. Splashed across the bottom half of the front page was a picture of the previous day's triathlon. The photo showed a wide shot of my ass in pink fatigues, as I toppled over while doing the Scorpion Handstand.

The headline read:

INSPECTORS CITE SAFETY VIOLATIONS AT MOUNTAIN CAMP WHERE WOMEN'S DEATHS OCCURRED

By Lainey Lanston

The article stated that state inspectors had fined Body Blast for numerous safety violations. To make things totally humiliating, the cutline beneath the photo identified me by name. By now, I knew, that photo had been clipped and posted on the wall of every newsroom in the tri-state area.

"Son of a bitch!" I crumpled up the newspaper, then smoothed it out again to reread the article. This was bad—I'd missed an important angle on the story, plus I looked like a blithering idiot on the front page. I imagined Lainey laughing as it rolled off the presses.

Beatty looked at me across his desk. "Whaddaya got to say about this, Gallagher?"

"Well, we ran something different last night. Our story was about the lawsuits against the camp."

"You call lawsuits breaking news?" Beatty made a gargling sound in the back of his throat, like he was about to hawk up a loogie. "And what did you have about the safety violations? Nada. Zilch. *Bubkes*. We pay you to get out front on these stories, Gallagher—to report your stuff with a little pizzazz. Are you not feeling pizzazzy these days? Or did you miss this one 'cause you're all cuddly-cozy friends with the owner of that camp?" The escalating pitch of his rant meant that Beatty was building up to one of his full-blown hissy fits, the stuff of newsroom legend.

I opened my mouth to protest, but Beatty cut me off. "Are you going to be able to get the goods on this story? Maybe I should put Thompson on this assignment, move you over to features for a while."

"I *am* working on a big story—a related story—about Darwin Innova."

"Darwin Innova? I remember him playing in the pros. For the Prowlers," Beatty grunted, turning down his rage from boilover to a show-me simmer. "Whaddaya got on him?"

"I've got the real reason he left the Prowlers team—their management pressured him to leave because he had sex with an underage girl. And I also know that he harassed the first woman who died at Body Blast—Libby Fowler—right before she died. And I witnessed Marnie Taylor coming out of his office crying on the night *she* died. I'm piecing it all together right now."

Beatty's eyebrows rose, which meant I'd gotten his attention. "Well, see if you can work all that into something solid. In the meantime, follow up on this piece the *Ledger* ran, and don't miss anything else." He glanced down at my derriere shot in the newspaper, and added, "And keep your butt off the front page from now on."

"Yessir."

On my way out of Beatty's office, I got buttonholed by Thompson the reporter.

"Hey, did you screw something up?" Thompson's

eyes were glowing with excitement. "You did, didn't you? Don't worry about it—we've all been hauled on the carpet before."

"No, I did not screw anything up," I retorted. "I was just strategizing with Beatty about a story."

God, how I hated Thompson. I especially hated the way he wore lizard-skin boots and faked a Texas drawl, even though he'd grown up in New Jersey.

"Well, I've got the lead story tonight," he declared. "City Council's announcing a new anti-gang program. I just came off an interview with the chief of police. It's gonna be *huge*."

"That's so great, Thompson," I replied with a wide smile. "Did you get that huge scoop off the press release they sent out yesterday?"

He shot me an indignant glare, then turned tail and slunk back to his cubicle. Seconds later came the sound of his Tony Lamas thunking on top of his desk.

God, how I *hated* Thompson.

I spent the rest of the day developing a follow-up story about the safety violations at Body Blast. To get the "goods" on the story, as Beatty would say, I put in a call to Riley.

Riley sounded contrite when he called me back. "I'm sorry, Kate—I would have told you about those violations, except I didn't know what that reporter—Lainey—was calling me about," he said. "Honestly, I think she blew the whole thing way out of proportion. The inspector told us to replace a couple of tiles and fix some carpet in the gym that had gotten worn—that was all."

"That was *all*?"

"Yeah. The newspaper made the report sound like a big deal, but it really wasn't."

Riley faxed me a copy of the inspection report, which supported his claim that only minor violations had been cited at the camp. I felt a gleeful surge in my fingers as I wrote up a script that blew Lainey's "scoop" out of the water. It felt good to correct the record about my friend, and it assuaged some of the guilt I was feeling for having broken the original story about the deaths at Body Blast.

Beatty sat next to me in the newsroom that night when my piece aired, which included a cut shot of the inspection report. When it finished, he patted me on the shoulder without saying anything. The pat meant that I'd been upgraded from newsroom goat to golden girl.

After the six o'clock broadcast that night, I set off for Marnie's memorial service. By the time I hit the road, the sky had already darkened to a deep navy ribbon, with a handful of stars peeping through. In contrast to the previous nights, the air was positively balmy. I reveled in driving with the convertible top down.

I pulled up in front of Marnie's parents' house. "House" was a bit of an understatement. Perched high on a bluff overlooking a golf course, the Taylor home was a sprawling, country French Provincial–style estate that had pale green shutters and a slate-shingled roof. I hadn't realized that Marnie came from such a wealthy background.

A line of globe lights illuminated a white gravel driveway, where several cars were already jammed in. I hunted and pecked along the curb until I turned up a sliver of space between a Mercedes sedan and a Lexus, into which I squeezed the slim TR6. After gripping the steering wheel for a moment to steel myself, I got out and crunch-walked across the gravel to the front door.

A circle of young smokers had claimed a patch of gravel near the looming double doors of the main entrance. Age-wise, they looked like college students—

Marnie's friends, I supposed. I nodded in passing to the smokers, who between drags were draping each other with hugs and leaning into the circle for support, like a tangle of postadolescent puppies.

As I was stepping through the propped-open front door, a whispered voice drifted across my wake— "That's Kate Gallagher, Channel Twelve," the voice said.

I tossed a half smile toward the whisperer, but inwardly groaned—this was one time that I would have preferred to remain completely anonymous.

One thing I wouldn't have to worry about that night was my nemesis, Lainey Lanston. I'd spoken earlier in the day with Fergus, who'd told me that the sports reporter was traveling with his team to cover a big game—there was little likelihood that she would ditch that assignment for a memorial service. There didn't seem to be any other reporters around, either. Cameras were excluded from the memorial service, and that was evidently enough to keep the media pack at bay.

Inside the front hall, two older ladies with black ribbons attached to their lapels greeted me and pointed the way to go. I followed a short corridor to the living room, where Marnie's family sat on a long mohair couch, accepting condolences from a line of mourners. In the middle of the grouping was a man who had a full head of silver hair. I recognized him as Marnie's father—Dr. Hal, Fergus had called him—from having looked him up earlier that day on the Internet. His face was flushed and swollen. A single pillar candle in a tall glass container burned on the coffee table in front of him.

Between quiet, subdued greetings from the mourners, Dr. Hal Taylor erupted in loud statements to the room at large.

"Why did I let her go? *Why?*" he said at one point, his voice rising.

"Don't blame yourself, Hal," a woman to his right urged, squeezing his hand. She looked like an older version of Marnie, only slim and wearing subdued but stylish clothes. I wondered if she was Marnie's mother.

Oh, God, I shouldn't be here, I thought. But it was too late to leave.

When I reached Dr. Hal's side, his eyes were closed. I hesitated, not sure what to do next.

Ahead of me, a man took the hand of Marnie's mother. He held it, saying nothing—it was a moment of silent, sympathetic *presence.* So, feeling intrusive and awkward as hell, I reached for Dr. Hal's hand. I held it gently, not saying anything at first.

Then, finally, I said, "I'm so very, very sorry about your daughter."

Dr. Hal opened his eyes. "Thank you for coming," he said. "Do you work with Marnie at the women's shelter?"

"No, I'm Kate Gallagher," I said, bracing for an outpouring of grief. "I was Marnie's roommate at the camp, Body Blast."

Hal blinked and pulled in my hand and held it close to his chest. "Marnie mentioned you when she called home that last night," he said. "Can you stay awhile? I would like to speak with you a little later on. About . . ."

I could read the unsaid part of that sentence in his eyes. He wanted to know what his daughter's last night on earth had been like.

"Of course."

Hal nodded and released my hand. His eyes closed again.

I moved down the line, greeting the rest of the family, touching their shoulders and saying little. Then I migrated with a flow of people down another hallway to a huge dining room.

Compared to the hushed and mournful atmosphere where the family sat, the dining room felt like a decompression chamber. People were chattering in loud voices, swirling around a long table that was laid out with every type of food imaginable. A couple of people who had just entered the room carried covered dishes, and added them to the spread.

Looking over all that food, I felt a stab of guilt that I'd arrived empty-handed. At the very least I should have brought a Black Forest cake. That would have been just the right thing.

But the crowd in the room probably didn't even notice my cakeless arrival. The audio level around me had reached a high pitch, a nervous roar that was fueled by that overanimated way people have of expressing themselves in the wake of an unexpected death.

"Dreadful, isn't it?"

A brittle voice cut across the din from my left side. It came from a middle-aged woman who had her hair done in a flip-out bob that would have looked more appropriate on a much younger person. She stared disapprovingly at a gelatin carrot ring that had collapsed into shredded orange ruins.

For a second, I couldn't tell whether she was referring to Marnie or the carrot rubble. "Yes, very dreadful," I said nonspecifically, hedging my bets.

"So young," she said, sighing.

Ah. Marnie, not the carrots.

"Much too young," I agreed. "How did you know Marnie?"

"I'm her father's sister-in-law, Flo," she said, extending her hand. "His *ex*-sister-in-law, I guess I should say. Her uncle Charles and I are divorced. But Marnie's still family no matter *what* I think of Charles. And what about you?"

"I haven't met Charles," I said, while depositing a chaste portion of grilled chicken pasta onto a plastic plate.

"No, I mean how did you know Marnie?"

"I was her roommate at the—"

I stopped because Flo's attention had shifted to the far end of the table, where someone was setting down yet another foil-covered dish. Her features froze into an expression of outraged disdain, as if she'd spotted an offering that was even more offensive than the carrot rubble.

"What's this?" she said. "*This* one has plenty of nerve to show up here."

Following her stare, I instantly recognized the person who had set the dish on the table. It was Marnie's boyfriend—her *ex*-boyfriend—Antonio. He wore a black *guayabera*—a traditional Latin-style dress shirt—over dark pants, and his shoulders were slightly hunched. His crabbed-over posture made it seem as if he was expecting bouncers to materialize any second and haul him away from the table.

"I'm *sure* Hal doesn't know he's here." Flo lowered her voice to a stage whisper. "He couldn't stand that boy. Antonio Torres," she said, rolling the double R's in an exaggerated way.

"Why?"

Flo leaned in toward me, nodding her head in a conspiratorial way that made her hair bounce up and down. "Well, for starters, he probably swam across the border," she said. "He's from Guatemala—they're not exactly our kind of people."

I winced at that. My great-grandmother used to tell stories about how Irish immigrants hadn't been "our kind of people" in Boston society, either. Maybe it was because of the family tales about being snubbed by the Louisburg Square set, but I have a natural tendency to identify with cultural underdogs.

Flo scanned the room. "I should find someone . . ."

she said, looking as if she were trolling the crowd for some burly mourners to cart Antonio Torres off the premises.

"Maybe I can talk to him," I interjected. "I think I can probably do it quietly."

Flo raised her eyebrows. But then she nodded with a shrug.

As I approached him, Antonio was pulling the foil off his dish, releasing a plume of spicy beef aroma, mixed with fresh corn.

"That smells wonderful," I said to him.

"My mother's tamales," he said in a small voice, staring down at the dish. "Marnie really loved them." Underneath his black shirt, I noticed, he wore a gold necklace the weight of a bicycle chain. On his right hand was a pinkie ring studded with diamonds.

"Lamento mucho para su pérdida," I said, digging deep into my recent study of Spanish language tapes to express my condolences. "I'm Kate Gallagher, by the way."

"Gracias." Antonio looked confused. "Have we met?"

"I saw you when you dropped Marnie off at the Body Blast camp, a couple of days ago," I explained. "I was her roommate there."

At the word "roommate," Antonio flinched. Silently, he folded the foil into a careful square. Then he nodded.

"She should never have gone to that *maldecido* place," he said. "I should have dragged her back with me to Durham."

"You mean you should have dragged her back that night, when you were talking to her outside our window?" I said. By posing that question so boldly, I was placing all my chips that I was right about the pile of menthol cigarettes I'd found. The kind of cigarettes *he* smoked.

Antonio rocked back as if I'd slapped him with a hot tamale. "You heard us talking?" he said. "Marnie said you were *dormiendo*—dead to the world. What did you hear us saying, anyway?"

"I heard enough," I bluffed, because in fact I hadn't heard a single word. "What I *don't* know is what happened between the time you were there and the time we found Marnie—dead—on the sports field."

Antonio's expression stiffened. His eyes slipped off me and focused on something over my shoulder. "This isn't the right time to talk about it," he said.

I turned to follow his gaze.

Flo was bearing down on us like an avenging succubus-in-law, the wings of her hair lifting in the breeze. She had two unhappy-looking men in tow. Apparently I hadn't evicted Antonio quickly enough, and she'd dragooned some reinforcements.

Planting herself directly in front of Antonio, Flo crossed her arms.

"You have no business being here." Her box-cutter voice sliced across the noise of the crowd. "Haven't you done enough to this family already?"

The crowd around us fell quiet. People faded back, leaving a margin of space around the confronting parties. It was as if a helicopter searchlight had picked out the three of us—Flo, Antonio, and me—bobbing in a sea of mourners wearing black.

Antonio gathered himself. "I came to pay my respects to Marnie's family," he said, with a simple dignity.

"Well, you can take your respects and—"

"And I will thank you very much, on behalf of the Taylor family."

The new voice, deep and authoritative, silenced Flo's raspings. Dr. Hal—Marnie's father—stood framed in the doorway of the dining room, watching us.

Dr. Hal stepped forward. "Someone told me you'd come. You've had a loss too, son, I know." He extended his hand to Antonio.

"Thank you, sir." Antonio's voice cracked as he replied.

Dr. Hal looked at Flo. "My dear, Penney says they could use some help chopping things up in the kitchen," he said. "Would you mind?"

Flo stared down at the rug, her lips pursed. After a long, stiff beat, she said, "Of *course*, Hal." Brushing past us, she flip-bobbed her way out of the dining room.

Hal looked from Antonio to me. "Penney is Flo's ex-husband's new wife," he said, a faint smile appearing on his grief-battered face. "She'll deal with her."

Soon after that, Antonio announced that he was leaving. Avoiding my eyes, he told Dr. Hal that he'd only come to extend his condolences to the family.

I desperately wanted to follow Antonio outside, to learn more about the final conversation he'd had with Marnie on the night she died. But I'd promised Dr. Hal that I'd stay behind to talk with him.

After Antonio left, Dr. Hal turned to me. "Let's talk for a moment outside." He led me through a pair of French doors to a patio and swimming pool area that overlooked the golf course. In the far distance, a handful of diehards were finishing up at a green, backlit by a pool of artificial light.

Dr. Hal and I sat down on a wrought iron bench. Then he stared up at the night sky for a long minute, as if trying to make out a pattern in the stars. "I just can't figure out what happened to our baby girl, Marnie. Beyond all our grief, her mother and I are simply *confused*," he said, still gazing at the stars. "The authorities haven't been able to explain much of anything to us. They seem to think it was some kind of accident, but I'm not at all satisfied with their response so far."

"That's understandable under the circumstances, sir."

Hal looked directly at me. "I've seen your work—I know you're an excellent reporter—is there anything you can tell me about her? About what *really* happened?"

"I don't have anything solid yet," I said. "But believe me, I know the cops are working hard to figure it out."

This seemed like a good opportunity to ask Hal what he knew about Darwin.

"I understand you know the program director at Body Blast, Darwin Innova," I said.

"What?" Hal half turned on the bench to lock eyes with me. "*Darwin* works there? I had no idea," he said, sounding shocked. "Why didn't he let us know? Why didn't he come talk to us yesterday when we went up there?"

"I don't know. You're not in touch with him anymore then?"

Hal shook his head. "The last time I heard from Darwin was seven years ago."

"I heard you and he were fairly close, back then."

"Yes. I *thought* we were, anyway. I was a booster for the university's Alumni Association when he played on the football team. He even spent one summer living in our guesthouse, trying to recover from that knee injury."

"Why did you lose touch?"

Hal shrugged. "I never figured it out," he said. "One day he was staying in our guesthouse, and the next day he just seemed to vanish. I know it hurt Marnie's feelings—he was so protective of her, like a big brother. He always watched over her and her friends while they were swimming."

"How old was Marnie that summer, when Darwin was living here?"

"Let's see, she was twelve, maybe? That's right. Marnie was twelve years old that summer."

I asked Hal about Marnie's friends, thinking that it might be good to talk to them at some point. He gave me the name and number of her best friend, Beth.

"Beth was here earlier, but then she got paged to go deal with some crisis at the women's shelter," Hal said. "She and Marnie worked together there. Marnie was incredibly passionate about that place."

Flo's rantings had made me curious to learn what Hal really thought about Marnie's relationship with her former boyfriend, Antonio. "Flo seemed to feel that you weren't all that keen on Antonio's relationship with Marnie," I said. "What did you think about them being together?"

Hal blew out a sigh. "I wasn't too happy about it, frankly. I thought Marnie was way too young for a serious relationship, and they were from such different backgrounds," he said. "But the young man came to my home to pay his respects. And while he's under my roof, my policy is that he'll receive respect in return."

The stylish woman I'd seen earlier in the living room appeared at Hal's side and slipped her hand through his arm. Her eyes were red and swollen. Hal introduced her as Sylvia, Marnie's mother. Sylvia wore a black velvet ribbon around her neck. Dangling from the ribbon was a three-by-five-inch picture frame.

"This is Marnie at her high school graduation." Sylvia held out the frame with fingers that trembled slightly. It showed a picture of a smiling Marnie in a cap and gown, clutching a bouquet of red roses.

Sylvia turned the picture frame over and added, "And on the other side is a shot of her from a while back. That one was taken when she was twelve."

The picture on the other side of the frame was of

a much younger Marnie. Wearing a miniskirt, she was half-doubled over and grinning into the camera, as if someone had just tickled her. In this younger version, Marnie's figure was sleek—svelte, in fact—and she wore ridiculous earrings and too much eyeliner. But that didn't hide the fact that Marnie had been a total knockout. Lolita-esque, even.

"Marnie was only twelve years old in this shot?" I asked Sylvia.

"Yes, isn't that incredible? Everyone said she looked so much older. This picture was taken just before she put on all that weight, later that year." Her mother sighed. "But I never bugged her about dieting. No matter what her weight was, she was such a beautiful person."

When Hal rose to say good-bye to some guests who were leaving, I requested a picture of Marnie that I might be able to use in a follow-up story. Sylvia retrieved for me another copy of the photo that showed Marnie in her cap and gown.

During my discussion with Marnie's parents, an ill-defined thought had settled down into a dark corner of my brain. It hunkered there, chomping away on a vague idea. But I'd need some solitude to bring its shape into focus.

Still thinking about Marnie's pictures, I said good night to the Taylors, then made my way back to my car.

The streets around the Taylors' posh neighborhood were mostly empty at that hour—obviously all of Durham's CEOs and neurosurgeons were tucked in for the night. Street lighting was apparently unfashionable among the upper crust, so there were pools of pitch black in the wide gaps between homes.

I was starting to get lost when a car with too-bright halogen lights rolled up behind me. The beams pierced my rearview mirror. Annoyed, I flipped on the night filter. Even though I was going at a good clip and there was plenty of room to pass on the left, the car stayed right on my bumper. It was a tailgater.

I debated whether to turn on the flashers and slow down—my usual fuck-you tactic with tailgaters—or speed up.

"Okay, asshole," I said, downshifting. After checking the road, I popped the clutch and simultaneously hit the gas, whipping the car around in an abrupt U-turn. It's a maneuver that's called banging a U-ey in Boston. A bit of overkill for a tailgater, but after the emotional tension at the Taylor home, I felt a serious need to blow off some steam.

As I straightened out the wheel, I heard an engine rev behind me, followed by a squeal of tires burning on asphalt. In the side mirror I watched the other car—it was too dark to tell what kind it was—mirror my one-eighty turn. The halogens zoomed up on my tail again, flashing on and off like two angry lightning bugs in synchronized pursuit. The shrill blast of a horn cut through the air.

My tailgater had caught a bad case of road rage.

He was raging at me.

Chapter 10

Exercise and Sex

Let's talk turkey, shall we? Women who exercise have better sex lives, according to the latest research.

Women who are couch potatoes think about having more sex. Women who exercise actually have more sex.

'Nuff said.

—From *The Little Book of Fat-busters* by Mimi Morgan

The headlights flashed again, punctuated by more horn blasts. I felt vulnerable because my car's convertible top was down—if this punk cut me off, he might spring out from his car and attack me. I briefly considered returning to the Taylor home. But then I remembered a security post I'd passed on the way into the neighborhood. I decided to head back there and get some help. But first I'd have to get myself unlost.

Power-shifting again, I shot forward, then proceeded to lead my halogen harasser in a good imitation of Mr. Toad's Wild Ride. Dogged every foot of the way by the chase lights, I careened through the dark, empty streets. After a near miss with someone's mailbox, I finally spotted the security area ahead.

The halogens faded back into the darkness as I pulled in front of a guard shack, which was bathed in a comforting halo of light. Through a window, I spotted a guy in uniform reading the newspaper. He lowered his feet and the paper when I hit the horn, then came out with a concerned look on his face.

I flung open the car door. "I think someone's following me," I said, gasping for breath.

"What did he—"

The security guard broke off as a black Escalade—with ultrabright halogen lights—emerged from the darkness behind us. It rolled to a gentle stop behind my TR6.

I recognized the driver behind the wheel. It was Antonio. His window was partway rolled down, and he stuck his arm through it and started waving it.

"I just want to talk to you for a second," he called out to me. His palm was turned up, almost like a pleading gesture.

Scowling, the security guard reached for a radio on his belt. "Is that the guy who was chasing you?" he said.

I stared at Antonio for a moment, then turned to face the guard. "Wait a second," I said. "You know what? I think this may have been a misunderstanding. Can you just stand by while I talk to him?'

"Lady, I spend my whole life just standing by," the guard said. He shot Antonio a not-our-kind-of-people look that would have made Flo proud.

"All right, thanks," I said.

I approached the SUV. "You just scared the hell out of me, Antonio," I said, inhaling an acrid whiff of menthol cigarettes. "Why did you come after me like that?"

Antonio cast a wary glance at the guard, who'd rooted himself a few feet away, his right hand hanging near the radio at his hip.

"I was waiting for you in my car outside Marnie's house and fell asleep for a second," he said. "Then I saw you driving away and followed you."

"Why?"

Antonio kept a tight grip on the steering wheel. "To explain," he said. "What you heard by the window between Marnie and me that night—it's not what you think."

That's when I realized why Antonio had chased me down, wanting to "talk." He thought I'd overheard his midnight conversation with Marnie. If what he'd said had been incriminating, he might be afraid I was going to report it to the police.

He thinks I know something. The thought raised goose bumps on the back of my neck.

"Okay, then. So tell me exactly what your conversation meant."

Antonio rubbed the side of his brow as if a sudden migraine had come on. "I'm *Guatemalteco*. From Guatemala. People from my country are *apasionado* . . . we have strong feelings, you know?" he said after a moment.

When I nodded, he continued. "When Marnie broke up with me, I got angry. But I never would hurt her. *Nunca, nunca*. Not ever."

"But she *did* get hurt, didn't she?"

Antonio bent his head and stared at his lap. "Yes," he said. "But not by me. Not to hurt her body, anyway."

"What do you mean, not her body?"

A dark flush crept up the side of Antonio's neck. "Well, I know my words hurt her. That night, I was so angry. I told her that no other man in the world would ever love a . . ."—he swallowed hard—". . . *un puerco gordo*."

From my Spanish tapes, I knew what *puerco gordo* meant—"fat pig."

"Jesus," I whispered. In perhaps her last conversation on earth, Marnie's boyfriend had called her a

Porky Pig. But had he done something even worse than that to her?

Antonio rested his forehead against the steering wheel. "I've been to the priest many times. I've asked God to forgive me," he said. "But even if He does, I can never forgive myself."

Antonio's words sounded heartfelt, but they weren't convincing. Something Marnie had said about Antonio ricocheted through my head.

He's Mr. Nice Guy until he doesn't get what he wants, she had told me. *Then he acts like what he really is—a bully.*

Looking past Antonio into the car's interior, I caught the outline of a black handle resting on the carpeted floor of the passenger side. The handle was attached to a compact, lethal-looking pistol. From my days spent shooting on the police practice range with my father, I recognized it as a Beretta Cougar. It was an extremely expensive model, known for its light kickback and accuracy.

Antonio has a gun! screamed through my brain. Reflexively, I glanced toward the security guard, only to discover that he'd abandoned his vigil and wandered back to his newspaper inside the shack. A taut, palpable tick of time clicked by. An image of the guard shack's window being blown apart by gunfire swam before my eyes.

A trickle of sweat ran down my right palm. "So after you spoke to Marnie outside the window that night, you just left the camp?" I forced my voice to stay level. I didn't dare let my eyes go to the gun again.

Antonio lifted his face to look at me. "I drove straight back to Durham. Do the police . . . do they think someone killed her?"

"The police seem to be treating it as an accident so far."

Antonio focused on my eyes. "And you. Do *you* believe it was an accident?"

"I'm a reporter, not a cop. Their opinion is the one that counts."

Antonio's eyes narrowed. The look of a penitent seeking absolution vanished, replaced by a jet of flame. "Then since you're not a cop, I suggest you keep out of their business," he said.

"Actually, Marnie *did* tell me that you drove her up there to the camp because you had business in the mountains," I responded. "Exactly what kind of business are you in, Antonio?"

After a pause, he said, "Construction. I lay Sheetrock."

"Ah." How could a Sheetrocker afford to tote around a high-end pistol, plus drive a sixty-thousand-dollar SUV? Not to mention the thick gold chain he had hanging around his neck.

Antonio said quietly, "What else did Marnie tell you about me?"

"She didn't tell me all that much. Just that you lied to her about a few things."

His fingers tightened on the wheel. "Like what?"

"She wasn't specific. What's to tell?"

"There's nothing to tell. I never lie."

"Then there's nothing she could have told me, is there?"

Antonio shifted back in his seat, like a trigger being cocked. After a tense silence, he said, "It's unwise for you to play games with me, *chica. Tenga cuidado.*"

"I'll take that under advisement."

With a hard stare, Antonio pushed a button on his armrest. The tinted window glass closed silently between us. When his face disappeared behind the black glass, the SUV's engine revved. Then it took off with a burn of rubber.

Tenga cuidado: Antonio had said, "Be careful." It was a warning.

And the gun was a threat.

The message light on my answering machine was blinking when I arrived home. I'd driven straight back following my encounter with Antonio, trembling most of the way.

The voice mail was from my boyfriend, Lou. He'd seen me on cable TV and surmised that I was back in town.

Lou's message sounded warm and affectionate as he asked me to call him back. The message was full of his usual Lou-energy, but there was an unmistakable subtext: *Why hadn't I called?*

With a surge of guilt, I tapped in his number. In my haste, I fat-fingered the numbers and had to dial again.

"Hey, gorgeous," Lou said, picking up. "You're back?"

"Oh, yeah," I said. "I'm sorry I didn't call before—I got caught up in developing updates for the show. I've been running around like a mad hamster."

My explanation sounded weak, so I covered by launching into the saga of Marnie Taylor's death.

"Hal Taylor's daughter has died? That's terrible. I met him and his wife at a couple of AMA functions," Lou said. "I'll send them flowers tomorrow."

So Lou knew the Taylors, if only slightly. Was there anyone he *didn't* know? It was an intimidating thought. Lou was a few years older than me, and wildly successful in his law practice. It always seemed as if he was light-years ahead of me in terms of experience and contacts. Relatively speaking, I was the promising young student, but he was always the teacher. I was afraid I might never catch up.

"So are you done now with that story about the

Little Camp of Horrors?" Lou asked, after I described what I'd been doing.

"Not yet. I'm looking into a new angle to that story that's really interesting. A second woman from Durham—Libby Fowler—died during a hiking trip at the same camp last October. I've heard that the cops think she was murdered. From the little digging I've already done, I'm wondering if there might be a connection between the two deaths—Marnie's and Libby's, I mean."

I held my breath, waiting for Lou to announce that he knew *Libby's* family, too. But he didn't. Instead, there was a pause.

"Sounds a bit far-fetched, doesn't it?" he said.

"Far-*fetched*?"

Lou's chuckle crackled over the line. "Hold on," he said. "Don't get your dander up. You really think there's a serial killer in the mountains, preying on weekend Amazons?"

"I'm not *saying* that both women were murdered, or even one of them," I snapped. "But I have to report the story. That's my job. Jesus, Lou, give me a break, will you?"

My words tumbled into a little crevice of silence. I'd never snapped at Lou before. I'd never even *felt* like snapping, in fact. But there it was.

I expected Lou to sound hurt. Instead—and this was even worse, because it sounded dismissive—he laughed again.

"Well, I'm sure Beau Kellerman's ace investigative reporter knows precisely what she's doing," he said easily. Beau Kellerman was the general manager of my station, WDUR-TV Channel Twelve. Beau was someone *else* Lou knew, of course. They played golf together in exotic places like Scotland.

When I didn't respond, he added, "You're usually off on Wednesdays, right? Can I steal you away? My firm's sponsoring a big gala. I'd love to have you by my side."

"Of course," I said in a chastened voice. In fact, it would be difficult to get away from work midweek, but Lou was worth it.

"Great," he said. "I'll have Kurt pick you up in the chopper."

"What time should I meet him at the heliport? Are we just talking about dinner?"

"Actually, how about meeting him at ten a.m.? I'll have a surprise planned for you."

"That sounds exciting," I said. "So what should I wear to the gala?"

"It doesn't matter."

Ooh, but it *did* matter. I'd been to Lou's events before. They always drew out Atlanta's social luminaries. And the female luminaries—especially the trophy wives—intimidated the absolute hell out of me. They wore clothes by designers I couldn't even pronounce, much less wear. And their shoes were pointy and spiky enough to serve as lethal weapons. No way could I stay vertical for even ten minutes in those kinds of shoes. Thank God for Ferragamos. They're designer-y enough to pass as "nice" shoes, and they're actually comfortable. Maybe I'd wear my new silk wraparound dress from Saks. With the Ferragamos and my diamond stud earrings (a gift from Lou, of course), I could probably pull it together. I'd have to call Charlene the pet sitter to let her know she was back on duty, as well.

It was weird how I could feel on an equal footing with anyone in the world when I was working as a reporter, but at a disadvantage in party situations. Probably this was because I'd always defined myself through my accomplishments: first school, and then work. Somewhere along the way, I'd neglected to hone the skill of making small talk at social gatherings.

"Word salad" is what I called party chat. But I'd have to learn to enjoy gala parties if I decided to marry Lou. He went to social functions practically every week and seemed to thrive on them, whereas I was always glancing at my watch by nine p.m.

I said to Lou, "I'll have to be back at the studio the day after the party, so—"

"Can't you wrangle the rest of the week off? I have a client dinner Friday night that I want you to come to."

"I'd like to, but the news director is really on my tail about this story right now. I have to go back to Body Blast this weekend, in fact."

"I think you could get away if you really wanted to. I could square it with your big boss, Beau."

I winced. "No, *please* don't talk to the GM of the station about me. Even if you two are golfing buddies, trust me, management doesn't think kindly of boyfriends writing absence notes for their reporters."

"Well, is it okay if I ask for a little more flexibility on your part, going forward?"

"Meaning?"

"Meaning sometimes your work consumes you at the expense of everything else."

"Ouch." I paused. "Do you think that's fair, Lou?"

"Well, think of it from my angle. I have a very demanding career, but I always try to put you first."

"I know you do, and I love you for that." I felt a surge of warmth in my cheeks. "But Lou, you call the shots because you own your firm. I'm just a worker bee, with a bad-ass queen for a news director. But now that I know how you feel, I'll work on it, okay?"

Lou sighed. "Okay, Ms. Independence," he said. "I'll see you on Wednesday."

We said good-bye without our ritual exchange of I love yous. I prepared for bed, then tossed and turned, chewing over my conversation-gone-wrong with Lou.

I didn't like the way it made me feel—Lou didn't seem to understand what it was like to have to claw one's way up the career ladder.

Rejecting that uncomfortable train of thought, I returned to the computer in the dining room to do some research on Marnie's boyfriend, Antonio Torres. When I entered his name in a search, I got back a gazillion hits. The links mostly went to Spanish language sites, and few provided useful information, much less pictures. I realized I wouldn't be able to get usable information about the man unless I had more to go on. I cursed myself for not having memorized his license plate during our run-in that evening.

Now, drop-dead tired but still not sleepy, I threw myself across my bed. After a purring Elfie settled herself into the crook of my shoulder, I zoned out while watching a cable news program.

Around two a.m., I awoke to the blasting sound of a TV commercial that was hawking some kind of a roll-on headache potion. By the time I fumbled through the sheets and dug up the clicker, the TV had switched to a program called *To Catch a Predator*.

In that night's episode, the program's host and the police were lying in wait for a twenty-something male who thought he'd set up a date over the Internet with a thirteen-year-old girl.

As the police swooped onto the would-be molester and handcuffed him, I thought of Marnie's picture from when she was twelve, and how gorgeous she'd been. And about how Darwin had been living at the family's guesthouse that summer, "lifeguarding" her at the pool. About how he'd resigned from the Prowlers team after getting involved with a fourteen-year-old girl. And about how, soon after he mysteriously vanished from the Taylors' lives, Marnie had piled on weight.

The darkling thought that had been lurking in the

back of my mind ever since Marnie's memorial service stepped forward into the bluish glow of the television set.

What I thought I saw was disturbing: When Marnie was twelve years old, Darwin had molested her.

Chapter 11

Risky Business

Psychologists used to believe that risk-takers—especially in sports—suffered from a mental disorder. They couldn't fathom why anyone would willingly expose herself to risk.

Nowadays, we understand that most risk-takers are emotionally stable. Risk-takers seek to master particular areas in life—including business—by pitting their skills against calculated odds. By testing themselves in order to master a goal, risk-takers achieve a high degree of satisfaction. They are often extremely successful in their careers.

So you go for it, girl—take a risk!

—From *The Little Book of Fat-busters* by Mimi Morgan

The next morning, I sipped coffee with nonfat creamer at the kitchen table, with my thoughts still focused on Darwin. If he had molested Marnie, that would have been when she was *twelve years old*, for God's sake. Could he really be such a monster?

While my brain thrummed along those lines, I did a scan of the morning paper. The *Ledger*'s editors hadn't bothered to correct the misleading article that Lainey had written the day before about the inspections at Body Blast. True to form for most news media, they were simply going to ignore the fact that they had run a hatchet job.

My cell phone beeped to indicate that I had a new message. My father had left me a voice mail to ask whether I'd seen a network news story about how to escape from an automobile that was trapped underwater. Dad said he was sending me an escape tool by express mail. It would be useless to remind my father that I drove a convertible—he'd just tell me to keep the tool in my purse in case I needed to escape from someone *else's* car.

I smiled and tried not to roll my eyes. My father was forever sending me these types of warning messages and missives. One time, when I took a cruise around the Hawaiian Islands, he'd sent me instructions for escaping from a volcano, just in case the Haleakala volcano happened to erupt during my eight-hour excursion trip to Maui.

I knew he issued all the warnings out of love and concern for me—my dad had turned into a world-class worrywart at about the time my mother died when I was young—but sometimes I wondered whether all his pressure for me to "stay safe" had actually contributed to my becoming something of a risk-taker.

I started my research for the day by calling Beth, Marnie's friend, whose number I'd gotten from her father.

When Beth answered her cell phone, she told me that she was volunteering that day at the women's shelter where Marnie had also worked. The shelter was called Rescue Retreat. At first she refused my request to come to the shelter to talk with her about Marnie.

"We don't publicize the location of the shelter," she explained. "We have to keep it a secret so that the women here feel safe."

I assured Beth that I wouldn't bring a crew, or even

divulge the shelter's existence in any of my stories. After a tough back-and-forth negotiation, she finally gave me the address.

Rescue Retreat was located in a residential section of Durham that could best be described as "struggling." Housed in an old converted Victorian, the shelter was surrounded by a cinder-block wall, which was topped off by coils of barbed wire. Security cameras dangled from the gingerbread trim of the peaked roof. The overall effect was a bit like an elderly lady who had taken up martial arts after being mugged.

After parking along the street and getting buzzed in through a daunting maze of gates and Plexiglas barriers, I stepped into the backyard.

Inside the grounds of the shelter, bedlam reigned. A half-dozen toddlers were playing and rolling around a grassy area that looked like it had been scavenged by goats; they were being watched over and occasionally screamed at by a group of tired-faced women who sat in an assortment of mismatched chairs on the deep-set back porch.

A young woman who had been folding clothes got to her feet as I advanced up a cement walkway toward the house. She was dressed conservatively with a green silk scarf covering her hair.

"I'm Beth," she said, offering me her hand but no smile. "You're Kate Gallagher? You look different on TV."

I never knew whether that remark was a compliment or a slam. "Yes, hi. I'm Kate," I said. "Thanks for letting me meet you here."

Beth waved in the general direction of the chairs on the porch. "I'll be just a minute. We're about to put the kids down for a nap," she said. "Have a seat. If you can find one, that is."

I glanced around. Every chair on the porch that

wasn't already occupied was piled high with toys, odd pieces of clothing, and packages of diapers. But then a space opened up as a couple of women rose and started herding the children inside the house, followed by Beth.

I smiled tentatively at a frizzy-haired woman who was sitting in a rocking chair. She nodded back, but her expression was so sad and preoccupied that I didn't venture any small talk. What would one say as an icebreaker at a shelter, anyway? *What are you on the run from?*

Minutes later, Beth returned to the porch. She swept the toys and packages of diapers off a ladder-backed chair, then sat down.

As if by an unspoken signal, the frizzy-haired woman rose from her rocking chair and shuffled inside, leaving Beth and me alone. With all the children gone from the yard, the atmosphere on the porch felt oddly muted. Afternoon light peeked through a bit of gingerbread trim that edged the porch's overhang, throwing a snowflake pattern of sun dapples at our feet.

I expected Beth to lay down some ground rules for our discussion. When she didn't, I got straight to my questions. "So, I'm just trying to learn more about Marnie Taylor for my story about her. Were you and she friends for a long time?"

Beth nodded. "We were friends ever since the third grade," she said. "But we really became close friends in the ninth, when we both started volunteering here, at Rescue Retreat."

"The shelter here seems like such important work. How did you and Marnie start volunteering at such a young age?"

Beth picked up a teddy bear that had fallen to the floor. She sat it in her lap. "Marnie and I went to a private high school that made you do community service. They gave us credit for it," she said. "But Marnie really got into it. She wanted to make a career working with abused women, especially young girls. She brought me into the program."

"Why did Marnie want to work with abused young girls in particular, do you think?"

Beth looked away. "I think she had her reasons."

"I think she had her reasons, too, Beth."

Beth shifted her gaze to the bear in her lap. "Maybe."

When she didn't add anything else, I leaned in. "I respect the work you do here, Beth, so I'm going to be very direct. I've been wondering whether Marnie experienced some abuse, herself, when she was young. In fact, I suspect that something happened between Marnie and Darwin Innova—the former pro football player—when she was twelve years old."

Carefully, Beth set the bear back on the floor. "Marnie made me promise never to tell," she said, avoiding my eyes.

I placed my hand gently on top of hers. "Beth, Marnie's dead. You don't have to keep silent anymore."

She didn't reply, so I continued, "It's not just Marnie's past with Darwin that I'm looking into—I'm also trying to find out whether he had anything to do with her death."

"What?" Beth looked at me with a horrified expression. "You mean, you're thinking that Darwin might have *killed* her?"

When I nodded, she let out a little sob. "Oh, God. Marnie's dad told me she died in an accident. Wasn't it an *accident*?"

"It might have been. But I saw Marnie with Darwin just a few hours before she died. She was crying when she left the office. She was very upset, but she wouldn't talk about what happened."

"Oh, God. *God.*" Beth buried her face in her hands.

I waited.

After a moment, she said, "Marnie went to that camp to get in shape—it was just so she could get into that stupid sorority. I kept telling her, 'Would you *forget* about the Tri Kaps, already?' Now look what happened to her. It's so horrible."

"Beth, please tell me—what took place between Marnie and Darwin when she was twelve years old? Did he hurt her in any way at all?"

With her hands still covering her eyes, Beth nodded. "Marnie was terrified that her dad would kill Darwin, if he knew what happened back then."

"Did Darwin molest her?"

Beth lowered her hands from her face. Avoiding my eyes, she stared out at the lawn without blinking, as if looking into the past. "Darwin was living at her family's guesthouse that summer," she said. "Even though she was only twelve, Marnie was convinced she was in love with him." She looked at me. "Can you imagine? A twelve-year-old who thought she was in love. How ridiculous."

"It's dangerous when a predator takes advantage of those feelings," I said.

Beth nodded vehemently. "That's exactly what Darwin was, a *predator*," she said. "He was twenty-three, for God's sake. But Marnie thought they were going to get married or something. Then one day, Darwin just up and disappeared. After that, Marnie gained a lot of weight and got kind of depressed. But everything turned around when she started doing community service here. That's when she realized that the whole situation with Darwin had been wrong."

"Did you know that Darwin works at the camp where Marnie died?"

Beth's eyes widened. "I *did* know that," she said. "She called me from the camp that night. Oh, my God, she was totally freaked. She finally confronted this jerk after all these years, and he just blew her off. After everything he did to her, he had the nerve to treat her like she was some kind of pest. Like she was *stalking* him."

I remembered that Marnie had been making a call on her cell phone when I left the room the night she died. It must have been Beth whom she had called.

"Do you know if Marnie was planning to see Darwin again later that night? On the night she died?"

Beth shook her head. "No, she was talking to me about filing charges against Darwin, even though it was so many years later," she said. "I thought she should go for it—I mean, after all, they charge priests years after the fact, right?"

"So no one has ever reported what Darwin did to her back then?"

"No. When you're that young, you don't know what to do, right? Neither Marnie nor I did, anyway. She was so terrified that she'd get Darwin in trouble. But *he* was trouble. He took her childhood away. And when it was over, she just wanted to forget about the whole thing, to put it behind her. She also felt guilty, like it was all her fault somehow."

"*Her* fault? Meaning . . . ?"

"The summer it happened, Marnie and a couple of the girls in our group were raiding their parents' liquor cabinets, getting a little crazy. She thought she brought it on herself. It was just a passing phase, but she ended up really getting hurt."

Beth leaned forward and looked into my eyes. "Do you really think it's possible that Darwin killed her?" she asked me. "Marnie's dad told me it was an *accident*. I didn't think—"

"If someone killed her, I'm hoping the police will look at Darwin as a suspect."

I felt a renewed rush of sorrow for Marnie, who'd

endured sexual abuse from Darwin, and then, years later, verbal abuse from Antonio. She'd spent her adolescent years trying to help other girls, only to have her own life snuffed out at an early age.

A quiet, steely resolve hardened in the marrow of my bones. No matter what else happened, I resolved to see to it that Marnie's story was told. After I informed the police about her experience with Darwin, I'd tell the world on the nightly news. I didn't have enough evidence—yet—to accuse Darwin of murder. But with Beth's interview and Fergus's information about Darwin's being forced off the Prowlers due to an affair with an underage girl, I had more than enough to expose the bastard for the vermin that he was.

The police, I soon discovered, had zero interest in my theories about Darwin.

Driving home from my meeting with Beth, I put in a call to the SBI's Raleigh headquarters to find out who was in charge of the investigation into Marnie's death. From my work on previous crime stories, I had a couple of contacts over there. However, I was dismayed to learn that one of them had retired, and the other was away on vacation.

I had one other cop contact—a Durham homicide detective named Jonathan Reed. But he was local, not the SBI. Plus, our connection was complicated on a personal level. Six months earlier, Jonathan and I had started a fledgling "thing" that had sent me into raptures at the time. But then our romance had mysteriously fizzled away. After all this time, it would feel much too awkward to call on him. And anyway, the last time I checked, I'd heard that Jonathan, who was originally from the UK, had returned home for an extended visit.

I called the operator at the SBI, who routed me to

the Community Relations office; I wound up talking to a peppy-voiced young guy who sounded like a recent graduate of the Dale Carnegie School of Public Relations. He promised to find out who was working on Marnie's investigation and get back to me. Like *that* would happen anytime this century.

But PR Dale surprised me. By the time I returned home to my apartment, I had a message on my landline's answering machine from someone at the SBI—an investigator named Powell—returning my call. Powell's gruff-sounding message made it sound like I had better have a damned good reason for burning up his precious investigator's time.

When I called Powell back, a receptionist put me on hold. Elfie had jumped onto my lap and curled up by the time I heard the sound of being clicked through.

"Powell here."

I was startled to hear some pops of gunfire in the background. He must have been standing near a firing range. "Hi, Investigator Powell, this is Kate Gallagher," I began. "I'm with—"

"Channel Twelve, I know. You called about that girl who died in the mountains this week? Marnie Taylor?"

"Yes. I discovered some information that—"

"Before you get started, let me just tell you that you can save your camera batteries. I've seen your work. This isn't your kind of story."

"Why not?"

"You cover murders, right?"

"Among other things, yes. Are you saying that Marnie Taylor wasn't murdered?"

"On the record? I can't say anything."

"Well, let me tell you what I've learned, and then perhaps I can just get a confirmation from you." I launched into explaining what I'd learned about

Darwin—that he'd molested Marnie when she was twelve years old, and that she'd confronted him about his past behavior just before she died. "I talked to a friend of Marnie's who knew about their relationship at the time," I explained. "And I have paperwork proving that Darwin had an affair with another underage girl. That affair was the reason he had to leave the Prowlers football team."

The only sound coming from the other end of the line was more gunshots, so I plunged ahead. "And I've learned that there was another girl who died last October during a camping hike—Libby Fowler. Turns out she complained to the owner of Body Blast—the day before she fell down a ravine to her death—that Darwin harassed her. What do you think about all that?"

"I'm afraid I'm not at liberty to share what I think with you, Ms. Gallagher. But just in case you're worried, please rest assured that we're able to handle our own cases here at the SBI, including the deaths of Ms. Marnie Taylor and Ms. Libby Fowler."

I didn't have a pair of fishing boots high enough to wade through the exaggerated politeness in Powell's reply, so I cut to the chase. "But isn't it true that you're investigating both women's deaths? I just need a confirmation of that for the story I'm working on."

"Both cases remain open." Powell's tone took on an annoyed edge. I suspected he hadn't meant to say anything about Libby's death. "And that's all I can tell you, frankly."

And frankly, that's a whole lot of not much, came my thought-retort.

"Just 'open'? Or under investigation as suspicious?" I pressed.

"Both cases—Marnie Taylor's and Libby Fowler's—

are *open*. That's all I can confirm. And that's all I have time for today, Ms. Gallagher."

I heard a pop in my ear. Whether that was another burst of gunfire or Powell hanging up on me, I couldn't tell.

I sat for a moment and stroked Elfie's fur. She blinked up at me, her blue eyes glowing like aquamarines in the late afternoon sun that streamed through the window sheers.

Although getting information from Investigator Powell had felt like trying to pull out someone's teeth sans Novocain, at least I'd gotten him to confirm that the SBI had open cases for both Marnie's and Libby's deaths. Getting confirmation from reluctant officials, even of minor facts, is often the most grueling part of the reporting job.

Next, I put in a call to Riley, to arrange my return trip to Body Blast that weekend.

When he came on the line, Riley sounded so depressed that I decided not to add to his burden right then by telling about the information I was developing about Darwin. After all, I didn't have anything solid yet. Sharing my theories about Darwin might only ring false alarm bells. Instead, we talked about Riley's boyfriend, Khan.

I said, "Things were so crazy while I was there for the triathlon that I never asked you what happened with Khan and those files you were worried about, the ones that were missing. Did they ever turn up?"

"Khan had them," Riley said. "He said he was reviewing them so that he could go over them with me."

"That's plausible, I guess."

"I don't know." Riley sighed. "Despite all his flaws, I really care about that guy. But I also feel like something's weird with him right now."

Then he added, "By the way, I hired that accountant to go over our books, like you suggested. I should have the results by the time you get back here. I'm afraid Khan didn't take the idea of an audit too well—he's been giving me the silent treatment."

"How can you tell? The man doesn't talk anyway."

At least I managed to make Riley laugh before we hung up.

Chapter 12

The Many Benies of Yoga

Everyone knows that yoga helps you tone your muscles and increase your flexibility. But did you know that yoga also lubricates your joints? Joint lubrication is very important as you get older (and if you don't believe me, just go check out the booming market for glucosamine). And if you love massages, you'll be happy to learn that yoga makes you feel massaged on the inside. There's a reason for that—when you do yoga, you are actually massaging your internal glands and organs, even the prostate (which men will love).

Yoga also helps you rid your body of toxins. What could be better?

So go out and have yourself a Namaste day.

—From *The Little Book of Fat-busters* by Mimi Morgan

Early Wednesday morning, Lou's private helicopter whisked me away to Atlanta. I was too preoccupied to engage in much conversation with the pilot, Kurt. But silence never seemed to trouble Kurt. A man of few words and a military background, he struck me as the kind of guy you'd have to torture to extract a single leaf of word salad.

When I got to Lou's house, a sprawling estate that took up a significant portion of one of Atlanta's seven hills, I learned about the surprise that he had in store for me. As soon as we crossed the threshold of his magnificent master bedroom suite, he marched me into the walk-in dressing room (which was almost the size of my living room back in Durham). A lineup of garment bags hung from hooks on the walls, with exotic-looking fabrics billowing out from the bottom of each bag.

"For me?" I asked, feeling confused.

Lou nodded. "I don't know anything about women's clothes, but I borrowed a fairy godmother who does," he said, waving at the bags. "Cherize?"

A woman who was leggy and tall as a giraffe appeared in the doorway between Lou's dressing room and the bedroom. She wore a smile that seemed to stretch wider than her hips.

"Cherize is a former supermodel who owns the hottest designer boutique in town," Lou said. "She'll get you squared away for the party tonight."

"Well . . ." I murmured, before adding a reluctant "Thank you." To me, trying on clothes in front of a supermodel—former or no—sounded about as appealing as trying on swimsuits in public. Didn't Lou *know* that?

"You're welcome," Lou said, checking his watch with a distracted look. "Come here. 'Scuze us a second, Cherize."

He pulled me into the closet and reached into his pocket, then pulled out a dark blue box that I recognized. It was the engagement ring.

"I know you haven't given me your official answer yet, but could you please wear this tonight? I'm afraid I've already let the cat out of the bag to my partners, and all the wives want to see the bling."

"Oh, you already told them we're getting married? But . . ."

But I haven't accepted yet, a voice wailed in my head.

Lou stared at me. "Whoa," he said. "Are you trying to tell me something? This isn't a turndown, is it?"

"No, no, of course not." All at once, my head fogged up and I couldn't think clearly. Then I added, "Of course. I'll wear the ring tonight." I watched him slip the ring onto my finger. It felt oddly heavy.

Lou kissed me on the cheek. "That's beautiful, sweetie. I'll be the happiest man in town tonight." He checked his watch. "I have to run to a quick meeting right now. But I'm leaving you in good hands." He steered me back into the bedroom toward Cherize, then left.

Cherize looked me up and down. "This is going to be fun," she said. "Why don't you undress, and then let's try on the Galante first."

I pushed away my feelings. "I hate to scare you, Cherize, but I think designer sizes stop where I begin. I'm a fourteen," I said, unbuttoning my blouse. "And even that may be a tad optimistic in the hip zone."

Cherize waved her hand dismissively. "Don't worry about that." Then she let out a gasp that almost made me slide off the chair. "Look at that *ring.*" She snatched up my hand. "I've never seen anything so gorgeous. That's the Lucida setting from Tiffany's, right?"

"I think so," I said. "I mean . . . well, it came in a Tiffany's box."

"Honey child, you have hit the *jackpot.*" Cherize squeezed my hand in a spasm of vicarious joy. "All the deb moms are fit to be tied that you've snagged Lou. Watch out tonight when you turn your back—they'll have their knives out. The Atlanta social set can be pretty scary."

"I'm probably better at handling knives than debutantes."

Cherize disappeared into the dressing room for a second, then came back with the first garment bag. It rustled like taffeta as she unzipped it.

"Keep your eyes closed while I slip this over your head," she ordered.

I closed my eyes obediently. As Cherize guided the dress over my head and shoulders, I wriggled my way up through a tube of netting, feeling like an earthworm doing the shimmy-shaky. Then there was a swishing sound as Cherize arranged another layer of fabric around me.

"Okay, now look in the mirror," Cherize said.

"This thing feels way too . . . *oh*." I caught my breath.

Staring back at me from Lou's mirror was a creature transformed. It was me, only me in a shimmering gossamer dream of a dress. It was so *flattering*. I didn't look overweight at all in this dress. The top layer, which was made of some kind of finely shredded silk, glowed with the radiance of fractured opals. It nipped in and out at just the right places, and skimmed over the spots where the sartorial gods declared that things should be skimmed. The underlayer of netting kept everything else under control. For once, I would be able to face a fancy-dress event without my hip-smoothers.

"How does he *do* that?" I said, my eyes widening.

"There's nothing like really knowing how to sew and fit." Cherize grinned. "So now let's try the—"

"No, no, *this* is the dress," I declared. "I don't have to try on anything else. In fact, I think I'll wear this dress for the rest of my life. They'll have to bury me in it."

"Okay, then," Cherize announced. "Now for the shoes."

"Oh, that's all right," I responded quickly. "I don't need shoes. I brought a pair of black Ferragamos with me."

Cherize looked horrified, as if I'd just announced I was going to wear her designer confection with a pair of Ugg boots.

"Absolutely not—only *these* shoes can go with this dress." She reached for a stack of shoe boxes that was leaning against Lou's giant sleigh bed. After another rustling sound, this time of tissue, she extracted a pair of shiny, pointy shoes. Placing them on a fan she created with her palms and fingers, she raised the shoes for my inspection as reverentially as if they were ruby slippers.

Reluctantly, I tried on the shoes. They were the right size and—okay, they made my calves look sleek and fabulous—but talk about toe jam. It felt as if all five toes were being squished into a cubic area the size of a pencil point. I resolved to smuggle the Ferragamos into the party for a quick switcheroo later on.

After Cherize's dress fitting, Lou's driver arrived in a town car and spirited me away for another part of the surprise, a trip to a day spa and salon. By the end of the day, every square inch of me had been steamed, plucked, pummeled, sprayed, and waxed. The only thing that was missing was a layer of Armor All on the exquisite updo that a stylist crafted from my hair. I kept my head very still the rest of the afternoon, afraid I was going to shake something loose and collapse it like a bad soufflé.

That evening, back in Lou's bedroom, I put it all together—the dress, the shoes, the jewelry, the makeup, and the updo—and turned to face him.

Lou's jaw dropped. "Oh, my God." He danced a circle around me in an imitation of a Zorba the Greek dance, then reached forward to brush the side of my neck with his fingers. "I'm going to have to do math equations in my head or something to control myself tonight. Otherwise, I'll have to drag you off to the powder room and ravish you before dinner. Screw that—let's do it right now." He pulled me toward him, pressing against me.

I could feel the bulge beneath his belt grow to indelicate proportions. "Don't upset the updo," I warned him, smiling. But inside, I was taken aback. Lou was responding—and boy, was he *ever*—to the new, slicked-up version of me that he'd created.

But unfortunately, the new me didn't feel like "me" at all.

Halfway through the charity gala that night, two words came in answer to Lou's marriage proposal. They rose high in the dome of my brain, shining as brightly as a pair of Christmas comets: *not ready*.

The hour was just before nine p.m. All evening, I'd been longing to get some time alone with Lou, to discuss Marnie's death and my thoughts about what had happened to her. But he was caught up in major host mode, schmoozing with the movers and shakers of Atlanta's charity circuit. I'd spent most of the evening attached demurely to his side, serving up enough word salad to fill the Superbowl.

I excused myself from Lou and the rest of the group. In search of temporary refuge, I made a hobbled retreat in my toe-killers to the buffet table. Along the way, I had to dodge eye-daggers being hurled my way by a member of Atlanta's deb brigade. Word was that this particular deb had been stalking Lou for months, but hadn't made any headway despite wearing outfits like the one she had on tonight. From the front, she was Southern princess perfection, but the back of her dress hinted at her bad-girl side—it plunged deep enough to reveal the leading edge of her butt cleavage. With any luck, her next dagger would boomerang and lodge itself there.

I'd made it to the food table and was calculating the caloric damage that would be inflicted by some yummy-looking cheese puffs when I heard a voice whisper in my ear.

"Word to the wise," the voice said. "Go for the puffs. They're beyond nirvana."

I turned. Lou's gregarious law partner, Sid, stood just off my left shoulder. He and his wife, Anna, were cosponsors of the gala.

"That's all the encouragement I need." I speared a couple of cheese puffs and landed them on my plate.

Sid looked delighted. "Kate, you're my kind of gal," he said. "Anna and our girls won't eat anything with carbohydrates—or much of anything *else*, for that matter." He stole a cheese puff from my plate and popped it into his mouth.

"I just wanted to say how happy we all are that Lou has lassoed you," Sid continued, half-chewing as he spoke. "Anna's already lining up some spots for you on her boards."

"What boards?"

"Oh, you know—the opera, the Shriners' hospital. I probably don't even know half the *fakakta* boards she's on. I only write checks and go to parties and eat. But Anna's happy to be getting some fresh blood. I tell you, it's a full-time job, raising all this money for charity."

I bit into a puff—which *was* heavenly—and looked across the room at Anna. Dressed in killer plumage that made her look like an exotic bird, she was holding forth in the middle of a cluster of people. Anna was one of those women who were *electric* at social events. She'd spent most of the gala moving between groups, energizing conversations and introducing people to each other. Anna and Sid were about ten years older than Lou. *Twenty* years older than me.

I felt a sinking sensation in the pit of my stomach. *Not ready*, whispered the voice inside my head. Not ready to leave my job and move to Atlanta. Not ready to haggle over whether or when I would work, as Lou and I had earlier that week.

Not ready, therefore, to marry Lou.

After the gala, I gave Lou the bad news. Sitting next to him in front of the fireplace in his library, sipping a glass of wine, I told him that although I thought I could make a life with him someday, I needed to do some things first. Like explore my career and—more importantly—explore *life* a bit. I needed to achieve a solid sense of myself before I merged that self with him, I said. Marriage would have to wait a couple of years.

Everything I said sounded perfectly reasonable—and it was true—but I found myself dragging in stitchy breaths to keep from getting upset. My words as they poured out kept twisting and running ahead of my thoughts.

Lou said nothing the entire time I was speaking. When I finished, silence spun out between us. The expression on his face was one I'd never seen before. It looked as if a dark energy was gathering behind his brow, some powerful emotion that he could barely contain. I felt a shiver of apprehension as I watched the expressions flicker across his face.

When Lou finally spoke, he began in an even, lawyerly tone. "I've probably pushed you too fast, just because *I'm* ready to settle down right now," he said. Then his voice flattened. "So look—I'm going to give you the emotional space you seem to need so desperately."

"I don't think I need that much—"

Lou raised his hands in the air and made a pushing back motion. "No, you do. And I'm prepared to give it to you—starting tonight."

"Tonight? Wait, Lou. I'm not saying I want us to break up, all I'm saying is—"

"I know exactly what you're saying." With a rough

gesture, he dug in his pocket and pulled out his cell phone. "I'm calling Kurt. He'll take you back to Durham."

"Right now? Kurt's probably watching Leno, or asleep."

"Kurt requires little sleep."

As Lou started punching numbers, I put a restraining hand on his. "Lou, would you hold on a second? I think you're overreacting."

"No, I'm not." He shook off my hand and put the phone to his ear. "Hey there, Kurt-man. I need you to make an express delivery to Durham for me. Yeah. Thanks."

Then he looked at me straight on. "You know, I could have my pick of the most beautiful women in Atlanta. Debutantes, models—anyone. But instead, I chose you."

"Oh? What you're really saying is that you *settled* for me, isn't it?"

"No, I'm just saying that it never mattered to me that you're heavy. I wish you'd appreciate that a little more. I did ask you to marry me, after all."

"A fat sow like me really *should* be more appreciative, Lou. I totally get that. Thanks for letting me know how you feel."

In a haze of confusion and hurt, I got to my feet, pausing just long enough to visualize dumping the contents of my wineglass onto his head. Then I made a dignified retreat to the upstairs bedroom to pack my things.

By the time I was dropped off in Durham like an abandoned kitten two hours later, my upset over being unceremoniously air-dumped by Lou had morphed into righteous rage.

After letting myself into my apartment, I stormed around the living room.

"How dare he? How *dare* he?" I made an impassioned case to Elfie the cat, who hunkered down on the couch and stared at me with wide, concerned blue eyes. "He thinks I should be *grateful* to marry him, because I'm fat? Well, fuck him and the helicopter he rode in on."

When Elfie blinked, I added, "It's a good thing I found out what a jerk he is before we got married. A very good thing!"

I racked my brain for someone I could call at two a.m., then decided to hold off. All my friends were now in their mid-to-late twenties, with real jobs and families. Maybe they wouldn't appreciate being rousted out of bed for a sobfest, the way we had during college. This thought made me suspect that I was a loser as well as fat and boyfriendless; I burst into tears.

At that point, the emotional stress must have gotten to me. Like a somnambulant sleepwalker, I woke up in front of the open door of the freezer, staring thoughtfully at a box of frozen Whoopie Pies that a friend had sent me from Maine. The moment was enough to set off alarm bells in my head—I knew from hard experience that Freezer Stare Syndrome is always followed by an eating binge. I was dancing at the edge of a major diet meltdown.

To avoid a Whoopie Pie Waterloo, I microwaved some low-fat popcorn, made a cup of sugarless hot chocolate, and then beat a hasty retreat to the bedroom. After what seemed like hours, I finally fell asleep in a debris field of jagged popcorn bits.

But there was this to cling to: Even though my love life was apparently over, at least there wouldn't be hell to pay at the scale the next morning.

Chapter 13

Busting Those *?#@! Weight Plateaus

When you're losing weight, you'll inevitably hit plateaus, when no weight loss shows up on the scale. Oftentimes this happens when you're converting fat to muscle, which weighs more than fat.

To break through a plateau, a simple solution is to take up treadmill walking, or make a slight change in your treadmill routine. If you're doing the lazy woman's holding-on-for-dear-life walk, start walking hands-free. Another easy change is to increase the percentage of your incline by one degree. Walking is a steady calorie burner, and it builds nice lean muscles.

Of course, this solution works only if you're following your eating plan. You <u>*are*</u> *still* following your plan, aren't you?

—From *The Little Book of Fat-busters* by Mimi Morgan

"Your weight is . . . one hundred seventy-five point seven pounds." My Bad News Bear body composition analyzer sounded smug as she announced my stats the next morning. "Your weight change since last weigh-in is . . . an *increase* of point four pounds."

That's a strange law of the universe, I thought as I slunk away from the scale—when you take heroic measures to avoid a binge, as I had the night before, the gods of Fat smack you down with a gain. Other times they'll grant you a mulligan for no good reason at all.

To avoid dwelling on my previous night's catastrophe with Lou, I threw myself into work. It was a measure partly born of necessity. My abortive trip to Atlanta had put me behind schedule on my reporting. I spent the bulk of the day producing background interviews that I'd need to develop my story about Darwin.

First, Frank and I met with Marnie's friend Beth from the Rescue Retreat. I arranged to meet her at her parents' home instead of the shelter, so that I could talk with her on camera about Marnie.

We did the interview on the back deck of Beth's house, which was one of those McMansions in a newer subdivision. Beyond the deck lay a strip of emerald lawn that was so narrow, it probably got a bikini wax every week instead of a mowing.

Beth wasn't wearing a scarf today, as she had been during our meeting at the Rescue Retreat shelter. I was surprised to see that underneath the scarf she was a flaxen blonde—something about her serious demeanor during our previous meeting had pegged her as a no-nonsense brunette in my mind.

The interview was excellent. Beth broke down in tears as she talked about how Darwin had taken advantage of Marnie. Her sound bites would give the story an emotional punch.

But best of all, Beth provided eyewitness testimony—from Marnie herself.

"I thought I'd lost this, so I didn't mention it the other day," Beth said as she handed me a small, fabric-covered book. The cover of the book had images of fairies floating across it.

Inside, the pages were filled with crabbed, schoolgirl-style handwriting.

"Is this Marnie's diary?" I asked her.

"No, it's mine," Beth said. "But Marnie wrote some stuff in there about Darwin. She wouldn't put anything in her own diary about it, because her mother was kind of a snoop. But that summer, when everything went down with Darwin, I let her write in my book for a while. There's a picture of her and him stuck in there, too. It's pretty gross, though."

As I flipped through some pages, a snapshot fell into my lap. It was a photo strip, the kind you take in a booth at a mall. The frames showed a very young Marnie sitting in Darwin's lap. Through her T-shirt, you could see the outline of his hands, holding her breasts. In one of the stills, someone had slashed out his face with strokes of red Magic Marker: It was evidence of a young girl's betrayal and rage, long ago.

"Is it okay if I take this photo with me, and the diary?" I asked Beth, as the interview wound down. "I'll get them back to you."

When she hesitated, I added, "I'll take good care of it. Plus, the police may want to look at it." Although they probably wouldn't want it anytime *soon*, judging by my recent smackdown by Investigator Powell, I thought.

"Okay." Beth still looked worried. "I just want to make sure I do the right thing by Marnie now. If that guy Darwin killed her . . ." She broke into a sob. "You won't make her look like a bad person in the story, will you? *Darwin* started the whole thing."

I stood up to give her a hug. "Sweetie, Marnie was a good, good person," I said. "It's Darwin who's bad."

After leaving Beth's house, my next destination was the home of Marnie's parents, Hal and Sylvia Taylor. They refused to do an on-camera interview, so Frank dropped me off at the station so that I could pick up my car.

As I passed through the studio's lobby, the receptionist handed me a plain manila envelope that someone had left for me. There was no return address, but I could tell from the contents that it came from Fergus. Inside the envelope were copies of records. They revealed that the management of the Prowlers football team had settled out of court with the family of a fourteen-year-old girl. The payments to the family amounted to more than seventy-five thousand dollars. That settlement, plus Darwin's slimy conduct with Marnie, would be enough for me to portray him as a serial abuser of underage girls.

Given their earlier reluctance, my visit to the Taylor home was going to be the toughest part of this assignment. I was going to have to talk to her parents about something bad that had happened to their daughter, under their own roof.

I wasn't looking forward to it.

As they had during their daughter's service, Hal Taylor and his wife Sylvia sat side by side on their mohair couch. Sylvia clutched a ball of tissue in her right hand. The couple listened as I told them everything I'd learned about Darwin, about what he'd done to their daughter Marnie when she was a young girl.

"I have a picture that shows them together, and some of Marnie's writings," I said, leaving out my source. "She described everything. There's no doubt about what happened. Darwin had sex with her that summer, when she was twelve years old."

When I finished speaking, Hal's head was bowed into his hands, and Sylvia had folded herself against him. The room got so quiet, you could hear the tiny *thwack* of a golf ball being hit onto a green in the distance.

"What you're telling me is that I let a monster into my home." Hal's words, when they finally came, were slow and careful.

"Well, Darwin, he—"

"No." Hal shook his head vehemently. "No, I cannot accept that I let a *monster* into my home, into Marnie's life."

"You didn't know, then, that Darwin left the Prowlers because he had an affair with a fourteen-year-old girl?"

Sylvia looked at me with a surprised expression, then at her husband.

Hal's face turned dark. "I heard something about that, after the fact," he said. "But teenagers, sometimes they're— I guess I just assumed she was one of those *Girls Gone Wild* types. From a bad family, perhaps. I never thought the incident had anything to do with *us*."

Abruptly, he stood up and strode across the fine Oriental carpet of the living room. Moments later came the jarring sound of a door being flung open, then slammed shut.

Sylvia gave me a stricken look. "I should go look after Hal," she said, getting up from the couch.

"I think I should probably leave."

Sylvia extended her hand, palm up, to stop me. "No, stay here, please, Kate. I'll just be a moment. I would like to talk to you some more."

I sat on the chair and waited alone in the Taylors' living room, staring glumly at the heavy, champagne-colored cut velvet drapes, which were drawn tight over the window.

It seemed like an eternity before Sylvia returned. When she finally reappeared, she sat down on the couch again and looked at me square on.

"I have to know," she said in a surprisingly strong voice. "Do the police think that man killed my baby girl? We'll talk to them, of course. We'll press whatever charges we can."

"I don't know the answer to that yet, unfortunately. I know that Marnie confronted Darwin on the night she died. I told the police that I saw Marnie crying when she came out of his office. They haven't given me any sense of which way their investigation is headed. But when I put my information on the air, believe me, it will pressure them to pay attention."

Sylvia smoothed out her ball of tissue in her lap, as if she were arranging a baby's blanket.

"I'm so sorry," I added, after another moment passed. "I know that what I've told you must only be adding to your grief."

Sylvia stiffened. " 'Grief' doesn't capture what we're feeling right now," she said. "They'd have to invent a new word."

I nodded, trying to project silent empathy.

Sylvia glanced toward a cabinet that had a flat screen television hanging on the wall above it. "We have so, so many videos of that summer, when Marnie was twelve," she said. "I'm sure there are lots of pictures of *him* in there—please, can you just take them away? Give them to the police, or burn them? I can never touch them again. It would be like touching something evil."

Sylvia's words had just managed to crystallize in my mind what the true center of my story was—it was a vindication of her daughter. By using Marnie's own words from her diary, I hoped to keep her from being relegated to playing the role of Darwin's victim. She'd become part of his takedown.

"I'll do everything I can to make sure that Darwin never harms another young girl, ever," I promised Sylvia. "When this story runs, everyone will know exactly what he is."

"Hal said it best." Sylvia's face crumpled. "He's a monster."

After I returned to the studio, I holed up in my cubicle for a couple of hours to read Marnie's entries in Beth's diary. They laid out a damning history of the way Darwin had abused her trust when she was underage. Then I moved to an editing booth and reviewed the family videos that Marnie's mother had given me.

It wasn't long before I struck broadcast gold. Buried in the footage was a shot that showed Darwin poolside at the Taylors' house. He was surrounded by young girls (whose faces we would digitally mask).

Darwin and the girls were playing some kind of chase-and-tickle game. The leer on his face made him look like a fox in the henhouse. It would be the perfect shot to use while I was telling the viewers that he'd been involved sexually with underage girls. From the sports archives, I dug up some shots of him playing football with the Prowlers, which we would also use in the piece.

I needed one more thing to complete the story: an interview with Darwin, to confront him about his past with Marnie. Frank and I would have to do an "ambush-style" interview, which meant surprising Darwin with hostile questions. I'd have to stage the interview away from Body Blast—I couldn't abuse my friendship with Riley by confronting Darwin at the camp. Probably all I'd get in response to my questions would be some expletives that we'd have to bleep out. But only the visuals really mattered.

As I rewound the tape, it occurred to me that it was a good thing I worked with a camera instead of a gun. It was a good thing I didn't *believe* in guns, in fact.

Because if I had a gun, the moment I got Darwin in my sights, I'd be sorely tempted to blow the bastard's face off.

Chapter 14

Perception Is Everything

You know it's good for you to exercise, but did you know that people think you're more attractive simply because you exercise? Studies suggest that even if you're overweight, people view you as more physically attractive if they think you work out regularly.

So if I were you, I'd start toting your free weights into the office—even if you don't plan to use them. It also won't hurt to glance at your watch every once in a while and announce that you're late for your racquetball game!

—From *The Little Book of Fat-busters* by Mimi Morgan

My last task that day was to do some more research on Libby Fowler, the first woman who had died at Body Blast. I knew that she'd complained to Riley about Darwin's advances, right before she fell from a cliff under mysterious circumstances. Maybe Darwin really *was* a sociopath. Maybe he'd murdered both Marnie *and* Libby. That idea lent additional urgency to the story. If he was some kind of weirdo psychopath, he needed to be stopped.

I beat up the phone for a while, digging around to find out where Libby had lived and attended school. Then, with the help of a friendly girl I located through her college sorority chapter, I turned up the names of some of her friends. I left messages for several of them.

One of her friends, Irene, returned my call to her office nearly immediately. That was typical. People normally get back to me right away—there's something about getting a call from a reporter at their local TV station that piques their curiosity.

When I told Irene I was working on a story that involved her friend Libby, she said she already had plans for the night, but I cajoled her into meeting me for a few minutes. Irene said she could meet at Mr. Max's near her office in East Durham. It was a beer, peanuts, and sawdust-on-the-floor place favored by Durham's singles crowd.

When I entered the restaurant just before six p.m., a tiny brunette waved at me from a table across the room. It was Irene.

After we introduced ourselves, Irene ordered an appletini and I asked for a light beer, out of respect for watching my liquid calories.

"I'm sorry I can only stay a minute," Irene said, after we'd gotten our drinks and rebuffed a couple of bar lizards who launched sorties in our direction. "But I'm so glad you're looking into Libby's death. I think there was definitely something wrong with the way she died."

"What do you mean by 'something wrong'?"

"Libby called me before her group left on that horrible camping trip," she said, taking a sip of her appletini. "She was venting about something that happened with a guy up there—Dirk, I think his name was? No, *Darwin*. I guess he made some kind of dumb-ass play for her. She hung up before I got all the details."

"Was that conversation the last time you heard from her?"

Irene shook her head. "I got a text message from her, right before her group left for the mountains."

"What did the message say?"

"Not much. All it said was, 'Remind me to tell you about major B-Ho blast. ML.' "

"ML—that means 'more later'?"

Irene nodded and stirred her drink with a little plastic straw. "But I never heard anything more from her later," she said. "The next day, she went off with that group to the mountains. And then . . .well."

"What does 'B-Ho' mean?"

"It was the nickname for our clique back in junior high—Longleaf Day School—we called ourselves the Bitch Hos." Irene rolled her eyes. "God, we were all so horrible, *especially* Libby. I'm surprised somebody didn't kill us back then, we were so mean."

"There was a group of girls just like that at my school," I said, making some notes in my reporter's pad. "I was younger because I skipped a couple of grades, so they saved their special tortures for me."

"Oh, I know. Girls can be such monsters. *We* certainly were."

I was making light of my experience to Irene, but in reality, the whole episode had been traumatic. What made the timing of their mean-girl treatment worse was that it took place right after my mother died. When I finally graduated from high school and started Wellesley College, I felt as if I'd escaped the isle of Bimbo Barbarians and landed on the shores of the Beautiful Brains.

Irene continued, "Once there was this one poor girl, kind of a loser, overweight, and we—well, it was like something straight out of *Carrie*, the way we treated her. You know, the tampon-throwing scene?"

I shrugged. "Well, present company excepted, if there's any justice in the world, all the mean girls should grow up to be tubby, pockmarked, and work at Chick-fil-A."

As Irene smiled and reached for her drink, I added, "So what Libby texted to you that night—'B-Ho'—that was code for your old junior high clique?"

"Right. Nowadays we simply say 'B-Ho' whenever we're reminded of something dumb from back then. I'm sure Libby was talking about that Darwin guy. He probably reminded her of some jerk wad from the eighth grade. You know, the ones who tried to impress girls by doing ollies on their skateboards. Libby told me he drives some kind of muscle car. Ick. How loser is *that*?"

"Did you tell any of this to the investigators?"

She nodded. "Libby's brother Theo put me in touch with the SBI," she said. "An investigator returned my call. He seemed interested in what I had to say about Darwin. He came out here to see me and did an interview—took notes and everything. He said they'd follow up. But since then I haven't heard anything else."

Our waitress approached to find out whether we were ready to order food. Irene had to go to her other appointment, but I hadn't eaten in hours. I decided to stay for dinner.

After Irene left, I ordered a mandarin salad, even though probably the only decent thing on Mr. Max's menu was the cheeseburger. As I waited for the food to arrive, I found myself studying the wall décor intently to avoid eye contact with other people, especially men. Eating alone in a singles place made me feel conspicuous as hell. It was as if I had a sign over my head that said, "Horny woman." I felt all the more uncomfortable because my work at Channel Twelve had turned me into something of a minor local celebrity. Wherever I went, people always seemed to be watching me. It was ridiculous—being on camera had nothing to do with *me*, really—but I always felt eyes tracking me wherever I went, especially in a place like this.

Evasive maneuvers proved useless at Mr. Max's, however. Soon after the waitress delivered my salad, she returned, carrying a tray with an oversized strawberry daiquiri on it.

"This is from the YCMS by the bar," the waitress whispered, setting down the frosted goblet with a wink.

I looked toward the bar, where the Young Cute Male Species in question was staring at me with brooding, expectant eyes.

"The cougars—that's what we call the gals over forty—call him Heathcliff," the waitress added. "But I guess they mean someone from a book, though, not the dog. Because, honey, he *definitely* ain't a dog."

"You know, that's nice, but I'm allergic to strawberries," I lied. "Please tell Heathcliff that it's nothing personal."

"You got it," the waitress said, vanishing with the daiquiri.

Seeing his offering rejected, Heathcliff frowned. He turned his back and melted into the jungle by the bar, where no doubt a cougar was waiting to pounce.

I remembered with a jolt that my parking meter was about to expire. I'd had to park on the street because the restaurant's undersized lot had been overflowing. In this part of town they ticketed until ten p.m., so I'd have to hightail it to avoid a fine.

After choking down a few more wilted bites of iceberg lettuce mixed with mandarin orange and dry chicken, I paid my bill and rushed outside. A brush of night air on my face felt cool and moist.

Under the streetlight, I saw a police cruiser pulled

alongside my TR6. A tall figure was sticking a piece of paper on the windshield. A parking ticket.

"*No-o-o* . . . dammit-dammit-*dammit* . . ."

I broke into a trot as I crossed the street. Maybe I could argue my way out of it.

"No *way* has that meter expired already," I wailed, hurrying up to the car. "I had at least five more minutes. The meter's timing must be off."

"I hope *my* timing isn't."

The voice spoke in a cool, British accent that I recognized immediately. It was Jonathan Reed. *Detective* Jonathan Reed, of Durham Homicide.

I gaped stupidly at Reed. "So, no ticket?" I said, then cringed inwardly. What a dumb-ass way to greet someone I hadn't seen in half a year—someone who'd saved my life once.

"No, that's not my department." He gave me a faint smile. "I recognized your car. I was just leaving you a note asking you to call. It's been a few months."

"Nine," I said, then flushed at the thought that Reed would think I'd been counting the months since we'd last seen each other. I started to add, *But who's counting?* But I couldn't add a single syllable, because the sight of him made me lose my breath, as if the blood pumping through my arteries had gone fizzy all of a sudden.

I recovered my breath with a delicate cough. "Why are you driving a cruiser tonight? Where's Homicide's Batmobile?"

"I'm running this car back to the station for a uniform who got sick. You look amazing," Reed said, scanning me up and down. "But then, I didn't have to see you to know that. I see you on the news all the time."

What seemed more amazing was that Reed and I had never run into each other during all those months.

Dressed in casual Brooks Brothers perfection, he looked just as I remembered him. Since my youth, which I'd spent surrounded by fashion-challenged roughnecks, I'd obviously become a pushover for perfect tailoring.

Reed and I had met during a murder investigation the previous summer. He was the cop in charge, I the reporter. From the very start, I'd developed a wild crush on him. Even today, if I so much as *heard* a male British accent, my pulse would skip a beat.

At the end of his investigation the previous summer, Reed had confessed that he was attracted to me, but then he insisted on putting our relationship on hold until the suspect's murder trial wound down.

When Reed wrote that little stipulation into our fledgling romance, I withdrew into a major F.U. snit. Then he pulled a disappearing act. I'd heard (by making some very discreet inquiries among my cop contacts) that he'd gone back to Great Britain for a few months. Still, every time I did a story at the Durham police headquarters, I kept an eye out for him. But as the months passed without any contact, I drifted deeper into my relationship with Lou. Eventually, I chalked up Reed as one of those baffling close encounters of the male kind.

Now Reed was staring at me with a sheepish expression on his face. "I've been planning to ring you, but I was afraid you'd tell me to buzz along," he said.

The word "ring" made me flash on an image of Lou's abandoned engagement diamond. I chased the image away.

When I didn't respond, he added, "Would you fancy having a dinner with me this weekend? Saturday?"

"This weekend? Oh." I struggled for a coherent reply. "Oh, this *Saturday*? This Saturday I'll be out of town."

"Ah."

Reed hesitated. It was clear that he was trying to figure out whether I was blowing him off.

And I was half-inclined to. How dare he show up after all this time, expecting me to be just *available.*

But instead of blowing him off, I launched into a breathless, rambling summary of my plan to return the next day to Body Blast. I told him about Marnie's and Libby's deaths, plus my theory that there was something odd going on at the camp. "But after I come back, I'd love to. Have dinner, I mean." I heard those words come sailing out of my mouth on a jet stream of air.

"Brilliant," Reed said. He looked relieved but also slightly agitated, as if he'd been stressing about asking me out. Why? He could have—*should* have—contacted me long before this.

I expected Reed to warn me to stay out of police business—when I'd gotten too involved in *his* murder investigation the summer before, he'd practically had me handcuffed and hauled away to the slammer—but he didn't. Instead, his expression turned thoughtful.

"The Smokies are a little out of my jurisdiction, but I'll ask around. See if there's any noise on the wire about it," he said.

"That'd be great. I talked to the SBI investigator—a guy named Powell—but he was about as informative as a stone wall."

"A friend of mine works over there," Reed said, stifling a grin. "Carla Manning. I can call her and pave the way for you."

"Thanks. I'd really appreciate it."

Reed shoved his hands deep into the pockets of his trousers. "So if I don't see you until next week, mind yourself up there in the mountains."

"I will, and thanks."

"Until a week from Saturday," he said, then leaned toward me and aimed a kiss at my cheek.

At the last possible second, his lips turned and pressed against mine. They felt warm and urgent. His hands emerged from his pockets, and his arms circled me, drawing me into him. Reed's nubbly jacket gave off a woodsy fragrance of KL, over a darker note of police headquarters.

"Sorry, but apparently I couldn't wait," he said, when the kiss ended and we both came up for air. "I want to explain about—"

"That's okay. We can talk about it next week," I replied quickly. I was feeling off balance—too off balance to listen to any explanation from him right then. That could wait.

Reed gave me a little salute. Leaning against the cruiser, he waited as I got into my car. In the rearview mirror, I could see him watching me as I drove away.

My hands felt sweaty on the leather steering wheel. Oh. My. God. Ten minutes in Reed's presence, and I could feel it happening all over again—the breathlessness, the brain fog. I hadn't finished processing the breakup with Lou, and here I was, setting up a date, for God's sake.

But I felt compelled to see Reed again.

I felt compelled, the way a luna moth is drawn to a flame.

Chapter 15

Ten-Minute Toning

I know it's hard—very hard—to start an exercise routine. But you can do almost anything for ten minutes, can't you? So here's what I want you to do today—I want you to engage in some kind of exercise, just for ten minutes. You can walk, run, dance, or swim; I don't care. And then tomorrow, I want you to do another ten minutes.

Here's the beauty of this approach—at the end of twenty-one days, you will have formed a ten-minute-a-day exercise habit. At the end of twenty-one days, I want you to add one more minute of exercise. Seven days later, I want you to add another minute of exercise. Build up at seven-day intervals until you have reached thirty minutes of exercise per day.

See where we're going with this? Slowly, almost imperceptibly, you will build up an exercise routine.

All it takes to get started is ten minutes. Miraculous, isn't it?

—From *The Little Book of Fat-busters* by Mimi Morgan

From the moment Frank and I set off for the mountains the next morning to get our ambush interview with Darwin, it felt as if the gods who ruled the day had woken up on the wrong side of Mount Olympus.

At ten a.m., we were motoring along in a little caravan of two through the foothills of the Great Smokies—I was out front in my car, with Frank trailing behind in the broadcast truck—when an accident ahead of us stalled the traffic. The backup caused the radiator of the temperamental TR6 to stage one of its seasonal hissy fits. Driving a vintage British sports car is like owning a great old house: It's full of charm and character, but you'd better know how to patch the plumbing. After we pulled to the shoulder and I resuscitated the radiator with a bottle of distilled water that I kept in the trunk (Frank got a few shots of the accident, just in case), we hit the road again.

A bigger challenge was dealing with a one-man Greek chorus also known as The Boss. Soon after we got underway again, my cell phone rang for the gazillionth time that morning. It was Beatty, our news director, calling to grill me about yet another detail of my Darwin story. Overnight, my piece had assumed a high profile in Channel Twelve's news lineup. Beatty had decided to develop a "three-sixty" broadcast about child molestation. My Darwin story would provide a news hook, while other reporters generated stories that covered different angles on child abuse—Crystal, the legal beat reporter, would do a law enforcement piece, and the features gal would work up something at the Department of Social Services.

In the middle of all this activity, Beatty directed his reporters like an anal-retentive maestro, making sure every instrument was tuned to perfection.

"You already got all the cut shots and local background you'll need?" he demanded for the umpteenth time.

Without waiting for a reply, he continued, "What about that camp, Body Blast? Is that where you're gonna nab him?"

"No—we'll get him off-site. I know where he'll be."

Earlier that morning, I'd called my friend Riley to tell him about what was going down. He sounded shocked, but agreed to send Darwin on an "errand" that afternoon that would send him straight into our rolling camera lens.

"And he'll never be allowed back at Body Blast," Riley said during that conversation. "I'll send him an e-mail informing him that he's fired. After what you've told me, I just hope they arrest him."

Now it was hard to stay focused on the cell phone and Beatty, who was still yammering in my ear about production details.

"Got it. Got it. It's under control." As soon as I clicked off, I realized that I'd accidentally hung up on Beatty. *Oops.*

Having my boss crawling up my ass only added to the pressure I already felt about the Darwin piece. Normally I don't get nervous while working on stories, not even high-pressure pieces. But my anger over Marnie's death—and the way Darwin had abused her when she was young—made this story feel different. This one felt *personal.* I wanted everything to go just right.

Two hours later, Frank and I had our stakeout ready outside the post office in Maggie Hollow, the tiny hamlet that was located a few miles away from Body Blast. I'd already heard from Riley that Darwin was on his way there on a faux errand.

When about half the population of Maggie Hollow turned out to goggle at the unusual sight of a TV news van, I had Frank stash it on a side street. Then he and I tried to make ourselves as inconspicuous as possible—always a challenge for camera crews in small towns. We finally sought refuge inside the office of a gas station across the street from the post office.

There, I was able to keep one eye out for Darwin's arrival while fending off goggle-eyed questions from the gas station's manager.

Twenty minutes later, a black Shelby Ford Mustang with white racing stripes squealed into the parking lot across the street. I recognized Darwin behind the wheel.

"That's him," I said to Frank, who was already on the move with camera rolling.

Together, we bolted out the gas station door and charged across the street toward Darwin.

Before we made it to the opposite sidewalk, I heard several squawking, staccato shrieks—it was a siren being tapped—shred the air.

A green and black truck with rooftop strobes flashing hove into view; it slammed to a halt in the parking lot, directly behind Darwin's car. The truck's side door was marked SBI. State Bureau of Investigations.

Two men in plain clothes—SBI cops, obviously—emerged swiftly from the truck. They took positions beside each of the Mustang's two doors.

The guy on the driver's side, who had his humongous back to us, flashed a badge through the window. Then he flung open the door, reached inside, and unceremoniously hauled Darwin out of his car.

Frank and I paused on the sidewalk about ten feet away from the confrontation.

With the camera still rolling, Frank glanced up from the camera's eyepiece and mouthed silently, *What's going on?*

I shrugged. "I guess someone else decided to do a takedown today, too," I stage-whispered to him. "Let's keep moving in, but slower."

With his free hand, the giant cop was jabbing his finger into Darwin's chest. Darwin was at least six feet tall, but the big guy topped him by at least half a head. Something told me it was Investigator Powell, the SBI investigator I'd spoken with a few days earlier.

The cop on the opposite side of the car caught sight of us and scowled. He pivoted, then made stiff, bow-legged tracks our way, as if he'd rolled out of bed with a bad case of crabs.

"Back off." He raised a vertical palm to block the camera's view. *"Back off!"*

"I'm with Channel Twelve News in Durham," I said. "Why are you arresting Darwin Innova?"

"I told you morons to move back," said Officer Crabs. "We're conducting official business here."

"Are you arresting him in connection with Marnie Taylor's death? I'm wondering, because I have information that he—"

"You have to talk to Investigator Powell for anything official. And he's kinda busy right now." Crabs jerked his thumb toward the other cop, who by now was folding Darwin into the backseat of the SBI truck.

I took a sideways step around Crabs. "Come on, Frank," I said, heading in the direction of the SBI truck. "Let's get a close-up of Darwin in the back of the truck."

Behind me, I heard a burn of feet moving on pavement.

Crabs grabbed me by the elbow, then spun me around to face him.

"God dammit, miss, I told you to back the hell *off*!" he yelled. "You want I should throw the two of you in the truck, too?"

While Crabs was busy snapping his pincers at me, Frank had a few precious seconds to get a tight-in shot of Darwin sitting in the back of the SBI truck.

I glanced sideways and looked at Frank, who gave me the "okay" nod. That was his signal that we had the crucial shot.

"Of *course* not," I said, shining a sweet-as-pie smile at Crabs. "I guess I just didn't hear you right. You gentlemen have yourselves a beautiful day."

Crabs's official police response gave us one more *bleep*, just for the record.

It took ninety teeth-gritting minutes to make the drive from the Maggie Hollow post office to the city of Ashland, where our sister station, Channel Three, was located. I had to hold myself back from speeding the entire way. It was one thing for me to take these mountain roads at breakneck speed in my TR6, but behind me, Frank was driving the news van, which had as much road-hugging capability as a tipsy elephant.

After we arrived at the Ashland studio and introduced ourselves breathlessly to the local news director, Frank and I jammed into a production booth. We were now in über deadline mode, scrambling to get the Darwin story finished and uplinked to the satellite by six p.m.

It was already a few minutes before five o'clock. I knew from hard experience that Beatty would already be pacing outside the satellite feed booth at our home base in Durham, waiting for our story about Darwin to download for that night's newscast.

After I finished narrating the script, Frank and I hovered like anxious mother hens while a preternaturally calm production editor—who seemed to groove on taking his time tweaking the visuals while we sweated bullets by his side—laid down the visuals.

"Let's lay in that shot of Darwin getting shoved into the SBI truck," I said to Zen Editor, who slowly adjusted a knob on the editing deck. "And you can use the crabby cop swearing at me over the part where I say that they wouldn't comment on why they were arresting Darwin today."

Once the completed disc with the story was in hand,

Frank and I headed for the TOC—which still stands for Tape Operation Center, even in this satellite and digital age.

Just as Frank was getting ready to uplink the finished story, my cell phone rang. It was Detective Jonathan Reed.

"Pardon the interruption," Reed said. "I tried to call you at the office, but then remembered you're out of town. Do you have a moment?"

Hearing Reed's voice, I felt a tiny beating in my chest, like the air in my lungs was being pushed by a butterfly's wings. "No. I mean yes, no interruption," I said, uncomfortably aware that my voice was pitched an octave higher than normal. "What's up?"

"I heard something just now that I thought you'd want to know," Reed said. "I checked in with my friend at the SBI, Carla. She says they've determined that the girl you spoke about—Marnie Taylor—died accidentally. It was a freak accident. It was definitely *not* a homicide."

I reeled back sharply, knocking the back of my head against the wall of the TOC. "Ouch. No way," I sputtered, reaching up with my hand to rub the back of my skull. "You're telling me that Marnie's death wasn't a homicide? I just can't *believe* it. Then what—"

"That's the SBI's conclusive ruling," Reed replied. "They've already completed the autopsy and run extensive lab tests. Their investigators believe that she was trying to climb some kind of wall on an obstacle course when she fell. Her death was simply an accident, evidently. There's no evidence of foul play at all."

I waggled my fingers frantically at Frank to get his attention. *Hold off,* I mouthed to the cameraman, whose hands had been poised to start the uplink. I snatched the disc from his hand.

With a shrug and a quizzical expression on his face, Frank parked his butt against the wall.

Reed's information spun my world on its axis. Until now, I'd been assuming all along that Marnie's death was suspicious. That was the tone of my story, if not its direct implication. Now it looked like her death had been an accident after all. Where did that leave me and the piece I was about to file? In Screwed City, was the most likely answer. I needed to change the story—fast.

"Is this information a problem for you?" Reed sounded amused. "In Homicide, whenever the evidence doesn't point to a murder, we chalk it up as a default win and head off to the nearest bar to celebrate. It means we have one less victim to worry about."

"Of course. I mean, of *course* it's a good thing that Marnie wasn't murdered," I said, almost peevishly. "But then tell me this—I saw a couple of SBI guys shove Darwin into their truck and haul him away. It sure as heck looked like they were arresting him. How do you explain that?"

"That's just how their Investigator Powell plays hardball when he wants to shake up an interviewee, evidently," Reed said. "Carla told me they're questioning Darwin about last fall's death of another girl at that camp, Libby Fowler. Her death was definitely a homicide."

"So Darwin *is* still a suspect, then?"

"Yes, but in Libby's death last fall, not Marnie's."

"Whoa, okay. Crap, crap, *crap*."

"Crap, you say?"

"Sorry, I didn't mean crap to *you*. I meant crap to me. I was just about to send in a story about Darwin for tonight's broadcast. Now I'll have to rethink it."

I heard a little chuckle come from Reed's end of the line. "You didn't imply that Darwin killed Marnie Taylor, did you?" he asked. "That would be quite the

National Enquirer of you—naming a suspect before the police call the crime."

"No, of course not—well, not *directly*. It's just that now I have to say that it's confirmed that her death was accidental, and that he's being questioned about the *other* girl's death, Libby Fowler."

"That's right, but to get that on the record, you'll have to call Carla at the SBI. She'll hook you up with all the information you need."

"Hmm. Carla doesn't know me. Why would she talk to me?"

"Because I asked her to. And probably because Investigator Powell's at the very top of her bad list," Reed said. "I guess he's not the world's greatest charmer with women. But Carla's not available right now. You'll have to call her in the morning."

"Yikes." I glanced at a digital clock on the wall. It was almost five fifteen. I already had one foot planted firmly inside the city limits of Screwsville.

I took in a deep breath. "Jonathan," I began, releasing his name on the exhale. Even though we'd traded that steamy kiss the other night, this was the first time I'd ever used Reed's first name, I realized. The three syllables of it—*Jon-a-than*—felt slippery and intimate as they passed across my tongue.

"Uh-oh. Ye-s-s-s?" He drew the word out as if he knew what was coming next: a hit-up.

"Look, I'm on a really tight deadline right now. So I'm hitting the panic button here. All I need from you is confirmation that Darwin is a suspect in Libby Fowler's death, which you've already told me. I won't name you; I'll just say that I heard it from 'a source who's familiar with the investigation.' "

Nothing came back for a second. "Carla will know I told you," he finally said. "You'll put me in the rough with her."

"Put you 'in the rough'? Oh, you mean she won't give you a good-night kiss tonight?"

"No, no, it's not like that at all with Carla and me." Jonathan sounded off balance, to my delight. Then he sighed. "Okay, then. I'll deal with Carla. You can say that I'm 'familiar with the investigation.' Brilliant."

"It *is* brilliant. Thank you."

"I hope it's worth it." Jonathan's implication seemed to be, *I hope* you're *worth it.*

"It's worth it, and I'll totally make it up to you. You'll see."

Even though we were discussing a news story, it felt like dirty flirting, talking with him this way. I loved it.

I was already on the move as I hung up; this was a major crisis—I needed to get the story completely rewritten and put back together in less than ten minutes. Otherwise, Beatty would scrap the piece, and my job would be toast. Even though he was five hours away in Durham, I could already feel the heat of Beatty's dragon flames singeing my neck hairs.

Frank had snapped to full alert while listening to my end of the phone conversation with Reed.

"Is there a problem with the story?" He dogged my heels as I rushed back in the direction of the production booth.

"A big-time problem."

Without bothering to knock, Frank and I burst back through the door of the production booth. Our dramatic reappearance startled Zen Editor, who'd been about to take a sip from a mug that had a picture of a lotus blossom on it. The editor jumped, spilling a few drops of steaming liquid on his lap.

"Sorry about that," I apologized to Zen while he beat at his pants. "But we've gotta totally redo this piece. And we've got only nine minutes."

"Nine minutes?" Zen's face drained.

I looked at Frank. "Call Beatty and tell him I have

some breaking info. I might be late, so he'll need to book a longer satellite window."

"Uh-oh, he's not gonna like this," Frank said, before heading out to make the call.

Time was so short that I didn't bother to input a new script on a computer—I just scribbled a few words on a loose sheet of paper. I ducked into a sound booth to voice the story, then returned to Zen's booth. The whole process took two minutes.

Frank popped his head back into the booth.

"Beatty didn't take it too well, but we got the extension," he announced. "You know, our arses are really gonna get mowed if we miss this deadline."

"Now you can tell me something I *don't* know."

Even Zen caught the tension. He tripled his speed as he laid down the visuals over the new audio.

When he finished, there was more bad news: The new version of my story was five seconds shorter than the first one. And in TV news, five seconds might as well be five minutes. We'd have to recut all the video to make it fit.

My cell phone screamed. Without even looking at the caller ID, I handed the phone to Frank.

"Tell Beatty I'll have it to him in three minutes," I said, keeping my eyes on the screen in front of me. "Tell him all I need is three goddamned *minutes*."

"I'll try." Bending his head over my cell phone, Frank ejected from the booth again to jawbone our news director.

An image of Darwin played across the monitor.

I tapped the screen with my finger. "Okay, pause it there," I said to Zen. "This'll work. Let's use this shot of Darwin on the Prowlers sideline, scratching his balls. I want you to insert it at the in-cue: '*Innova played for the Prowlers until he quit the football team, claiming a knee injury*.' I'll have to chop five seconds off the anchor's lead-in."

"Ah, okay. Oh, *shit*," Zen said, fumbling with the controls as he missed the in-cue.

"There's no time for 'shit.'" Punching a button, I corrected his mistake. My past life as a field producer served me well in crises like this.

"Sorry." Zen's forehead was oily with sweat. From the looks of him, the poor guy looked like he'd need to head to the nearest meditation bar after work, for a stiff shot of Dharma Juice.

At 5:33 p.m. and twenty seconds, exactly, I burst out of the production booth, completed story in hand. Hurtling down the short hallway back to the satellite feed room, I barely avoided one woman, who flattened herself against the wall to avoid a collision.

Inside the TOC, I shoved the disc with my story into the machine's slot and punched in the coordinates for Channel Twelve in Durham. Then I lifted my eyes to the acoustic tile ceiling and said a little reporter's prayer: *Please God, don't let there be any sunspot activity that balls up this transmission and torpedoes my career.*

Two minutes and forty seconds after I pressed SEND, Frank appeared in the doorway of the feed room. He brandished my cell phone in his hand.

"Jumpy Rob says it made it," he announced. "And he says it's good."

Jumpy Rob was Channel Twelve's perpetually stressed-out studio producer. They had our story.

I blew out a relieved sigh. "Thank goodness."

"You got that right." Frank sagged against the doorframe. "Beatty was really chomping for our hides this time."

I took up a spot across from Frank and leaned against the opposite side of the doorway. Framed in the opening like a pair of bookends, we gathered ourselves together and shared a moment of recovery.

Once we recaptured our breaths, Frank and I migrated out to the newsroom. We set up camp in a couple of rolling chairs near the assignment desk, which had a good view of a bank of televisions that monitored national, state, and local news.

I clicked the TV closest to us to Durham's Channel Twelve, so that we could catch our story as it came across the air.

Four minutes before six o'clock, with a jolt I remembered a promise I'd made to Libby's brother, Theo Fowler. He'd asked me to call him with any new information about his sister's death—he didn't want to hear it from the news, he'd told me. I needed to call him.

Frantically, I scrabbled through the contact list on my phone. With one eye on the clock on the wall—it was 5:57—I retrieved the number to Theo's used car business.

Thankfully, Theo was still in his office. I filled him in on the bare bones of the story that was going on the air in less than five minutes: that the SBI was questioning Darwin because he was a suspect in his sister Libby's death.

Theo seemed grateful that I'd called, but I could hear the anger rising in his voice. "I knew all along that guy Darwin was no good. I *knew* it," he kept repeating. "Accident, my ass. That's bullshit. He killed her. He pushed her off that cliff."

"Well, for the moment the SBI is just questioning him, evidently—my source says he hasn't been arrested, yet."

When I hung up with Theo, Frank and I watched the Channel Twelve Action! News show as it came on the air.

"It looks really solid, Kate," Frank said to me. "They'll never know we patched it together at the speed of light."

Frank was right—our story looked good. Overall, the news team's effort had produced the kind of show that Beatty would probably submit for an AP award, later on. Led by my piece about Darwin, the three-sixty report provided a mosaic of stories that showed various aspects of child abuse and exploitation issues. My story ended with the dramatic shot of Darwin being driven away by the SBI for questioning about Libby's death. Even though her death was unrelated to the child molestation angle, it added a strong visual underscore to the piece—a final, damning indictment of his character.

Word had evidently gotten around about our story, because a little semicircle of Channel Three reporters and production assistants stood near the television, watching our show as it came across instead of theirs. Channel Three's news director—whose manic energy field made him seem unnervingly like Beatty—nodded approvingly as he watched our stuff. But he seemed to be getting a glower on, too.

I knew what the glower meant—why hadn't *his* reporters gotten the Darwin story? Darwin worked in their backyard, after all. Because Channel Three was our sister station, they'd be able to run all our stories as part of our reciprocal arrangement.

But I could already tell that some reporter's ear was going to get chewed off the next day.

Thank goodness, the sacrificial ear wouldn't be mine this time.

Chapter 16

The Skinny on Protein Shakes

Protein shakes are so overrated. Odds are you're getting enough protein on a daily basis. But if you think you need more, consult a nutritionist. Then, you should get your added protein from real food, not from those high-calorie shakes (which taste nasty anyway). The so-called nutrition companies want to sell you all kinds of shakes and bars and God knows what, but it's much better to whip up an egg-white omelet with veggies.

—From *The Little Book of Fat-busters* by Mimi Morgan

Frank had to get the news van back to Durham that night, and I was eager to see what was happening at Body Blast, so after the show we turned down an offer to go out to eat with a couple of the local reporters. Instead, I hit a drive-through in Ashland before making the drive back to the camp. I ordered a salad, then—after a pause to consider—added an Oreo cookie shake (it *had* been a supremely stressful day, after all).

Body Blast was lit up like an airport when I arrived around nine p.m. Inside the main lobby, two bodybuilder types were flexing in front of the fireplace, heatedly debating the merits of a bodybuilding supplement called CLA. Everything else seemed oddly normal. It made me wonder whether any of the campers had gotten wind of what had gone down with Darwin, or my news story. There wasn't a television in the lobby, so maybe Riley had been able to keep the whole thing quiet.

No one was at the front desk, but one of the drill instructors, Hillary, was floating near the stone fireplace with a watchful expression on her face. I almost didn't recognize her—since the last time I'd seen her the week before, she'd chopped her long hair into extra-short layers. The shaggy new pixie cut was gamine but startling, like she was channeling Joan of Arc.

"Wow, love the new haircut." I smiled as I approached, lugging my duffel bag behind me. "It's very urban chic."

"Oh, thanks." She ran a hand through her feathery chop and headed toward the front desk. "I just needed a change, I think. I'll check you in."

"Where's Riley, do you know?"

Hillary frowned as she handed me a key. "I haven't seen him—or Khan, either, for that matter—for hours," she said. "It's kind of odd for them both to disappear for so long. But then, this whole *day* has been odd."

"What do you mean?"

"Oh, I don't know." Hillary's eyes swung around the lobby, then returned to me. "We're just so short-staffed right now. The program director—Darwin—vanished into thin air this afternoon, leaving us hanging on some stuff. Then Riley took off."

"So people here haven't heard anything about Darwin?"

"Heard *what*?"

"You didn't see the news, then?"

"We never see the news. Riley won't let us have TV—it breaks the workout focus."

It suddenly occurred to me that Riley would most likely prefer to be the one to tell his staff about Darwin; I hadn't even had a chance to update him yet.

"Well, it's a bit of a long story," I said. "I'm sure Riley would prefer to explain it to everyone tomorrow."

When I started to leave, Hillary stopped me. "No, please," she said. "I want to hear about it—I won't tell anyone else. Is it okay if I walk you to your room? It'll be kind of confusing to find the way after dark, anyway."

"Okay." Maybe I could learn something useful, I rationalized.

"Hang on a second." Hillary pressed a button on a phone that was sitting on the counter. Moments later, a twenty-something guy, whose forearms packed enough muscle to fuel a bout of 'roid rage, emerged from a narrow door behind the desk area.

"Sorry, Hill. I was just giving that new sports massage oil a test drive," he said, wiping down a gigantic bicep with a white towel.

"No problem, Gordon," she said to him. "I'll be back in a sec."

Hillary led the way down an outdoor walkway, which kept branching off in different directions. "It's so easy to get lost on these walkways after dark," she told me. She lowered her voice to a whisper, even though no one else was in sight. "So what's *up* with Darwin, anyway?"

"He's being questioned by the SBI about Libby Fowler's murder."

Hillary stopped in her tracks. With a confused expression, she said, "Libby?"

"Yes. The SBI is questioning Darwin about her murder."

Hillary's frown returned. "But Libby and—and

Marnie, too, I guess—they were both *accidents*, I thought," she said. "Everyone thought that."

"Well, Marnie's death *was* an accident—evidently, although I'm still not convinced. But according to the SBI, Libby's death was a homicide."

"And they think Darwin had something to do with it? I just don't believe that. Why would—whew." She reached up with her hand as if to instinctively pull on a long lock of hair, but grabbed only empty air below her new pixie chop.

"It must be a shock, I know."

"More than a *shock*. I don't like Darwin, but . . ." She shook her head. "I don't even think we should have reopened the camp for the weekend. This whole thing has all been a little too nutso for me."

We'd stopped in front of a tiny wood-shingled bungalow. Hillary let us in through an exterior door, then to my room, which was the first door on the right of the hallway.

My new room had knotty-pine walls that smelled woodsy and wonderful. There were two narrow beds, but no sign of a roommate's gear lying around. The emptiness reminded me that on this visit, Marnie wouldn't be here.

"We're a little light on bookings this week, so you've got a single this time," Hillary announced, glancing around the room. "In fact, there's only you and one other girl in this entire building."

That sounded fine to me right about then. I definitely did not feel up to doing the getting-to-know-you thing with a new roommate. But I wondered what the drop-off in bookings would mean for Riley's business.

Hillary opened her mouth as if to say something, then glanced away. "So, the police must be pretty sure that Darwin killed Libby?"

Instead of answering, I said, "You were on that

camping trip, right? What happened between Darwin and Libby, exactly?"

Hillary shot me an evaluating look. "I'm not sure if I should even be talking about this. No offense, but you *are* a reporter."

I pretended to check through my pockets. "Don't worry, no hidden cameras on me tonight. I'm off duty." Which wasn't *exactly* true.

When Hillary laughed uncomfortably, I added, "The truth is, Riley has asked me to help him figure out what's going on around here, and it's not just about Darwin. Darwin's only one piece of the puzzle."

"Yeah, Riley did tell us that you're helping him." Hillary took a deep breath. "Actually, there *was* some tension between Libby and Darwin, on that Wilderness Challenge."

"Such as?"

"I didn't know what was going on at the time," she said. "But later on I heard that Libby had complained to Riley about Darwin. I guess it was some kind of sexual harassment thing?" She rolled her eyes. "Like *that* was unusual. Here's the truth about Darwin: He was all over any female with two legs."

"So I guess none of the women on the staff liked him?"

Hillary shrugged. "Well, except for maybe Erica. They seemed to get along okay. The rest of us can't believe that Riley kept promoting such a jerk. It's because of his reputation from football, I guess." She gave a cynical laugh. "Don't you just *love* the old boys' network?"

I shrugged. "So what happened the morning that Libby fell down into the ravine? Who discovered her body?"

Hillary's face shut down. "Um, I don't know."

"Well, how did the morning unfold? What did you see?"

"Actually, I kind of hate to dredge all that stuff up again," she said, edging toward the door.

Then, apparently having second thoughts, she stopped. "Erica and I were the first ones up—that's what I *thought*, anyway—because our job was to go around to the tents and get all the women going," she said. "And I guess Riley or Darwin must've been getting the guys up. But when I got around to Libby's tent, she was gone. Her tentmate was still asleep. She didn't have any idea where Libby was. In fact, she didn't even know that Libby had left the tent."

That part of the story jangled a memory bell in my mind. It reminded me of the way Marnie had left our room, the night she died on the obstacle course. I hadn't even known that she'd left the room during the night. I decided not to tell Hillary about the angle of my story that included Darwin's sexual abuse of Marnie when she was a girl—I preferred getting information to giving it.

"What was Libby's tentmate's name?"

"Joycie Woo. She owns a clothing shop in Durham, and she's a regular here. Joycie really has it together with her body. Not like Libby."

"What do you mean, 'not like Libby'?"

"Well, Libby was totally out of shape, even though she was thin. And you'd think she'd never been outdoors before, the way she kept freaking out about bugs. Then she got sick, so I helped her get up the mountain."

She leaned toward the hallway. "Well, I better go relieve Gordon," she said. "I'll see you bright and early on the field tomorrow. You won't have to take the Eval again—we'll go right into core training."

"Okay, thanks."

In the doorway, she paused again. "So Darwin's in the news in a bad way. And *you're* a reporter." The implication hung in the air.

When I didn't reply right away, she added in a light

tone, "Well, I guess we'll all have to watch out for you, then." But underneath, there was a wary note.

After Hillary left, I unpacked a few things and thought about what she'd said, about people having to watch out for me. What was it Pike had accused me of being last week? A turkey vulture. Ouch.

You know, you really are *in danger of becoming a vulture,* my most negative inner voice—I call her Harsh Hannah—piped up to inform me.

No, a few necessary evils come with the territory of getting important stories on the air, the reporter in me retorted, a tad snippily.

*I just don't want to see you turning into a bully,*Hannah rejoined. *The world doesn't need any more broadcast blowhards.*

After banishing Hannah to the nether realms of my gray matter, I opened my laptop on the bed to check my e-mail. There was nothing urgent, so I headed back to the main building. I was eager to touch base with Riley. But his office was buttoned up and dark.

On the way back I made a perfunctory stop by the lemongrass tea bar in the lobby, but the idea of an herbal infusion right then was totally unappetizing. What I *really* could have used right about then would have been a hefty slice of Entenmann's Cheese Twist, even though that was on my verboten list. But all the bar was offering that night was a plate of high-fiber scones that, taste-wise, might as well have been a platter of Brillo pads.

To make things worse, I was fighting off a sudden, overwhelming bout of fatigue. The day and the deadline pressure of producing the Darwin story had completely worn me out. I headed outside and along the pathway toward my room.

It was getting late—already ten p.m.—but the night air was surprisingly warm on my face. Especially considering that just last week, there'd been a snowfall.

Hillary was right about my new room's location—it was difficult to locate after dark. Within a few yards of the lobby building, the surrounding light and sound dropped off dramatically. Flat evergreen needles mashed under my feet and released a citruslike scent as I trudged along. The soothing fragrance reminded me that it was a good thing that I was back at the camp. I needed to refocus my efforts to tune my body—my earlier dive into the Oreo shake and sudden onset of strudel thoughts were warning signals that I was just one bite away from a total dietary meltdown.

Soon, I realized that I'd managed to take a wrong turn off the complicated network of pathways. I found myself standing at the end of a deserted cul-de-sac, next to a prefab storage shed that looked like a fake red barn. The only light, amber and flickering, came from a solitary light pole. The bulb made a slight hiss as it sputtered.

Feeling disoriented and slightly spooked, I looked left and right, trying to remember the way back.

"What are you doing here?"

The voice—slurred and hoarse—shot from the silence behind me.

Squeaking out a mouse shriek, I spun around. In the middle of the pathway, just a few feet away, loomed a hulking shadow.

I was debating whether to scream when the shadow stepped forward into the tangerine light. It was Khan.

Riley's partner swayed unsteadily on his feet. A damp troposphere of beer fumes—mixed with tobacco—rolled off him in waves.

"I *said*, 'What are you doing?' " Khan demanded again.

"I'm getting lost, apparently."

What's this guy's problem? I wondered. This was

the second time that he'd snuck up and scared the bejesus out of me.

"Lost, huh?" Slowly and deliberately, Khan closed the gap between us. When he was just inches away from my face, he tilted his head slightly to one side and loomed in, almost as if he were homing in for a kiss. But I knew Khan was gay, so *that* couldn't be what he had in mind.

Fending off a noseful of brew vapors, I tried not to gag as I waited to see what he had to say.

Finally, Khan spoke. "You were the one who talked Riley into getting that damned audit of our books." He turned his head slightly right and spat on the cement walkway, near my feet.

"That's right. Riley doesn't understand the numbers. He needs to know what's happening with the business."

"Who the hell are you to say that? It's not your business," he snapped. "I'm his partner. You stay out of it."

"Riley asked me for help."

"Oh, 'Riley asked me,' " Khan echoed in a mocking tone. "Well, isn't that just the sweetest little thing." "Sweetest" came out "shweest."

I sighed. Khan was obviously too stir-fried to carry on a reasonable dialogue. "Look, Khan, if you have a problem with the audit of the Body Blast books, why don't you take it up with Riley?"

He listed to port. "Maybe I don't have a problem with the audit," he said, jabbing a finger into my chest. "Maybe I have a problem with *you*. The way you're always buzzing around Riley these days. What are you, anyway, some kind of fag hag?"

"Oh, please."

When Khan yawed again, this time to starboard, I stepped deftly around him. Without looking back, I walked away. My footsteps rasped along the concrete path.

In my wake came only silence at first—there was no sound of Khan pursuing me. But then, like a following sea, his voice carried across the night air.

"Hey, Prom Queen," he called. "I know you've always had the hots for Riley, ever since he took you to that high school dance, way back when. He told me all about it one time when we were stoned."

That stopped me. "That's *totally* ridiculous," I snapped, wheeling around. "You—"

Khan yelped out a high-pitched note. It sounded like a hyena's bark. "Riley's not bi, you know," he said. "Maybe he was back then, but not anymore. He doesn't even look at women now."

So that's what was really going on—Khan was jealous. *Brother, that's* all *I need right now,* I thought: *a green-eyed boyfriend on a bender.*

"You need to go someplace and cool off, Khan." I flung the words over my shoulder as I turned away again. "And you need to sober up."

"Pheh, that's what they all say," came the mumbled reply. Then a brief silence, broken by another yip-yelp. "Like that's *news*, Prom Queen!"

I focused on keeping my pace casual and unperturbed as I walked away.

Khan's taunts faded into the distance. But they kept erupting, punctuated occasionally with cackles. "News at eleven! Brought to you by Kate Gallagher, the Queen of Hots for Riley!"

One thing was certain: Khan was *so* much more appealing when he didn't speak.

After navigating my way back to the correct path, I trudged up to the outer door of the bungalow. As I reached for the door's handle, I caught a whiff of something. I paused to sniff: It was smoke. And not Khan's tobacco smoke. It smelled as if someone were burning a pile of leaves close by. A faint crackling noise came from somewhere above my head.

I backpedaled a couple of steps away from the doorway and looked up toward the roof. Against the inky black backdrop of the Carolina hemlocks, one edge of the timbered eaves seemed to be faintly glowing. It looked as if someone had drawn a bright line across the wood with a fluorescent, yellowy orange paint.

Not paint, though—it was a line of flames, a flickering thread that was licking its way slowly across the roof.

The bungalow was on fire.

For a half second, my breath caught in my throat. It took me that long to register what I was seeing.

Then, sound burst from my throat, louder than I'd ever thought possible: "Fire!" I sucked down a huge breath of air, then released it in another scream: *"Fire!"*

I looked wildly around me. The surrounding area was deserted-looking, black.

Someone may be inside, was my first thought. *Get them out.*

One thing my dad—police captain and preacher of personal safety—had drummed into me over the years was how to respond in a fire situation.

Using the back of my hand, I felt the top of the door and the crack around the doorframe, to make sure that the fire wasn't lurking on the other side. The door felt cool. I opened it slowly and carefully.

The smell of smoke in the short hallway was much stronger, almost choking. I pulled my shirt over my nose and mouth, then spotted a fire alarm along the left side of the wall. I pulled it. A buzzing noise—like a hundred alarm clocks going off all at once—hit my eardrums.

Thick, black smoke was boiling from underneath the first door on the right—from *my* door, I realized.

But I didn't have time to check into it. I remembered that Hillary had said only one other person was checked in to this building. But which room?

I ran down the hallway, coughing and banging on doors. They were locked, so I started kicking them.

Several doors down, after I kicked and raised a ruckus that rivaled the fire alarm, a woman stumbled out of her room. She must have been asleep, because she looked at me with a dazed expression and didn't seem to register what was happening.

"We've got to get out of here," I said to her. "Come on."

"W-wait, I gotta put on something," she said, slapping at her thighs. She was wearing only a T-shirt and bikini bottoms.

"No time!" I grabbed her by the shoulders. Then I half herded, half pushed her past the oily black smoke toward the exit door.

Together, we staggered into the cool, clear night.

Coughing and bending over to brace my hands on my knees, I gulped down huge lungfuls of sweet, pure mountain air.

Chapter 17

Too Much of a Good Thing

Back when I was losing weight, I went through a period in which I was actually addicted to exercise. Here are the warning signs that you are exercising compulsively:

- *You don't allow minor injuries to heal before reinjuring them with more exercise*
- *Women experience amenorrhea, which is the cessation of the monthly menstrual cycle*
- *You withdraw from work, social life, and family to focus on working out*

If you're experiencing any of these symptoms, I suggest you consult your doctor and a nutritionist—and maybe a therapist—to get yourself back on a healthier track.

—From *The Little Book of Fat-busters* by Mimi Morgan

"The fire started here, in Ms. Gallagher's room."

The park ranger—Pike, I remembered his name from last week—used a tone that made his words sound like an accusation.

It was early the next morning. Ranger Pike, Riley, and I were walking through the bungalow to survey the fire damage to the building. Most of the damage seemed superficial, primarily smoke residue. *Except* for my room, where we now stood.

My room was a disaster zone. That much was obvious, even though there was barely any visible light. The electricity was shut off, and only feeble patches of gray morning filtered through the smoke-blackened window.

Pike probed the room with a torch flashlight that he held in his hand. The beam revealed a starburst pattern of scorched and charred wood that was concentrated around the window frame. Everything else in the room was soaked and sodden.

I looked from Pike to Riley. "But how could the fire have started *here*?" I said. "I was only in here for a second last night to drop off my bag. And by the time I came back, the fire had already started."

"Maybe it was something electrical?" Riley suggested. Overnight, he'd developed a permanent-looking worry line on his brow.

The night before, Riley had arrived at the scene—along with a small brigade of Body Blast employees and campers—moments after I escaped from the bungalow fire with Ms. Bikini Bottoms. A short while later, an engine responded from a nearby substation, and the crew quickly knocked down the blaze. Khan never showed up—I figured he'd probably passed out under a pine tree somewhere.

After the fire was put out, Bikini and I were offered clothing and lodging in other rooms. But I elected to spend a rough night on an undersized couch in Riley's office.

That turned out to be a big mistake. I rolled off the couch early the next morning, still wearing an odd mixture of hand-me-down Body Blast sweatpants and a long-sleeved T-shirt that from all appearances must have belonged to an orangutan-weightlifter, judging by the way it billowed at the shoulders and hung long over my wrists. I still hadn't had a chance to shower or brush my teeth. I might even have BO, I thought as I caught a waft of something close-in and sour-smelling.

But my *odeur du corps* didn't appear to be the reason that Pike was glaring at me now.

"The fire inspector is coming back within the hour. He'll check out the electrical," he said to me. "But are you sure you weren't smoking? Last week, I recall, I found you standing next to a pile of cigarette butts. You seemed quite interested in them."

"But I told you then, those weren't my cigarettes. I don't even *smoke*," I said, trying to keep a defensive note from creeping into my voice.

The beam of the ranger's flashlight traced the edges of the room's small, square window. In the middle of the windowsill, the light paused on a small pile of blackened debris.

Pike stepped to the window, bent down, and brought the light in close. He peered at the charred remains. Then, leaning down even closer, he gingerly poked at them with the edge of the flashlight.

"You can forget about the cause being electrical," he announced, straightening up. "This is an incendiary device. I'm going to have to ask both of you to leave this area, right now. But don't go far."

"An *incendiary* device? What kind?" I asked him.

Pike glared at me, then nodded toward the window. "An old kind, but effective," he said. "A pack of matches tied up with a rubber band, attached to a cigarette. The arsonist lights the cigarette, which burns down until it lights up the matches. Fortunately, the fire didn't wipe out all the evidence."

Pike looked from me to Riley. "If this was done by anyone connected to you, we'll be talking to you about insurance fraud, I promise you. And as of this very second, the entire building and surrounding perimeter is off-limits to you, your staff, and your customers. No mistakes, or I'm shutting you down immediately. You got that?"

"Got it," Riley said.

"We're just lucky that no one was hurt or killed. *Killed* would have meant a murder charge." On the word "murder," Pike's eyes raked through me as if I were a heap of dead coals.

As the ranger was talking, his flashlight beam caught the edge of my laptop, which was sitting in the middle of a pool of water on the sodden bed. The laptop—and all my notes about the case—were probably a total loss. *Hosed*, I thought bleakly.

"Okay. Come on, Kate." Riley extended an arm.

I followed him mutely outside, feeling like a hound that had been kicked in the ribs. I didn't know which was worse—the idea that someone had deliberately set a fire in my room, or Pike's none-too-subtle implication that my name—and Riley's—topped the list of arson suspects. It felt like having a blister rubbed raw to be wearing the shoe on the other foot, to be the person *accused* of something. It occurred to me that I'd probably have more empathy for the targets of my investigative stories, from now on.

Riley led me outside and down a path to a curved cement bench that was tucked underneath a stand of trees. "Let's sit down here for a second," he said, then took a closer look at me. "Hey, hon, you don't look so good. You need to find a bathroom or something?"

"No, I'm okay." I pressed my fingers against my stomach and tried to ignore a sudden urge to vomit. "Riley, you *know* I didn't start that fire last night. All I did after I arrived was talk to Hillary for a second in my room. Then I parked my gear and left."

He waved off my protestation. "It hurts me that you even think you have to say that. I can't understand how Pike would suspect either one of us, frankly."

"Because statistically, insurance fraud is the number one reason for arson-set fires," I said to him. "In fact, it's typically the *only* reason for arson fires. I learned that while I was working on a story a while back."

"But that would mean *I* set the fire, not you."

"Well, it started in my room, and you're my close friend, so that makes it seem like . . ." I let the implication hang in the air.

"Like we're in cahoots . . ." Riley dropped his head into his hands. "Oh, my God."

I sat for a moment, thinking. "Remember last week?" I finally said. "You told me there had been another fire, a couple of months ago. You said that fire started in an equipment shed that had previously been burglarized. Right?"

Riley looked at me warily. "What about it?"

"Well, when they investigated, was there any sign of arson?"

When he didn't reply, I pressed, "What?"

"Actually, we never reported that fire." He sighed. "I know we should have, but we were able to put it out really fast. Our operating license is up for review in August, and, well, because Libby's murder is still being investigated . . . I just didn't want to draw attention to any more problems."

"That sucks, Riley. If there *was* any evidence, it's probably long gone now. You'd better tell Pike about the other fire ASAP."

Riley set his chin. "I don't think I can do that," he said. "They'd shut us down for sure."

"Are you *insane*?" I half turned on the bench to stare at him. "This is an arson investigation. That's an unbelievably serious charge. And you've already got a murder investigation on your hands. You can't afford to fool around right now—you've got to tell the authorities what you know, and let the business chips fall where they may. Worse comes to worst you shut down, then later on you reopen when the smoke clears."

"So to speak," Riley said with a weak grin. He twisted his hands, which were hanging between his knees. "You're right, of course. I'll tell Pike about the shed fire."

"Good."

"Do you think Darwin could be behind it? The fire last night, I mean?" Riley asked. "I mean, on top of all the trouble he's in with the police, I gave him the boot yesterday, and you ran that story about him on the news. He must want to kill *both* of us right about now."

I thought for a moment. "Someone could have told him where my room was," I said. "That's possible, I guess. But if the two fires are linked—if the shed blaze was arson, too—what motive would he have had to set the earlier one?"

"Dunno about that."

We sat silently on the bench for a moment and gazed over the sports field, which unfurled in the distance below us. Morning workouts were underway. People were huffing around the perimeter of the field in little ragtag groups, and the sound of a whistle blast reached our ears, carried on an updraft.

"You were going to tell me something yesterday, before I rushed off to do the Darwin interview," I said after a while. "What was on your mind?"

After a moment's hesitation, Riley sighed. "Our books here at Body Blast are way, way off," he said. "That accountant—the one you introduced me to?—says that the receivables for Body Blast are being overreported. Significantly. The truth is, we're almost broke. I'm probably going to have to lay some people off."

"Khan's been skimming?"

"Yeah. And it's not just a screwup—it's deliberate, the accountant says. That's why I wasn't around all afternoon yesterday. Khan and I were having a knock-down, drag-out over it."

"What did he say when you confronted him?"

"I had to practically beat it out of him, but he finally admitted everything. It's because of his gambling, just like you said a while back. He's gotten himself into some trouble with a loan shark. I guess the guy's been threatening him unless he comes up with thirty thousand, fast. Khan actually had the nerve to ask me to lend him the money, can you believe the gall? Like I have *that* kind of dough on hand—thanks to him, we're running on a shoestring right now." Riley groaned and hunched forward on the bench. "Aargh, why do I always fall for bad boys? It's like my curse or something."

Riley's information about the state of finances at his business only worsened my fears. If his business was teetering on the edge of a financial meltdown, it only increased his motivation for fire insurance fraud, from an investigator's point of view.

"I bumped into Khan last night, right before the fire broke out," I said, making a motion as if lifting a cup to my lips. "He seemed pretty pissed, in every sense of the word."

"You mean wasted?"

When I nodded, Riley swore under his breath. "It figures that he'd swan dive into a saki bottle after our fight," he said. "God, he's *so* incredibly pathetic when he's all jugged up. This is the first time he's ever brought it into the camp, though."

"How much money has he stolen?"

"About 40K, from what the accountant can figure so far."

"Yikes. What are you going to do about it?"

"Legally?" Riley sighed. "Nothing, unless he refuses to pay me back. But we'll have to break everything up business-wise. I can't have a partner I can't trust. Beyond that, I don't know. I told him he has to get some help, or it's over between us. And I really mean it this time."

I thought about what Riley had said about Khan needing to come up with more money for the loan shark. "What if Khan was planning to rip off the insurance money?" I asked him. "Do you think he could have—"

"No way." He stared at me. "You mean, did *he* start that fire? No way would he do anything like that. Not in a million years."

"But last week you didn't think he was stealing from you, either."

"That's true."

"Or," I said, thinking it through some more, "maybe the loan shark is making good on his threats. Did Khan say who he owes all his gambling money to? Is it just one person?"

Riley nodded. "Guy has a really weird name," he said. "It sounded like Evil Eggplant."

A chill ran through me. "Do you mean Yves Laplante?"

"That sounds right. You've heard of him?"

"He's a French Canadian guy who runs a string of pawnshops, the biggest in North Carolina. But his real business is black market gun dealing and loan sharking. The DA keeps trying to convict him, but nothing sticks—he's got such a violent reputation that people are afraid to testify, I think. About three months ago, he was brought up on some charges. I covered the trial. But he managed to beat that rap on a technicality."

"What was he charged with?"

After a beat, I delivered my reply. "Arson and insurance fraud."

Riley buried his face in his hands again.

Chapter 18

Go for the Burn . . . *Not*!

Back in the day, our mothers suffered while sweating along to Jane Fonda tapes. "No pain, no gain," was the mantra circa 1980.

Nowadays, we know that the opposite is true. A little soreness here and there doesn't hurt when you're learning a new exercise, but repeated over-stressing of your muscles can actually tear them down—and that's the opposite of your goal! Proper workouts build your muscles gradually and precisely.

Along with headbands and hideous hair, "going for the burn" is so yesterday.

—From *The Little Book of Fat-busters* by Mimi Morgan

After Riley headed off to confess to Pike about the shed fire, I grabbed a chance to take a quick shower in the gym. I didn't push to tag along with Riley, mainly because I wanted to be spared another j'accuse-atory encounter with the park ranger. Plus, I desperately needed to do some exercise if I was going to salvage anything body-wise out of the weekend.

After wolfing down a lumpy brown rice and scrambled egg concoction that the kitchen staff warmed up for me, I tramped down to the workout field.

Hillary's group had already departed on a hike, so I got put in Erica's Advanced Corps. Fitness-wise, it was instantly apparent that I was out of my league. But what made things worse was that every time Erica looked my way, she winced like someone who felt a tooth abscess coming on.

"Your external obliques need a *lot* of work." She punctuated the criticism with a disdainful sniff as she put me through yet another set of ab crunches and thigh lifts, which have to be my least favorite exercises in the universe.

I couldn't muster a comeback because I was in too much agony. *This is what the onset of labor must feel like,* I thought—like a giant lobster claw had grabbed hold of you around the middle and was squeezing you in half.

At the end of the first hour, I was exhausted, sweating like a pig and ready to beg for mercy. Erica and a couple of überfit guys—I called them the Hardy Boys—stayed on the field while the rest of the group took a hydration break.

I crawled to the edge of the field and threw myself down on the grass next to a couple of backpacks that had been stowed there.

I'd been lying there for several minutes, gasping like a flounder that's just been hauled in for the journey to someone's Red Lobster platter, when a burst of tinny music announced that a cell phone was ringing nearby. Startled, I looked around; the phone was sitting on top of the nearest pack with its flip-top open. The caller ID on the phone's LCD screen said MIKE CROWLEY.

At the sound of the ringing cell phone, Erica came hurtling off the field and scooped it up.

"Hey, Mikey." She turned away with her head bent over the phone, then spoke in a hushed tone. By straining my ears, I caught snatches of her end of the conversation. It sounded like they were talking about some kind of new workout program.

That's when I recalled something: When Marnie's lifeless body had been lying out on the exercise field, Erica had told me that the sports field was a dead zone for cellular reception. And now here she was, taking calls from her honey bear, if that's who this "Mikey" was. It made my antennae go up.

When Erica returned a minute later, she gave me a challenging look.

"You had enough yet?"

"Not yet." Jeez Louise, what was *with* this chick? Had I sat on her little gym-rat dog when I wasn't looking? That's the vibe I got. But apparently, it was directed only at me—by contrast, she and the Hardy Boys were carrying on like they were in Best Bud City.

Erica placed her fists on her hips. "Well, I think you should head back to the gym. You're totally unqualified for this group," she said. "You're holding the others back. I need to spend my time with the more advanced people."

"I'm holding my own. And by the way, I thought you said the other day—when Marnie died—that there was no cell phone coverage out here on the sports field."

"I *what*?" Erica looked confused. "Oh. I upgraded my cell phone service, that's all. You got a problem with that?"

"No, it's just that—"

"Forget it." Erica dismissed me with a wave of her hand and then turned away. "I'm busting you back to the beginner's level. You can go work out your triceps until Hillary's group gets back."

As she tromped back onto the field, it was all I

could do to keep from working out my middle finger—in her direction.

Riley looked puzzled when I tracked him down in his office and mentioned the phone call I'd just overheard. "Mike interviewed for a job here a while back, but then he got a better offer at one of those upscale gyms downtown," he said. "Mike's in touch with Erica, you say? Could they be dating, do you think?"

When I nodded, he added, "Funny, I'd envision him as more of a gym bunny fan. Erica's kind of . . . I don't know. Hard-edged, maybe. I always thought she'd make a fabulous dyke."

"A lot of their conversation sounded like it had something to do with the training business, but it was kind of coded. It sounded as if they were designing something together. Like a workout program, maybe?"

He frowned. "I just hope he and Erica aren't planning to run off with my clients—open their own place."

"What makes you think they'd do that?"

Riley hooted. "Trainers are notorious for poaching clients," he told me. "As soon as I find a decent one who builds up a client list, they start getting big ideas about opening their own place. And then, bam-o—they take off with half your list. And Erica's the best trainer I have."

Humph, not judging by me, I thought as I turned to leave. I'd just as soon train with Bridezilla the Hun.

At his office door, I turned back. "By the way, what kind of reception did you get from the ranger, when you told him about the shed fire?" I asked him.

"Ranger Pike was busy with the fire marshal." He stepped to the window and adjusted the blinds against the noonday sun. The motion cast horizontal bars of light and shadow across his face. "Pike wouldn't even talk to me—he just gave me a look like I was the scum of the earth."

"So you didn't tell him, then?"

Instead of answering, Riley kept adjusting the blinds, as if trying for a precise slant of light. "I'm scared at how ugly all this is getting," he finally said. "If Khan or his loan shark had anything to do with last night's fire, Pike may assume that I was in on it, too. Do you think he'd think that?"

"It's too soon to panic." I knew that didn't sound very reassuring. "But you might want to talk to your lawyer."

Riley grimaced. "At five hundred bucks an hour? I don't think so," he said. "So, what are you going to do now?"

"I'm heading north to the tri-city area for the rest of the day, to check out a few things."

My first order of business would be to track down an evil eggplant.

On the assumption that you shouldn't venture into a lion's den without letting someone know where to come pick up your carcass, I found a quiet corner in the lobby to call Crystal, the law beat reporter at Channel Twelve. I told her that I was heading to the town of Newton to track down Khan's loan shark, Yves Laplante.

As expected, Crystal lodged an objection.

"You're going to Laplante's place? By *yourself*?" Over our connection, I heard her take in a deep drag from a cigarette. "Are you out of your frickin,' *frickin'* mind? That guy has people killed," she said on the exhale.

"Keep in mind, though—he's never been convicted of anything."

Crystal's obscene comeback would have been stricken by the judge, if we'd been in a courtroom.

I visualized my reporter friend in her cubicle at Channel Twelve. Within easy arm reach, as usual, would be her crammed ashtray, which said YOUR CIVIL RIGHTS on the side of it. Even though we hadn't known each other long, I'd taken a real liking to the law reporter. An African American, tough-talking chain-smoker with a Harvard Law degree, Crystal didn't teeter around in tight suits and stilettos like most TV women. She strode through life wearing sensible shoes.

"Okay, so here's the deal—you're calling me the *second* you get outta that loan shark's place," she instructed me. "If I don't hear from you by three o'clock p.m. sharp, I'm sending in the Marines. Or at least I'll send in Frank. He's still looking for payback for that brick wall thing."

Three months earlier, when I'd covered Laplante's arson trial, one of his bodyguards had expressed his admiration for the media by slamming Frank into the wall of the courthouse.

"You can send Frank, but don't do it unless I don't call you," I told her.

On the other end of the line, Crystal chuckled. "And hey, speaking of calling—and *calling*—someone was trying to reach you big-time yesterday," she said. "I just happened to glance at your phone when it rung one time, and it said 'Detective J. Reed.' That's Jonathan Reed in Durham Homicide, right?"

"Right."

"I met him once on a story—talk about a hottie. *Ooh,* honey, even his accent is hot. If you don't mind a snoopy question, is he a story, or personal?"

"He's . . . personal. I think."

She paused, then said, "I guess that explains why I haven't *happened* to see that other caller ID in a while. That wannabe fiancé boy—Lou, right? Is he gone? Not that I'm snooping again, mind you."

"You know what? I'm just not up to talking about it right now." I could hear my voice crack.

"Okay. But girl, we're sooooo having dinner as soon as you get back from that butt-hole camp. I sense the need for a major hair-letting-down session. It will involve significant amounts of booze."

"That sounds great. This week, let's do it. Definitely."

"Don't forget, baby—call me by three." Crystal's last words came across as I clicked off.

Before leaving for Newton, I stopped in the lunchroom in search of a bite to eat. My conversation with Crystal had deposited a sad little pressure over my heart, which telegraphed itself to my stomach as a hunger pang. Excited as I was at the prospect of the date next Saturday with Reed, I worried that I hadn't recovered from my breakup with Lou. I couldn't bear to think about Lou very much; whenever I did, everything disappeared into a vortex of red rage. And inside the rage was hurt. That probably wasn't the best mind-set for launching a new relationship.

"Stick a fork in it, Kate," I muttered, banishing further analysis of my romantic imbroglio. I needed to have my head on straight if I was going to face the loan shark, Laplante.

I needed to sort out all the recent events that had taken place. Unfortunately, the loss of my laptop—and with it all my notes—in the previous night's fire had disoriented me. I was starting to feel fragmented. In an effort to regroup, I spent the next hour by myself at a table in the cafeteria, hunkered over my BlackBerry while I chomped down a raw veggie and navy bean salad.

Ignoring the crunch of celery in my jaw as well as the chatter that was swirling around me in the cafeteria, I used the notes feature to recreate everything that had happened since my first arrival at the camp.

I tried to put it all into a rough semblance of a time line. There were so many moving parts to the story. Maybe if I put everything down in a brain dump, I could detect some critical paths that would help me figure out what was really going on at Body Blast.

Ever since Marnie's body had been discovered on the sports field, I'd assumed that she was murdered. But I was wrong, evidently. The SBI was saying now that her fall was accidental. That meant I could put to rest my suspicions that she'd been killed by Darwin, or by her volatile ex-boyfriend Antonio, he of the *puerco gordo* put-downs.

But there *had* been one homicide: Someone had pushed Libby Fowler off a cliff the previous October. And according to Reed's friend Carla at the SBI, Darwin was a suspect in that death. That was something I needed to do right away, I reminded myself—to follow up with Carla and get any information I could about the ongoing investigation into Libby's death.

Another troubling issue was last night's arson fire. I couldn't imagine any logical connection between the fire and Libby's murder, so I had to assume that they were completely separate incidents. And there'd been that previous shed fire, the one that Riley had never reported to the authorities. I suspected that the fires were somehow connected to the gambling debts of Riley's partner, Khan. Perhaps Khan's loan shark—Yves Laplante—set both fires to make good on his threats. Or maybe Khan had started them, hoping to rip off the insurance proceeds.

Then there was my friend Riley. I couldn't put my finger on it, but something about the way he'd been behaving recently was bothering me. It almost seemed as if he was holding something back. He'd pushed for me to get to the bottom of everything that was going on at Body Blast, so why was I picking up an evasive vibe from him now? My fingers felt heavy as I tapped a single word onto the screen with the stylus—"Riley?"

I stared at the blinking cursor for a long minute, chewing over the entry. Then, with an abrupt shake of my head, I erased his name. A passing vibe wasn't enough to merit an entry in my notes.

There'd also been those unexplained thefts at the camp—the break-in to the equipment shed that later caught fire, and the cash that had been swiped from Riley's office. Those incidents, however, seemed like garden-variety thefts that anyone could have done. Again, my primo suspect for those was Khan.

When everything was jotted down, I reviewed my notes. There was still a lot that was unexplained in the mix—starting with the connection between Marnie's death and Libby's.

There *was* no connection between the two deaths, according to the SBI; Marnie's was an accident, Libby's a homicide—finis, end of story. But I was still troubled by some unanswered questions. I'd never bought the idea that Marnie had ventured down to the sports field by herself before dawn on the morning she died. From everything I'd observed about her, she simply wasn't the hardy, morning-exercise type. Just like Libby wouldn't have gone crawling around a dark mountainside by herself, as her brother Theo had told me. Neither scenario for the two women's arrival at the scenes of their deaths made any sense.

What *did* make sense was that someone was with Marnie on the morning she died. But who? And why didn't that person report her fall? Why didn't they sound the alarm, if it had been a simple accident?

The question reminded me of a chain reaction collision that I'd once witnessed in the Callahan Tunnel in Boston. A drunk had come up behind a line of cars at high speed and smacked into the end car with such force that it set off a series of fender benders. All the damaged cars pulled into the emergency lane to sort out the insurance paperwork—except for one. A BMW with tinted windows had hesitated, then taken off with a squeal of tires. At the time I'd concluded that the driver didn't want to draw attention to himself by getting involved in the accident. He probably had something to hide.

Maybe the person who witnessed Marnie's accident had something to hide, too. But who? What person would need to hide by not reporting her death?

I could think of only one probable person: the one who'd killed Libby.

That person had something to hide, big-time.

At first glance, Yves Laplante's headquarters looked like any other pawnshop doing business in the ragged exurban edges of the city of Newton. With its blinking neon sign—PAWN—LOAN—EXCHANGE YOUR SCRAP GOLD FOR CASH—the storefront seemed to be just another stopping point for overpriced toys as they left the hands of their overextended owners in exchange for a fistful of dollars. But behind the dumpy stucco façade, I knew, functioned one of the most powerful criminal organizations in the tri-city area.

Here and there were visible hints of the real business at hand, however: the webwork of iron that covered every accessible portal and window; the security cameras that monitored any unfortified point of entry; the firearms stacked behind the plate glass window. The loan shark's waters were not to be entered lightly.

And I wasn't feeling particularly light at the moment. I'd driven two hours from the mountains to get here, merely in hope of finding Laplante on the premises.

Even if I located him, there was no good reason to believe that the loan shark would talk to me. This excursion had all the hallmarks of a risky crapshoot.

The only reason I was rolling the dice was in hope of getting a flash of reaction, some fleeting indication that Laplante was behind the arson fire that had destroyed my room the previous night.

By arriving unannounced and surprising him with questions, I hoped to provoke an outburst like the one I'd seen during his trial, when he erupted in a rage at the prosecutor. He'd called her every unique name for female genitalia that's listed in the slang dictionary. Maybe if he went off into another temper tantrum, he'd reveal something useful. Unless he killed me first, that is.

After parking my car along the street, I trudged up to the front door of the pawnshop. It was locked. I gaped awkwardly into the lens of the overhead security camera. After an eternity, it seemed, a buzzing noise sounded. The door released with a vibrating snap.

I stepped through the entry into a small tiled foyer, which was sealed off on two sides by three-inch Plexiglas.

Behind the barrier, at a desk that was strewn with gold chains, and chomping a stub of a cigar, sat an even squatter, stubbier man—Yves Laplante.

As he scrutinized me, Laplante's gaze went from evaluating to wary. He rose from his chair and approached the speaker portal between us.

"Ah, a visit by the Fourth Estate. What brings you about today?" He pronounced "about" Canadian-style, as "a boot." His hard, flat gaze scanned my outfit, a borrowed tracksuit topped off by a seersucker jacket of Riley's that I'd donned in a desperate attempt to look more professional. But it probably came off more like homeless-woman chic, I realized.

I summoned up a smile that felt too stretched across my face. "I have a couple of questions that I need to consult an expert about. I thought you might have some answers."

When Laplante didn't reply right away, I thought he was about to tell me to get lost. But then, lifting his shoulders in a shrug, he pressed a buzzer along the counter.

A young guy with pitted red skin and a boxy sports jacket materialized from a back room. Without saying a word or even glancing my way, he folded his hands behind his back and assumed a stance next to the chair that Laplante had abandoned. I wondered what kind of weapon he carried underneath his jacket.

Laplante punched another button. A narrow door between the office and the foyer popped open. He stepped through the door, bringing with him a sickly-smelling draft of cigar smoke. As he walked toward me with his big belly hanging over toothpick legs, he really *did* look like an ambulating eggplant.

On the ledge lip below the Plexiglas, I noticed a small ceramic bowl filled with packages of matches.

I reached for a pack. "Mind?"

"Knock yourself out. I prefer lighting up a different way." With a stretch of his lips that showed off a row of feral, wide-spaced teeth, Laplante leaned his butt against the wall. He pulled an engraved silver lighter from his pocket and relit his cigar. After filling his cheeks with smoke, he clinked the lighter shut.

Before he could exhale the cheek full of fumes, I told him I was researching a story.

Forming his lips into a thick O, Laplante blew a smoke ring in my direction. "And this has to do with me because . . . ?"

"Because it involves one of your borrowers, Khan Douglas."

Laplante's eyes narrowed. "Not acquainted with the man."

"My information is that you *are* acquainted, and that he owes you a lot of money."

"That's business. My business, not yours."

"There was an arson fire last night at the camp where Khan's a partner. I'm wondering whether he—or someone else—could have set it. I thought you might know something about it."

Laplante stared at me. His expression seemed caught between disbelief and annoyance, like a bulldog being challenged by a teacup poodle. Then he threw back his head and laughed. It was a mirthless sound.

"Anything's possible. What makes you think it was arson?"

"The investigators say so."

Behind me, the front door buzzed open. I smelled the person who was coming in before I saw him. A young guy wearing dust-streaked jeans and a T-shirt stepped through the door, his arms wrapped around a wobbly stack of cardboard boxes. Arriving with him was an almost overwhelming smell of BO. The black stench invaded the small foyer.

He looked from me to Laplante as if surprised to see us standing in the foyer. "Hey, Legs, we got the g-"

"Shut up. Take it around back," Laplante snapped. "I told you, moron, don't bring that stuff in through the front. And don't call me Legs in front of civilians."

"Sorry, Legs. I mean . . . shit. Sorry," Stinky mumbled, and then stumbled back outside.

Laplante looked on as he disappeared. "The idiots I have working for me these days. All my regular guys are in jail," he said, shaking his head. His eyes swung back to me. "On false charges, of course."

"Of course."

Laplante plucked his cigar from his mouth. "You've

shown some decent-sized balls by coming here. And I'm in a good mood today, so what the hell." He raised the cigar in the air as if it were a teacher's pointer. "Here. I'll give you a little lesson. You can call it Arson 101."

Snorting at his own joke, he added, "Arson 101. Hey, I like that."

Laplante pointed the burning end of the cigar toward his opposite palm. With a twisting motion, he ground the glowing tip into his skin. It made a hissing sound, releasing a puff of burnt flesh. He didn't flinch.

I forced myself not to reel back while Laplante continued in a calm, almost professorial tone. "If a fire is set by a professional, it takes the cops a while to find any traces," he said. "Sometimes—if you're lucky—they never do. But if they find evidence right away, you can bet your bottom dollar the job was done by a rank amateur."

"I see."

"You see." He paused. "You *see*?" His voice changed, becoming agitated. "Well, then see this, Ms. TV News Reporter—Ms. TV News *Distorter*—you can take what you *see* right back to the fire marshal. You can tell him that arson job wasn't done by any of my guys. And you can tell them to get the hell off my back." He was ramping up.

"You sound a tad upset."

"You're damned right I'm upset. I'm upset that you come here, trying to pin some kind of goddamned Smoky the Campfire on Yves Laplante. Probably some dope-smoker toasting their stupid marshmallows set it. How the hell should I know—I'm outa that whole line of business. Not that I was ever *in* it, y'unnerstand?"

"Hmm, I think I do understand."

Laplante slapped his hand across his chest, over his

heart. "I'm a businessman. I'm a legitimate businessman trying to run a simple pawnshop." He scowled. "Merde, the crap you people put me through."

I opened my mouth to speak, then closed it as his rant picked up steam. "The cops think they're tough because they wear uniforms—because they got badges." He jabbed the air near my chest with his cigar stub. "They think they're *tough*? I pay my driver more than they make. They're all a bunch of low-paid control-freak shitheads. They don't know how to make any decent money, so they get off on giving businessmen like me a hard time. The same goes for reporters. You're all a bunch of hyenas. You're scavengers."

"I'm sorry you feel that way about us, Legs."

He was too busy nodding in violent agreement with himself to register the forbidden moniker. "Compared to you losers, I'm a fuckin' *lion*. I'm the fuckin' lion, king of the jungle. And here, while I'm at it—"

He grabbed my wrist. "The lion's gonna give you a survival tip. Here's a little bit of jungle law." He twisted my hand over, forcing it palm up.

With his other hand, he dropped the cigar into the center of my hand. One end of the stub was ashy and still uncomfortably warm; the other end was moist and disgusting from being in his mouth.

Using both hands, he cinched my fingers closed around the cigar. "Don't let me catch you coming back around here," he said. "Not ever. You got that message through your little red-haired curly brain?"

Message received.

Chapter 19

Avoid Faux Foods

Don't be snookered by "fat free" foods such as cookies, muffins, and spreads. These faux foods are usually high in calories, sugar, and noxious chemicals. It's much better to eat one small, regular bagel with a little butter than one dripping with fake, gluey butter substitute.

Those faux foods are not only unsatisfying, they're also not good for you.

—From *The Little Book of Fat-busters* by Mimi Morgan

It took several rounds of scrubbing in the ladies' room of a nearby Waffle House to wash Laplante's spit and cigar stench from my hands. But it would take a whole lot longer to regain my equilibrium after the ugly encounter with the loan shark.

I couldn't tell whether Laplante was telling the truth about not being involved in the fire at Body Blast. He had a big local reputation as a cheat and a liar, and I'd be the last person he'd be straight with—except for possibly the cops. He'd made one honest-sounding admission, though, when he said that most of his "regular guys" were in jail. If he'd hired the arsonist, maybe he had to make do with a bumbler, like Stinky. Maybe that's why the arson job had been so easy for Ranger Pike to spot. The arsonist had botched the job.

Now that I'd spoken with Laplante, I thought it made sense to tell the fire marshal about Khan's gambling debts to the loan shark. Once I convinced Riley that it was best to get everything out into the open, I'd get him to make that call. Plus, I had a pack of Laplante's matches—perhaps the fire marshal could tie them in with the ones that were used to start the blaze.

After checking in with Crystal at Channel Twelve to assure her I'd survived my run-in with Laplante, I headed out for my next appointment—something a little more civil, I hoped. At four thirty p.m., I was scheduled to meet Carla Manning, the SBI agent, in a park in downtown Raleigh, near the SBI headquarters. We'd chosen to meet in a park rather than her office to keep her from being spotted talking to a reporter.

Traffic woes delayed me on the drive from Newton to Raleigh, so I was running a few minutes late by the time I arrived. After pulling into a metered lot, I dashed into the park, worried that Carla might have given up on me and left.

The park was centered around a small but beautiful duck pond. Afternoon light slanted through the surrounding trees and cast quivering sunspots onto the surface of the water. The circles of light shattered into diamonds whenever a cruising mallard webbed through them. A serene scene, to be sure, but right then my mood was far too unserene to enjoy it.

I scanned the area around me wildly, trying to identify anyone who looked remotely like an SBI agent. To my left, a pack of school-aged kids was clambering across the top of a jungle gym and swinging from bars, burning off after-school energy under the watchful gaze of several women who looked like nannies and stay-at-home moms.

The only likely-looking candidate for Carla was a young but professionally dressed woman who sat on a wooden bench near the edge of the duck pond. She was feeding peanuts to pigeons from a red-striped paper bag.

I approached her. "Carla Manning?"

When she nodded, I sat next to her on the green wooden slats of the bench. "I'm Kate Gallagher. Sorry that I'm a few minutes late."

"No problem. I guess we could have met at headquarters after all—no one would have made you out as a reporter," Carla said, eying my outfit.

I tugged the lapels of Riley's jacket closer together. "There was a fire at the camp last night, and I lost all my clothes. I really appreciate your coming, though."

Carla raised the peanut bag in a wry toast, then shifted around on the bench to focus on my face. She had an intense, quartz gaze that I suspected would be quite intimidating under the right circumstances, such as from the other side of an interrogation table.

She began, "Just so you know, I've given our friend Jonathan some serious shit for talking to you about the SBI's investigation into Libby Fowler's murder. I told him *I'd* talk to you. He shouldn't have." She cracked open a shell and launched a fat peanut, which was quickly absorbed by a swarm of pigeons.

"Please don't hold it against him," I said. "I talked him into it because I was up against a big deadline."

"You reporters always are." Carla shook her head. "I told Jonathan, 'Don't talk out of school just because you have the hots for this woman.' "

Twin plumes of heat rose in my cheeks. "Can I ask how the two of you—"

"Know each other? We met during a joint task force when he first came to the U.S." She shot me a sideways glance, and the edges of her lips twitched. "But to answer your *real* question—did Jonathan and I ever have a 'thing'—the answer is yes. Nowadays, though, it's strictly friendship."

I loved the frank way Carla spoke her mind. She reminded me of a slightly profane, slightly older sister. It was no surprise to hear that she and Jonathan had once been a romantic item. Despite her no-nonsense investigator's garb, there was something feline and compelling about her looks. I hoped I'd have a chance to get to know her better.

Before we went any further, Carla set some ground rules about how I could report her information.

"If you mention any of my information in your story, it'll have to be attributed to 'an anonymous source at the SBI,' " she said. "That'll really piss Powell off. Too damn bad for him."

"Then I gather you're not a member of Investigator Powell's fan club."

"Few women in law enforcement are. Powell can't stand for any female to be on the job, except for maybe as a meter maid."

"Gotcha. So, can you give me an update about what's going on in the investigation into Libby Fowler's death? Is Darwin still a suspect?"

Carla stared at me. "Jonathan trusts you, so I guess I can. But this next part is on deep background, okay?"

Information that a reporter gets on "deep background" means that you can report it, but you can't identify the source in any way. I wouldn't even be able to say that the information came from anyone at the SBI.

"Absolutely. I'll attribute anything you say to an 'anonymous source.' "

"Okay. Well, it's too soon to tell, but odds are that Darwin will be cleared in Libby's murder. The investigation's pretty much at a dead end right now."

I stared at her, surprised.

Carla shrugged. "There isn't enough evidence to pin

anything down," she said. "Right now our operating theory is that she was killed by someone she didn't know—it might have been someone guarding a hooch. And if that's what happened, we'll never find him. He's probably back in Mexico by now."

"A *hooch*? What's that?"

"That's the encampment where people live who are hired to protect the marijuana plants. On the big farms, they're mostly working for Mexican drug cartels."

" 'Hooch' sounds like a term out of the old Vietnam War."

"Unfortunately, suppressing crime on the public lands is getting to be like a war. For whatever reason, though, it doesn't get much media attention."

"Well, it will now. But I'm just wondering—how do you know for *sure* that Libby was murdered? Isn't it possible that she just fell accidentally?"

"The autopsy showed a pattern of bruises that meant she was struck on the back of her head. She didn't fall down that ravine—someone clobbered her, then shoved her."

"Wow. Do they have any idea what she was hit by?"

"Something long and solid—possibly a rock-climbing ax. Or a farming tool." Carla dumped the rest of the peanuts into a heap by her feet, which set off a flapping feeding frenzy. "Right now we're hoping that something new breaks," she continued. "That story you did last night actually jarred a little movement, so I guess I'll forgive Jonathan for spilling his beans to you. Libby's family called this morning to say they're offering a hundred-thousand-dollar reward for any tip resulting in a conviction. So maybe that'll lead us to something new."

"Great, I can report that. Only about the reward, I

mean. Is that okay?" I reached into the jacket's inside pocket for a pen and a new spiral notebook that I'd purchased on the way to the park.

When Carla nodded, I added, "What about Marnie Taylor, though? Her death seems similar to Libby's."

"There's no evidence to contradict the coroner's ruling in that one." She shrugged again. "No evidence, no case."

"But did you know that Darwin has a connection to Marnie?" I pressed, making some notes. "I told Investigator Powell about it. Right before Marnie died, she confronted Darwin about a relationship they had when she was underage—twelve years old, in fact. Powell kind of blew me off when I tried to talk to him about it."

"He included your information in his report, though. He just never found anything to suggest homicide in her case, based on the physical evidence. Powell's an asshole, but he's not a bad cop."

Before she left, I told Carla about my visit to Yves Laplante's office, and my suspicion that he was behind the arson fire at Body Blast.

Carla let fly with a long, impressed-sounding whistle. "You're lucky you made it out of there in one piece," she said. "Laplante and his boys play rough—he's way more dangerous than most people know."

"This time, he let me go with a warning cigar." I explained about the way he'd ground the burning cigar against his hand, then into mine.

Carla's eyebrows rose. "You want to press charges?"

"I don't think so." I shook my head. "Besides, I got what I needed out of the interview."

"Well, Laplante's days on the street as a free man are numbered, in any case." She crumpled the empty peanut bag into a ball. "We're gonna nail that asswipe this time. We're building a case against him right now with a little help from the feds—from the only agency he fears."

"The FBI?"

"No, the IRS."

I raised my eyebrows. "With everything he's done, Laplante will finally go to jail for not paying taxes?"

With perfect execution, Carla jump-shot the balled-up paper bag into a nearby trash can. "Hey, don't knock it. It's how they finally put away Al Capone."

I remained on the park bench for a long while after Carla left, to phone in her tip about the reward that was being offered for information about Libby's murder. Beatty asked me to do a forty-five-second write-up for a voice-over. But I wasn't on the hook for any audio or camera work that would have required a mad dash back to the studio that night.

"I'll get Thompson to get a sound bite from her family," Beatty told me. "All he's given me so far this week is excuses for why he's sitting around on his keister. You said the family member to contact about the reward is Theo Fowler?"

"Yeah. Let me know if you'll need a rewrite after you get the sound bite. Don't let Thompson do the rewrite. He's such a show horse, he'll probably tag on a stand-up to make it look like *he* broke the story."

"I hear ya."

After I hung up with Beatty, I bent my head over my notepad and wrote a short script for the anchor to read. When it was finished, I glanced at my watch to time the piece. I could barely see the second hand—it was only six o'clock, but already the nearby trees had enveloped the bench in soft, deep shadows. I checked the surrounding areas—the children and nannies were gone. Even the ducks had vanished into their nests for the evening. The only sound was the soft lapping of the nearby pond.

Once I timed the script, it took me only a few quick taps of the stylus to e-mail my story to the managing editor at Channel Twelve.

Seconds after I pressed SEND, a garbled, rhythmic noise intruded on the surrounding calm. It sounded like chanting.

I made out a humped, ragged profile standing near the water's edge. A woman. She was leaning against a shopping cart next to the water, staring while she swayed and muttered to herself.

If the homeless shift was taking over, clearly it was time to leave.

I'd just gotten settled back in my car when my cell phone rang. The caller ID read, DETECTIVE J. REED."

"*Hey* there." My voice cracked as I greeted him. How annoying—if I was going to forge any type of relationship with this man, I'd simply *have* to stop squeaking like Olive Oyl whenever he called.

"Hi, Kate—I heard you met with Carla today. She said everything went okay, by the way."

"Yeah, it did. And thanks so much for putting me in touch with her. She's really great."

"I know."

"I *know* you know. I heard you and she used to date." Oops, where did *that* come from? It wasn't like me to sound jealous or insecure.

"Well, that was a bit ago."

After a pause, I took a deep breath. "Um, can I start over?"

"Okay."

"Okay, here goes: *Hey*, Jonathan."

"Hey, Kate."

"That's better, don't you think?"

"Much better."

"I'm glad."

"Me, too."

That bit of awkwardness settled, we went on to discuss everything that had been happening since my first arrival at Body Blast. Being the homicide detective that he was, Jonathan had no trouble following me as I spooled out everything that had happened since I'd last updated him.

"The information I got from Carla today puts a new spin on everything, so I feel like I'm back to square one," I told him. "All along, I've been concentrating on Marnie's death, but evidently the real focus should have been on Libby. From what I hear, though, the SBI investigation is at a standstill."

"Well, don't feel like you have to solve it—it's their job, after all. And be careful. When you go knocking on doors like Laplante's, you're asking for trouble."

"I know. But I've been getting some decent stories out of this whole thing, plus I promised I'd help my friend Riley sort things out. It just seems like things keep getting worse for him. The arson fire, the murder investigation, money problems—now, to top things off, he's even got trouble in the romance department."

Jonathan chuckled. "I can't offer any advice there. I've got a pretty poor track record in the romance department, myself."

"Hmm, really?"

Before he could reply, I heard a beeping sound that indicated another call coming in.

"Hold on a second," I said, then clicked over to the other line.

"Kate?" It was Charlene, my pet sitter. Her voice sounded stressed. "I just stopped by your place to look in on Elfie again. Someone broke in."

I felt my heart seize up in my chest. "Is Elfie okay?"

"The door was standing wide open. Kate, I'm afraid she's gone."

Chapter 20

The Fastest Way to Killer Abs

Forget ab-rollers and other fancy contraptions. The best way to tone your midsection is the old-fashioned stomach crunch. As you do center-and-side crunches, keep your knees bent and resting on the floor, alternating sides. It also helps to do the crunches on a Swiss ball.

—From *The Little Book of Fat-busters* by Mimi Morgan

"Gone?" A burstlet of brain confusion kept me from grasping what the pet sitter was saying. "Charlene, do you mean she's *dead*?"

"No, no—I think she just got out. I've been looking for her outside for the last half hour; I came back in just now to meet the patrol officers. Please don't worry—she's probably just hiding someplace."

"Oh, shit, Charlene. Call me the second you find her. Did they steal stuff?"

"I can't tell yet. Everything in the apartment's in a horrible mess. They tore it completely apart."

"Okay, I'm actually in Raleigh, so it won't take me that long to get there. Call me the second you find her."

"I will, sweetie."

I clicked back to Jonathan. "Oh, God, my—my cat's

missing. Someone broke into my apartment, and she's gone."

"I'll head over there right now, to see what's going on,"

"*Would* you?" I heard my voice crack again, this time with tears. "I don't know how to thank you. Do you know where I live?"

"Yes. This probably isn't the right time to tell you, but I went a bit schoolboy this week. I've been coming up with all kinds of excuses to drive by your house."

"That makes me love you so much." The words spilled out of my mouth before I even knew they were there.

This time, there was no awkward pause on the other end. "Then I guess my drive-bys weren't in vain," he said. "I'll call you as soon as we find her. I'll talk to the uniforms, too, to make sure they follow up right."

"The patrol cops will probably get freaked out to see a guy from Homicide there." A wild giggle burst through my attempt to suppress a sob.

"You let me worry about that."

I broke every land speed record between Raleigh and Durham, worrying about Elfie every inch of the way. Who had broken in? Had they stolen her? *Harmed* her? The first person who popped into my head was Yves Laplante—it just seemed to be too much of a coincidence that my apartment had been ransacked the very day I visited him.

When I pulled into the parking lot of my apartment building an hour later, I saw a black and white patrol car parked catawampus in front of the entrance to the stairwell.

My cell phone beeped, but I didn't pause to answer it as I took the concrete steps two at a time. From the second floor landing, I could see that the front door to my apartment was ajar. Light spilled through it onto the floor of the corridor. Taking a deep breath to steel myself, I stepped through the door.

Inside the living room, the first thing I noticed was a maelstrom of debris. It looked like a Kansas twister had torn through my apartment. Then, more slowly, several people came into focus.

By the fireplace, with his back turned to me, Jonathan was deep in conversation with an earnest-looking young cop who was taking notes.

Charlene, the pet sitter, was seated at the dining room table with an exhausted expression on her face. Elfie was curled up in her lap.

"Oh, thank *God*! Where'd you find her?" I cried.

"I just tried to call you—I found her a few minutes ago. She was all hunkered down underneath a shrub." Charlene's cheeks had sweat drying on them, and her eyes were red as if she'd been crying. "I've been checking her over—she doesn't seem injured. She's been glued to me like this ever since I picked her up."

I made a churring noise at the cat.

Hearing my voice, Elfie raised her head and returned a meow. She rose onto four white paws and hopped off Charlene's lap. Then she wrapped herself around my ankles in circle eights while making anxious-sounding chirps, as if to say, "Where the heck *were* you?"

Jonathan broke away from his discussion with Earnest Cop. "Charlene, I guess you're stale scones as far as the kitkat is concerned, now that her mum's back," he said to the pet sitter, then looked at me. "We took prints, but we didn't move anything, because we need you to take a look around and see if anything's missing."

Gathering Elfie into my arms, I surveyed the room. All the drawers of my antique hutch had been yanked open, their contents tossed about; through the doorway to the kitchen, I could see shards of Mikasa strewn across the countertops.

Charlene rose from her chair. "Oh, Kate," she wailed, taking a step toward me. "I'm so, so sorry this happened on my watch."

"Don't be silly." I shifted the cat onto my shoulder and gave her a one-armed hug. "I'm just grateful that you came back tonight to check on Elfie."

"I fed her at ten this morning, but then I realized I left my bag of cat treats here and came back tonight to get them," she told me. "Just lucky, I guess."

"And lucky that you didn't run into whoever did this."

"Well, I think I *almost* did," Charlene said. "Like I told the officers, this place totally reeked of BO when I first arrived. It smelled like the person who broke in had just been here."

I inhaled. There was still a rank trace of body stench detectable in the air. I'd been too distracted by Elfie and the chaos in the apartment to notice it before. I realized I'd smelled that exact same odor earlier today—rolling off Stinky at Yves Laplante's office.

Charlene turned around and reached for her purse on the dining room table. "I know you need some time right now to go over everything with the police," she said to me. "Will you be okay tonight? Why don't you and Elfie come stay at my place?"

"Don't worry—I'll look after them," Jonathan interjected, before I could respond.

Charlene looked at him with her eyebrows raised, then back at me. "Well, I can see I'm leaving you in good hands." A mischievous glint rose in her eyes. "I'll come back in the morning to help you clean up."

"Thanks." I gave her another hug.

After Charlene left, I set Elfie down despite her mew of protest, then followed Jonathan and Earnest Cop into the bedroom.

The disarray in that room was, if anything, even more disturbing. My intruder had pulled all my lingerie from the drawers and strewn it about. The idea that a violent stranger had been pawing through my panty drawer made me feel violated in a weirdly disgusting way.

My jewelry box was resting on its side on the carpet. I checked through the contents. Nothing was missing—not even the diamond studs that Lou had given me. They must have been worth thousands of dollars.

"That's strange. They didn't take anything," I said. "Not even my good earrings."

"That's because this was a muscle call, not a burglary," Jonathan said.

"A muscle call? You mean a warning?"

"Exactly."

"Yves Laplante, do you think? He had a guy in his shop today who reeked of this exact same French scent—Pepé Le Pew."

Jonathan grimaced. "Possibly," he said. "Laplante likes to scare people. He likes to hurt them, too. If we come up with anything pointing to him, we'll return his little muscle call, police style."

As we headed back toward the kitchen, Earnest Cop's shoulder mike squawked out a burst of static. He spoke into the microphone, then looked at Jonathan with a concerned expression. "Sir, they're calling me on an eleven eighty," he said.

An "eleven eighty," I knew from growing up in a cop family, was a traffic accident with serious injuries.

"Get the hell going," Jonathan replied. "You can finish this report later. I'll follow up with you if there's anything major to add."

"Yessir." With one hand resting on his shoulder speaker, Earnest tilted forward and made a run for the front door.

Jonathan and I were standing in the kitchen. Among the broken dishes on the counter, I realized with a sharp pang, was my mother's china serving platter, the one with the little wildflowers. It had been her favorite dish to use on Sundays.

I pushed the feeling down. "Coffee?" I asked him with a wan smile. "If I can find anything intact to pour it in, that is."

Jonathan kept his focus on me. "You're pretending this isn't a horrible shock. Don't."

I squeezed my eyes shut. "It's just—those animals broke my mother's china dish. She served fried chicken on it to us the night before she died."

"Oh, I'm so sorry, I didn't know. Would you mind telling me how . . ."

. . . *your mother passed away?* I braced myself for the next words that were sure to come out of his mouth. That was a story I was in no shape to share right then.

Jonathan must have seen the expression on my face, because he checked himself. Then he added gently, "Which platter is it?"

I pointed with a trembling finger. "The one with the little f-fl-flowers . . ." Whatever more there might have been to that sentence was swallowed up by a huge, gulping sob.

"Uh-oh. Here it comes." Jonathan's arms came around me. His jacket felt scratchy and cool against my cheek.

As I leaned into him, he added in a gentle voice, "It's okay to let go."

I shook my head fiercely against his jacket. "I don't think I should. It'll be really loud."

"I'm a sturdy bloke. I can handle it."

My chest shuddered and contracted, and I melted against him. For a long moment, we stood wrapped together in the middle of my kitchen while I sobbed.

The moment was broken seconds later when I hiccupped down some air that came right back up in a loud belch.

The burp set me off into a near-hysterical fit of giggles, which quickly shape-shifted back into sobs. Reed held me firmly in his arms as I released some of the awful tension of everything that had happened—the fire at Body Blast, the loss of my laptop notes, the upending of my apartment, the near-loss of my kitty.

"You go have a seat in the living room," Reed said, when I'd calmed down. "I'll fix you up with a traditional British remedy—a nice hot cup of tea. You Americans have really lost the art with all your coffee worship. You have some tea someplace, I'm assuming?"

"Just some bags I use to make iced tea, I'm afraid. Nothing exotic."

"That'll do."

I nodded in the direction of a cupboard, then sat down on the love seat in the living room. Physically, it hurt my eyes to look around the apartment. My eye fell on the framed photograph of Lou, which had fallen faceup on the carpet. I crossed the room and reached down to pick it up, but then pulled back as Jonathan poked his head through the door.

"Don't start cleaning—sit," he ordered, then disappeared back inside the kitchen. I couldn't tell whether he'd noticed the picture.

Soon I heard the whistling sound of a teakettle, and a warm waft of cinnamon fragrance. A minute later he returned to the living room, balancing two mugs of steaming tea and a paper plate. Arranged on the plate were strips of cinnamon toast.

"Ooh, yum." I took a buttery, sugar-coated bite.

"It's the closest I could come to hot buttered scones

on short notice." Reed had taken off his jacket, uncovering a holstered, black Glock at his side.

"Drink." He handed me a mug. "I found these unscathed in the back of the cupboard."

"Thanks." The one he'd handed me showed a picture of me when I was five years old, posing with my mother and father. "Well, thank God, I still have this," I said, fending off a fresh breaker of tears.

"Thought that might cheer you up." Jonathan held out his mug at arm's length to examine. " 'The Healing Power of Pork,' " he read aloud. "Is there a story behind that?"

"Believe me, you don't want to know."

Jonathan set down his tea. "I'll start in on some of this mess," he said, getting to his feet.

When I started to rise, too, he said, "No, you stay put. I'll clean."

"Yessir." I gave him a little salute.

As he moved about the room, I remembered Lou's picture and added, "No, no, that's okay, Please don't bother to clean up. I'll get to it later."

Too late—he'd stopped by the fireplace and was staring down at the frame on the carpet.

After an awkward silence, I added. "That's Lou Bettinger. You remember him from when we first met, last summer?"

"Yeah, I remember him." Jonathan's tone was flat. "Big-time lawyer. A real slick operator."

After a brief, taut pause, he added, "Are you two seeing each other?"

"We were for a while. Not anymore."

"And you just hang on to his photo for old time's sake?"

"We broke up recently."

"Ah." He placed the photo facedown on the mantel, then returned to the couch. The air between us felt heavy all of a sudden.

"Well, after last summer I never heard from you again," I said, trying not to sound defensive. "I asked around. Heard you went back to England."

"I did."

"What brought you back?"

"You did."

"What?" I turned sideways on the couch to stare at him.

"I said, '*You* did.' "

"No, I heard what you said. I just don't understand. Why, when—" *When I never heard from you during all those months*, I wanted to add.

Jonathan picked up his tea. He stared deeply into it, as if reading the leaves at the bottom of the cup. "Remember when we were talking on the phone earlier this evening—right before you got the call from the pet sitter—I was telling you that I have a bad track record in the relationship department?"

When I nodded, he continued, "I had to go back home to settle some things. I was getting a divorce. I went back to sign the papers, and—and things got a bit complicated for a while. The whole thing took longer than I expected."

"Ah," I said. "I didn't know you were married."

He sighed. "Apparently, neither did she. A few years ago, I did one of those walk-in-on-another-bloke scenes. That's when I took the job in the States."

I absorbed that, then said, "I'm sorry to hear about that. But a divorce—that's not such a terrible thing, Jonathan. What makes you think you have such a bad track record?"

He shrugged. "Ever since my marriage blew up, I guess I've been a bit dodgy about getting involved again."

"When was your divorce final?"

"A week ago Tuesday." He paused. "It was final on the day I left the note on your car outside that restaurant, Mr. Max's." He reached forward with his fingers and touched my hand.

I stared down at the back of his knuckles. They looked tanned and firm resting over my pale, upturned palm. I'd always sensed that there was something held back—guarded, even—about Jonathan. Now I knew what it was: a wife back in England, the hurt of an emotional betrayal.

Still . . . "You could have dropped me a postcard of the Queen Mum in a hat or something. Let me know you were alive, at least," I finally said.

He sighed. "I'm sorry. I just wanted to be free and clear the next time we met. Was that too old-school of me?"

In response, I lifted the back of his hand to my cheek and pressed it there.

Jonathan's breathing quickened. The next thing I felt were his fingers in my hair. Then they were pressing lightly up and down the back of my neck.

I let out an involuntary gasp of pleasure. Right then and there I knew—the sex was going to be fabulous.

Jonathan pulled back. Unholstering his Glock, he set it carefully on the glass coffee table, followed by his pager.

I stared at the gun. "Does that ever break the mood when you do that?"

He gave me a sheepish look. "Since my marriage ended, there's only been one lady," he said. "And she packed an Uzi."

I knew he must mean Carla. "Well, I know how men *hate* being outgunned . . ." I murmured.

The next thing I felt was Jonathan's hands grasping my shoulders, gently turning me facedown on the couch. Then his voice whispered in my ear, "Don't move."

"Or you'll shoot?" My words came out muffled against the cushion.

Above me, I heard him chuckle; then his fingers massaged lightly into my hair, then deeper into my scalp and down my neck.

Tingles shot up and down my neck as my tightly wound muscles unlocked. The feeling was decidedly delicious.

"Oh, my God," I groaned. "Please tell me when it's okay to move, because otherwise I'll remain exactly like this, turning into a mound of Jell-O."

Jonathan didn't reply, just kept working his way down my back.

As it turned out, Jonathan never had to tell me that it was okay to move; as he worked his way down my body, the tension I was feeling was replaced by a slow-growing warmth. The heat built up in my central core, then unfurled slowly into my limbs. By the time it reached my fingertips, the burning sensation was white-hot and electric.

That's when I reached for Jonathan.

Things went swimmingly from there, romance-wise, until we neglected to account for the space restraints of the antique love seat upon which we were thrashing. At one point, Jonathan pushed, I pulled, and off we rolled from the love seat into a heap on the floor, with me pinned under him, our lips lock-jawed painfully together. Whereupon I squeaked like a mouse, which sent us both into laughing fits.

When we finally stopped giggling from that, I gasped, "Okay, never mind what I said about not wanting to face the bedroom yet. Let's go."

Jonathan rose to his feet, pulled me to mine, and collected his Glock and pager. Then we made tracks toward the bedroom.

But something in the earlier disturbance of my apartment must have upset the equilibrium of my vintage sleigh bed. As we came together in rhythm, there was a distinct squeaking sound coming from the vicinity of the headboard. It echoed our thrustings like a pesky metronome.

"Bother," Jonathan growled. With the smooth motion of a magician removing a tablecloth without disturbing the silverware, he yanked the mattress off the box spring and spun it onto the floor.

And there, on the displaced mattress on my bedroom floor, we carried on through the night.

Chapter 21

The ABN Rule

When it comes to exercise, my motto is ABN—anything is better than nothing. People often put way too much pressure on themselves to work out for hours, stick to a rigorous program—well, don't! You can be assured that your body will respond to any exercise you do, even a little bit. There are some days when I'm so busy that I can barely get in a ten-minute walk during the day. I celebrate those ten minutes—they're something I'm doing for my body and myself. I don't castigate myself that I didn't make it to the gym for my two-hour routine.

—From *The Little Book of Fat-busters* by Mimi Morgan

Our limbs were intertwined on the mattress the next morning, Saturday, when the first diffuse streaks of gray light filtered their way through the lace window sheers of my bedroom window.

I grabbed my blouse, which was lying crumpled on top of the bureau, then untangled my legs from Jonathan's. Elfie was curled up at the top of Jonathan's head, purring. Her tail hung down over his shoulder, like a Daniel Boone cap.

"I'd give anything for a picture of that," I said to Jonathan, who snapped fully awake without blinking, a habit of street cops. "Will this be a problem for you, wearing a cat hat?"

Jonathan reached up and gingerly stroked her tail. "I love little kitkats, actually."

"Well, she certainly seems to like *you*."

Jonathan's pager vibrated to life where he'd dropped it on the floor. It emitted several loud beeps.

Startled, Elfie scrambled off his head. "Bother it. I forgot they have claws." Jonathan winced, rubbing his temples. He reached past me for his pager.

As he examined the LED display I said, "Office calling?"

He groaned. "There should be a law against discovering dead bodies on Saturday mornings. They found a one eighty-seven under an overpass on the I-40. I wanted to take you out to breakfast this morning."

"We'll have time another day."

With one finger, he stroked the underside of my cheek. "Definitely, we'll have lots of time," he said. "Can I wash up someplace?"

I nodded toward the bathroom. "The WC is over there. Be my guest."

After he spent a moment in the bathroom, he popped out his head again. "Is this a talking scale you have in here?"

"Don't talk to it—she's one hard-ass bitch," I said.

"What are you—" he began, then stopped and grinned at me. Even though we'd spent the previous night performing all kinds of uninhibited sexual aerobics, I now had my back turned modestly to him as I fastened my bra. For some reason, as soon as the sun comes up, the Irish Catholic schoolgirl in me always takes over.

I glanced over my shoulder at him. "I need to follow up with a couple of people—starting with a woman named Joycie Woo," I said. "She was Libby Fowler's tentmate the night she was killed. I'm also waiting for a call from the DEA to see if we can get a ride-along on a search for drug operations in the mountains. Maybe Libby stumbled across something up there, and that's what got her killed. That's what the SBI seems to think, anyway."

Jonathan's expression tightened. "I haven't argued too much with your playing gumshoe—until now," he said slowly. "Frankly, I've held back because I want to get back in your good graces. But just be careful, okay?"

Playing *gumshoe*? I felt a slow burn coming on. Was I wearing a sign that said DISS MY JOB on it?

When my simmer reached the boiling point, I snapped, "I'm always careful. And you know what? I already have a Cop Daddy back home in Boston—I don't need another one."

When Jonathan didn't reply, I steamrollered ahead. "You have to understand—I'm an investigative reporter. This is what I *do*. I have to ask you to respect that."

"I do respect you." He paused. "I just don't want to lose you—I already almost let that happen once." Turning away again, he disappeared into the bathroom.

I huddled on the mattress in a ball of abject misery, listening to the bathroom water run behind the closed door. I felt like a total shit heel. Had I already blown things on Day One of our new relationship? That would be a new speed record, even for me.

When Jonathan emerged a few minutes later, he headed straight for the living room.

I sprang up from the mattress. "Wait," I said, taking a step toward him. "I'm sorry I raised my voice. I know you're just concerned."

Jonathan gave me a bemused look. "You call that

raising your voice? You'll have to take some biddy lessons to impress me."

As the knot in my stomach eased, he added, "I'm sorry I have to go rushing off right now. I'll call you later."

He leaned in for a kiss, then unexpectedly pressed his lips into my hair, tracing them across the top of my ear. The sensation sent an electric tingle down the backs of my thighs.

Leaning back, he said, "Okay, then. We've kissed and made up. Till later?"

"Yup, later." It was hard not to sound breathless as I closed the door behind him.

Distance-wise, Joycie Woo's clothing shop—called Planet Woo—wasn't far from my apartment. Style-wise, it might have been located on the far side of the galaxy.

There was one sour note on the way to Planet Woo. I stopped off at a newsstand-slash-coffee shop to grab a bran muffin and a latte light. On a whim, I grabbed a copy of the *Atlanta Journal*, sat down at a table to eat the breakfast fare, then opened the Atlanta paper to the "Social Butterfly" column in the *Living* section. My eye was immediately drawn to a headline:

ATLANTA'S FUND-RAISER EXTRAORDINAIRE RAISES $1 MILLION FOR LEUKEMIA RESEARCH

Underneath the headline was a picture of Lou. He was beaming into the camera and holding an oversized check. Standing next to him, wedged close enough to require the Jaws of Life to separate them, was Ms. Butt Crack Debutante, the one who'd given me the evil eye all night at the gala I'd attended the previous week. She'd evidently grabbed hold of the fresh opportunity to move in on Lou. In the photograph, she was insinuating herself around him like a snake.

I tossed the newspaper aside. "Congratulations, you two—I'm sure you deserve each other," I muttered.

Seeing that photo of Lou and Snake Woman had just given me something I'd felt was lacking in the aftermath of our breakup.

Final closure.

The first thing I encountered upon entering Planet Woo was a jaw-rattling din of Eastern techno-metal music. But probably none of the customers—all of them incredibly skinny, most of them Asian girls—heard the music as they browsed through the racks, judging by the number of iPod wires dangling in view. Most of the clothing offerings seemed to feature complex zipper work and decorative metal trim, enough to make a nice suit of armor if you melted it all down.

Every inch of the shop that wasn't crammed with clothing was mirrored, even the ceiling. The net effect was disorienting. I felt vaguely seasick as I looked around for the owner.

"Kate Gallagher?"

A thirtyish woman wearing a black crop top, lowriders, and a sparkling belly-button charm approached me with her hand out. "Hi, I'm Joycie Woo."

"Hi. Is it okay if we talk somewhere else?" I waggled my fingers toward my ear. "I can't really hear all that well . . ."

"Oh, sure. Let's go into my office."

She led me to a small, messy room off the main floor. When she closed the door, mercifully, the thumping music faded to a distant rumble.

"Have a seat right there." She waved me toward a guest chair, then sat down behind a small desk that was piled high with clothing. "So, I wasn't clear from my assistant what you'd like to talk about . . . ?"

"I want to talk about Libby Fowler. I'm looking into her murder."

"Oh." My statement seemed to take her aback. Her gaze slipped off me, then returned with a cautious look. "I don't really watch the news all that much. You're doing a story about Libby?"

When I nodded, she said, "Well, I told the investigators back when it happened—I have absolutely no idea what happened to Libby. And I . . . I really don't want to get involved publicly in any way. I have a business image to protect."

Like armored clothing and migraine music? I thought, but said, "I'm only looking for some background information, not an on-camera interview. No quotes or attribution to you, either. Don't worry."

Joycie seemed to relax slightly in her chair. "I guess that would be all right," she said. "What do you want to know?"

"You were her tentmate during the Wilderness Challenge at the camp, Body Blast?"

When she nodded, I added, "Had you ever met Libby before that trip?"

"No, that day was the first time we met—and the last."

"What did you two talk about, if you don't mind my asking?"

"To be honest, we hardly spoke to each other. What's going on with the police investigation these days, do you know?"

"As near as I can tell, they're nowhere close to solving it," I said. "What was your impression of Libby as a person?"

Joycie shrugged. "She was kind of hyper, but not horrible. I really don't think she should have gone on that camping trip—she was totally out of shape. She got altitude sickness or dehydrated at one point, and we all had to stop for her to throw up."

"She got sick?"

She nodded, then said, "Once we got the tents set up, Libby turned in almost right away. When I woke up the next morning, she was already gone. Everyone started looking for her. Finally, Riley or somebody found her in the ravine at the bottom of Pittman's Bluff. She was already dead, apparently."

"Apparently?"

"Well, I never saw much of anything. Riley and that other guy—Khan—came back and kind of hustled us all out of there pretty quick. I didn't even know for sure what happened to her until we got off the mountain. That's when the cops came."

"Did you happen to notice anything unusual about Libby's interactions with any of the people on the hike, especially the staff? Any tensions?"

"Well, she kept rolling her eyes behind Darwin's back the whole way up the hill," Joycie said. "I figured he'd probably made his Darwin the Hound Dog pass at her. I've been to the camp before—he comes on to practically all the women."

"Hmm. Other than Darwin, anyone else?"

Joycie shrugged. "Erica was giving her the cold shoulder. I don't know *what* that was all about. Hillary and Libby seemed to get along, though. Hillary looked after her when she got sick."

"Really?"

"Yeah. Hillary's into that whole empower-your-womanly-body thing. It's not my bag, though. I prefer working out with Erica. She's more hard-core."

Behind me, I heard the door open. A teenaged girl washed in on a wave of thunderous music. At first I thought the girl might be an android, because there was a startling outcropping of metal bolted to the side of her head. Then I realized that the Borgian attachment was a phone.

"Sorry to interrupt, Joycie, but we're having a crisis

on the floor," 'Droid Girl announced with a breathless air. "Two customers are wrangling over our last J-Woo original stud belt. When's the next batch coming in from Koreatown?"

"Tomorrow. I'll go out there and smooth it out." Joycie looked at me. "We're done here, right?"

"Just one more quick question."

While 'Droid Girl and Joycie had been talking, I thought back to my earlier talk with Libby's friend, Irene—about something she said the night she met me at Mr. Max's. Irene had said that during their last text conversation, Libby had said something about a "major B-Ho blast." Irene had figured that Libby was referring to something from junior high school. But she had never learned what Libby had been talking about.

"Did Libby happen to say anything about meeting someone at the camp from her past? Did she ever mention anything about a 'B-Ho blast'?" I asked Joycie, harking back to that earlier conversation with Irene.

"B-Ho blast? No—like I said, we barely spoke." With a distracted look on her face, Joycie rose from her chair. "I'm really sorry, but I've got to get out there on the floor and take care of business."

"No problem. Thanks for your time."

As I retraced my steps across the floor on my way out, I saw that the fight over the J-Woo studded belt had escalated. Two groups of girls were in a standoff. They were yammering at each other in impassioned voices, punctuated with pithy-sounding outbursts in Asian languages.

I made my escape before the Jelly Kelly bags started swinging.

I left my interview with Joycie with the phrase "B-Ho blast" rattling around my brain. Maybe it was because I didn't have much else to go on at this point, but I wondered if there might be some special significance to those words. Libby's friend Irene thought she'd been referring to Darwin—that maybe he'd reminded her of the boys in the eighth grade—but what if Libby had meant something completely different?

I was still sans laptop, so I headed to the studio to research the backgrounds of everyone who had been on the camping trip with Libby. I wanted to see if someone who'd been on that hiking trip might have crossed paths with her in her past—specifically, middle school. Thanks to my friend Riley, I had the social security numbers of all the staff, so researching them should be easy.

Just before entering the newsroom, I poked my head inside and glanced around warily. Crystal, the legal reporter, was working in her cubicle. When I caught her eye, she gave me the thumbs-up sign. Good—that signal meant that Beatty the news director wasn't around. This was welcome news; in Beatty's view, if you weren't out in the field actively taping with a crew, it meant you weren't "busy," and you were therefore fair game to be sent out on some cockamamie assignment. I wanted to avoid another Earthfest assignment at all costs.

It was only ten thirty a.m. As usual at this hour on a Saturday, the bullpen was mostly deserted; unless there was major breaking news, the office kept only a skeleton staff. The weekend producer normally filled out the bulk of the shows with network feeds and repackaged stories from earlier in the week, updated with fresh information that was written into the anchors' introductions.

I turned on my office PC, unlocked a drawer, and withdrew the file folders that Riley had given me with background about the Body Blast employees.

I spent almost an hour online, searching for any

information that might indicate whether Libby and any of the Body Blast employees might have known each other in the past.

I turned up one promising hit: Erica had grown up in Durham, like Libby, and they were the same age. But Erica had gone to public schools, while Libby, I knew from her friend Irene, had been at Longleaf Country Day, a private school. Still, they could have known each other back then. Maybe it was something more than Erica's award-losing personality that had caused her to snub Libby on the doomed Wilderness Challenge. Maybe the snub had originated from something in their past.

Leaning back in my chair, I raised my arms over my head and stretched my neck to unkink it. With the exception of a circumstantial connection to Erica, my hunch about "B-Ho blast" had hit a blank wall. Probably the SBI investigators were right—Libby had been killed by a druggie or some random criminal hiding in the hills. If that were the case, they'd probably never be found. I blew out a sigh that sounded like a horse's sputter.

"No luck today?" Crystal appeared at the opening to my cubicle.

"Not much right now, I'm afraid," I admitted, then launched into a summary of everything I'd been learning about Libby's death.

"The SBI investigators seem to think she was attacked by some illegal alien or drug criminal who was hiding in the mountains. But I can't let go of the idea that she knew her killer."

Crystal crossed her arms and stared at me. "Kate, you're the best investigative reporter this station has ever had. You're probably *too* good for this market—this is Channel Twelve, Boob Tube News. 'Crap is King,' remember? You don't have to actually *solve* the crime. That job belongs to the cops."

"But I just don't think they're on the right track in this case."

Crystal shrugged. "Getting obsessed with your job will drive you crazy in the end. Trust me, that's why I'm no longer a prosecutor."

"You were a prosecutor?" I heard the surprise in my voice. "I don't know why I thought you were a public defender."

Crystal rolled her eyes. "You assumed that because I'm a 'sistah,' " she said. "The truth is that I was always right in line behind the cops. But whenever I lost a case in the courtroom, I couldn't stop thinking that my mistake had let a monster back onto the streets. I'd lie awake at night, wondering, 'What if I'd just said *this*, or *that*, to the jury? Would it have made a difference?' " She shook her head. "Don't be like me, Kate—you have to keep things in perspective."

Crystal left my workstation humming the lyrics to "Dirty Laundry": *Kick 'em when they're up, kick 'em when they're down . . .*

My office phone rang. The caller ID said, DEA—AGT. GARCIA. Garcia was the agent from the Drug Enforcement Agency with whom I'd left an earlier voice mail message, requesting a ride-along on a drug farm bust.

When I picked up, Agent Garcia said without preamble, "Hey, Kate, Operation Bladerunner is doing an interagency drug bust in the Smoky Mountains, near where that girl you've been reporting about died. But it's going down right now—can you and a crew get to the heliport at RDU airport in two hours for a ride-along?"

"Yes, absolutely! We'll be there, thanks so much." I'd have to scramble to get a crew on such short notice. But a takedown of a drug operation in the North Carolina mountains was big, big stuff. Beatty would *plotz* when he heard about it.

"One caution note," Garcia added. "These seizures can be a little risky because we never know exactly what we'll encounter. You and your crew will have to wear armored vests. And you should take a Dramamine. There's some nasty weather closing in fast up there—it might be a rough ride."

"Understood." I glanced out the window nearest me. The only visible slice of sky was solid gray. My stomach clenched at the thought of the upcoming ride.

After noting down some logistical details and signing off with Garcia, I hurried across the newsroom to the assignment desk.

"*Hey*, Caldwell. I've got something hot." My blurted pronouncement startled Caldwell—the weekend producer who reminded me a bit of Ichabod Crane wearing a bow tie—into dropping his pen with a clatter onto the desk. "I need a crew, and I need one now. I just got the word from a DEA agent that we can go on a helicopter ride-along—they're doing a big drug bust up in the Smokies. We have to meet the chopper at the airport at thirteen hundred hours."

"A ride-along? Good stuff." Caldwell scanned the assignment board. "Damn, everybody's out in the field right now. Let me call in Frank—he's got the pager this weekend. Do you think you'll be able to get me anything in time for the six o'clock tonight?"

I checked the digital wall clock. It was eleven thirty a.m. We were scheduled to take off for the mountains by chopper at one, but I had no idea how long the operation would take.

"Well, it won't be smooth, but give me one of the satellite phones. I can at least phone in something for the anchor to read," I told him.

"We'll make it work." Caldwell made some notes on a legal pad on the desk. "If we don't have any visuals by then, we'll run your write-up over some stock footage, and then give 'em a big buildup for the full report tomorrow. The DEA's busting drug dudes up there, you say?"

"Yep, as part of an interagency task force. But one thing—after the ride-along, their chopper has to drop us off in Ashland. They're not coming back this way. So we'll need a rental car. And I need to stay overnight because tomorrow I want to grab some footage of where that camper murder took place—we'll show the exact spot where Libby Fowler was attacked."

"No worries—you and Frank can expense a motel up there."

"Actually, I think we can save the station some money. I'm sure we can stay at my friend's camp—Body Blast—which is near Ashland."

"Cool." Caldwell had the phone receiver to his ear and was punching numbers to track down Frank. "I'll call ahead and have a rental car waiting for you at the airport." He rubbed his hands together. "Hah! And they say the weekend reports are nothing but leftovers. We'll give 'em prime rib with this story."

Driving home, I drafted a to-do list in my head. I needed to call Charlene, the pet sitter, to let her know I was going out of town again. I hated to leave Elfie again so soon—she had still been acting clingy and stressed out earlier this morning. The previous day's break-in had obviously traumatized her. Maybe Charlene could take her home to her house for the night, but I knew how cats hate to be uprooted.

My cell phone rang. When I clicked on the line, I heard a muffled roar of traffic in the background. It was Jonathan.

"So what was that murder call you had to go out on this morning?" I asked him.

"It was a decapitated guy under the I-40 overpass near the University exit. I'm still on the scene. We found a machete thrown in the grass nearby."

"A *machete*?"

"Yes. This perp was an unbelievable idiot—he dropped his wallet on the ground. We did some checking around—looks like the guy who did it is the victim's cousin."

"Sounds like something for us. Will it put you on the spot if I call it in to the desk?"

"Knock yourself out. Who knows, maybe I'll be a hero and give the reporter a comment for the record."

I felt my lips curl against the phone. "Why do cops hate talking to the media so much?"

"Present company excepted, most TV reporters are like rattlesnakes. Worse, in fact—at least a snake gives you a courtesy rattle before it strikes."

"It's nice to know we're so beloved. Have you had time to find out anything new on Yves Laplante and the break-in?"

"The lab will report back this afternoon on the prints we took from your place. I already checked with our guys who work the extortion beat. What happened at your place sounds just like Laplante's MO."

I filled Jonathan in about my upcoming ride-along on the drug grower bust, then said, "My follow-up story will hook Libby Fowler's death to the dangers of drug operations in the mountains. I'll say the authorities suspect that she was killed by someone guarding one of the hooches."

"*Hooches?* I see you're picking up the lingo now." Jonathan sounded amused. "Just don't go tromping off into those woods by yourself, okay?"

"Well, today, we'll be with a ton of cops. And tomorrow I'll have Frank with me. I'm going to ask my friend Riley to show us where Libby was killed."

There was a little pause. "What makes you trust this guy Riley so much?" Jonathan asked. "From what little you've told me, it sounds possible that he's running a game on you."

"A *game*? What makes you think—"

"Take that arson fire that happened at his camp—what's it called, Body Blast?" Jonathan pressed. "Wasn't Riley the one who told you about the debts his boyfriend owes to Laplante? He sowed that thought in your mind, didn't he, that one of them might have been behind it? Maybe Riley was behind it, for the insurance money."

"I don't believe he's behind anything." I heard a defensive note creep into my voice. "Riley's been my friend since high school."

"And our headless vic here was cousins with *his* killer since birth. I'm just saying that it doesn't pay to be too trusting of anyone."

"Hmm." Even though I didn't share Jonathan's concerns about Riley, I was impressed that he recalled every detail from our previous conversations about the arson fire. That quality probably made him a good homicide detective.

Jonathan quizzed me some more about the ride-along, then asked me for the location where we'd be taping the next day.

"Why—are you putting pushpins in a wall map to keep track of me?" I teased him, before giving him the information. Then I added, "You know, I'm actually worried about leaving town again so soon. Elfie's still acting freaked out. I think she hasn't gotten over last night's break-in."

Jonathan made me an offer I couldn't refuse. "Why don't you let me stay over at your place tonight? I can look after your little kitkat—she seems to have taken a fancy to me," he said. "I can also deal with Laplante if by any chance he decides to send his goons back."

"That's so sweet of you, Jonathan. Thank you. Thank you so *much*." I felt my voice well up at the edges, like a creek about to spill over its banks. "I'll leave a key for you with the manager."

As I hung up from our conversation, another surprising thing happened—this time, it was an unexpected thought: *He's going to make an excellent father someday.*

I stopped off at my apartment just long enough to call the assignment desk with the news about the decapitated man, pack up a few things, and do some triage in preparation for Jonathan's stay-over. I refreshed Elfie's cat bowl, changed the litter, and picked up the worst of the mess in my bedroom and bath. Then, after a second's hesitation, I arranged my favorite red satin teddy so that it looked artfully tossed across the slipper chair next to my bed. Let him get a good gander at *that.*

It was hard to imagine Jonathan spending time in my home—cooking in my kitchen, playing with Elfie—without me there. What exactly did it feel like? There was a comforting, almost familial feeling to it.

It feels like someone's coming home, I finally decided.

Chapter 22

The Sweetest Spud

A fantastic food—and fantastic <u>*for*</u> *you—is the sweet potato. Sweet potatoes are loaded with the following fitness-enhancing properties:*

- *Carotenoids, plant compounds that repair cell damage generated by workouts*
- *Vitamin E, an antioxidant vitamin that protects your heart and blood vessels*
- *Potassium, which is critical for muscle energy*
- *Fiber, which is filling, and helps keep your digestive system on "schedule"*
- *Copper, which helps your body utilize iron*
- *Quercetin, a powerful antioxidant that may help to prevent certain types of cancer*

—From *The Little Book of Fat-busters by Mimi Morgan*

At one p.m., Frank and I stood huddled at the edge of the helipad at the Raleigh-Durham airport. Between the takeoffs and landings of planes on the nearby runways, we scanned the overcast skies for any sign of an incoming helicopter. I strained to see through the clouds and tried not to think about the last time I stood at this particular spot—it was when

Lou's pilot had picked me up for my breakup trip to Atlanta.

Agent Garcia had told me that the chopper was going to touch down just long enough to pick us up, so we were prepared to move fast. Frank's camera was on his shoulder, ready to tape the landing shot.

At precisely one fifteen, a lull descended over the runway. From beyond the horizon, we heard a rumbling vibration. The sound grew steadily louder. Then a grouping of dark, long shapes lifted into the sky above the tree line—they were helicopters, six in all.

The formation advanced toward us, led by a smaller, wasp-shaped chopper. As it closed in, I could see missiles attached to the sides of the wasp leader.

"Hot damn." Frank let out a rebel yell and focused in with the lens. "That's an Apache gunship with Hellfires," he said. "Right behind him are the big mamas—Chinooks. The army uses them for troop transports and heavy lifting."

The oncoming choppers were aligned in a V-shaped row, like a flying wing. They pulled into the airspace over our heads, then hovered in place. By now, the propeller noise was deafening; I got whapped around by a violent upsurge of wind and dust that made it feel as if a cyclone had overtaken us.

Without warning, the chopper that was positioned directly over the helipad broke the formation. Its nose dipped down so fast that I ducked reflexively. Just above the tarmac, it leveled off. While the giant copter bobbed in the air, a door located in the middle of the cabin slid back.

A man in black body armor appeared in the opening. He held on to the side of the doorway with one hand while motioning Frank and me ahead with the other. He was shouting at us, but his words got sucked up into the turbulence.

Clutching my overnight bag, I made a half-crouching run for the door, followed by Frank.

The armored man reached down, grabbed my bag, and heaved it across the inside of the cabin, then took hold of my hand and elbow. He yanked me up so hard I thought he was going to heave *me* across the cabin, too. Then another pair of hands pulled me down—hard—onto an orange canvas jump seat, and fastened a safety harness around my shoulders. While other hands secured Frank and the equipment, the cabin door slammed shut.

"Hang on to your stomach, little lady—here we go," a male next to me shouted over the din in a heavy Southern accent.

I felt a sickening pitch and yaw as we lifted into the air. It was already clear that I was going to regret not having taken a Dramamine.

As soon as I recovered my breath, I took in the surroundings. The huge cabin resembled the inside of an eighteen-wheeler, barren except for some tied-down equipment, a double row of opposing seats, and a pair of steel cables that hung from enormous wheels bolted into the side of the craft. Two rows of men sat facing each other, about twenty in all. They were soldiers, judging by the green uniforms they wore underneath their body armor. Each man had a rifle secured vertically between his knees. I recognized the guns as M60s, the air-cooled machine guns that are standard army issue.

I extended my hand to my neighbor with the Southern accent. "I'm Kate Gallagher, from Channel Twelve in Durham." I practically had to scream my introduction to be heard. "Are you guys with the army?"

The soldier's face split into a toothy, farm-boy smile. "No, North Carolina National Guard RAID unit, ma'am," he said. "Me and my men just came back from a couple of tours of the sandbox."

"Sandbox? You mean Iraq?"

"That's right, ma'am."

I pulled out my notebook and pen, then said, "Can I get your name please, sir?"

"Lieutenant Robert Joe Henderson. But you can call me—"

The soldier seated on my other side reached over me and thumped the top of the lieutenant's head. "Quit show dogging the lady, KD," he said.

"Stick a sock in it, Crash," the lieutenant replied in an easygoing tone, then returned his focus to me. "These yardbirds call me KD—that stands for Kill Devil—because I come from Kill Devil Hills, North Carolina."

"Yeah, and because you really like to *kill* them devils in the hills!" Crash announced, to a round of snickers from the other soldiers.

Frank, who was seated directly across from us next to the cabin door, had reclaimed his camera and was taping our exchange. When he intercepted my look, he tossed me a microphone attached to a long cord.

I pointed the mike at Crash, holding it close to his mouth so that it would pick up his words over the chopper noise. "So you've gone from serving overseas to busting drug operations here at home in North Carolina—what's it like to make that kind of a switch?"

Crash looked pleased by the attention. "Hell, this little ole jaunt is like R and R compared to the 'Raq," he said. "Only thing is, you gotta be careful about who you blow away here in the States."

"Button up that loose trap, soldier," Lieutenant Henderson snapped. "That's a load of horseshit, and you know it."

"Yessir." Looking deflated, Crash lowered his gaze and began inspecting his weapon intently.

The lieutenant touched my wrist. "Pardon my language just then, ma'am. I just want to make sure you understand that North Carolina National Guardsmen are careful whenever we take any kind of offensive action. At home *or* overseas."

"Understood," I replied.

Lieutenant Henderson checked his watch, then announced in a shout that was loud enough for everyone to hear, "Listen up, dogs—hitting the drop zone in ten minutes."

"What are you dropping?" I asked him.

"Us." The lieutenant nodded at the rolls of steel cables hanging from the walls. "See those lines? That's how we deploy—we scale down from the chopper. It's called short hauling. It keeps us from having to beat our way through the snakes and poison ivy."

I stared at the cables. "Do you mean we're not landing?" Did that mean *I* was expected to "short haul" myself down a cord? Yikes.

"Oh, don't worry, ma'am. You'll land in the chopper after we deploy," Henderson said. "Once we secure the area, they'll bring you in. Then we'll load up whatever we find. That's why we're traveling in these big heavies today—our CO told us it's gonna be a really big haul."

"How much, any idea?"

"Don't know exactly. But I remember one great bust—we scored about sixty million dollars' worth of plant. It took us all afternoon to pack it up."

I glanced down the rows of men and machine guns. "It looks like you're expecting some resistance."

The lieutenant shrugged. "We never know, but we always have to be ready—last time out, some crazy hooch guard took potshots at us. That's why we always travel with that little attack chopper out front. He gives the dirtbags a warm Southern greeting if they try anything stupid."

Crash, who'd come back to life, nudged me in the

ribs with his elbow. "Wait till you see us drop—we swing down from the sky like Tarzans." He let out a yodel, which was picked up and echoed by the other soldiers. Soon the walls of the cabin were reverberating with jungle calls and screeching monkey imitations.

Lieutenant Henderson grinned at me. "The boys like to blow off a little steam right before a drop."

When the hooting and hollering died down, I told the lieutenant about the story I was doing on Libby Fowler's murder. "The cops say she may have been attacked by someone from one of these drug operations in the mountains. Whoever did it shoved her body down a ravine," I said. "Have you ever heard of something like that happening?"

The lieutenant's face turned solemn. "Nothing would surprise me. The cartels that run these farms are every bit as vicious as terrorists," he said.

Before I could answer, the chopper made a startling lurch, then bumped up sharply on an updraft. Soon it was dipping and rattling around like an old-fashioned wooden roller coaster. I bit my lip to avoid squealing with fright. I was determined to keep a poker face in front of these soldiers, especially in front of the one female in the row opposite me. She was staring at me with an amused expression, as if she were placing silent bets on how long it would take me to toss my cookies all over the floor.

"I guess we're hitting that line of thunderheads our CO promised us," Lieutenant Henderson said. "But it still beats the heck out of flying through a sandstorm, let me tell you."

Unable to see outside in the windowless cabin, all I could do was grip my fingers around the edges of my jump seat. And try not to retch.

A narrow door located at the front of the cabin opened. A soldier with a graying flattop stepped through it. Despite the bucking of the floor underfoot, he strode smoothly down the center of the cabin and surveyed the soldiers, who all straightened in their seats.

After shooting a brief glance my way, Commander Flattop announced, "Tar Heel Brigade. You hognose snake-troopers ready to drop and *roll* today?"

"Sir, yes, sir!" Their responses bounced back as a unified shout.

"Then get prepared. And use your rain gear—it's a wet one out there."

His order prompted a wild scramble. The soldiers removed their safety harnesses, then withdrew football-style helmets from underneath their seats. Crash and another man grabbed the loose ends of the steel cables from the walls and extended them toward the door.

Lieutenant Henderson patted my knee. "Well, I'll see you on the ground, little lady." He pulled on his helmet, tightened it, then handed me a folded square of green plastic. "Here, take this rain cape—you'll need it. Me, I don't like to wear anything that interferes with my shooting arm."

"Thanks so much, Lieutenant. And good luck to you guys, okay?"

Be careful out there, I wanted to add, but thought it would sound ridiculous under the circumstances.

"Thanks, ma'am." With a final flash of his country-boy grin, Henderson stepped to the doorway and yanked up on a handle. The door slid open with a hydraulic whine.

In synchronized order, the soldiers lined up in two long rows that led to the open doorway, where Henderson was waiting.

When the first pair of men were clipped to the cables, Henderson said, "Ready?" When he got shouted replies of "Ready, sir!" he thumped them across their backs. The men disappeared over the side.

Two by two, the soldiers attached to the cables and spidered down, cradling their M60s to their chests. The short haul went incredibly fast.

From my position opposite the doorway, I caught glimpses of evergreen branches and streaking rain. There were no visible treetops, which made me think that we must be hovering close to the ground. Then I heard an explosion, followed by automatic gunfire that sounded like Chinese firecrackers going off.

"Oh, Jesus," I whispered. "*Please* let them all come through this okay."

By the time I finished my whispered prayer, the very last soldier in line—Lieutenant Robert Joe Henderson—had vanished through the doorway, and the helicopter was pulling up and away.

Fast.

Chapter 23

Visualize Your Way to Strength

Studies indicate that you can actually think *your way to stronger muscles. You don't even have to exercise—all you have to do is visualize an exercise, and your muscle will actually respond.*

I can see a popular new class at the gym—instead of Spinning, everyone will be lying on mats, thinking *about Spinning. Sign me up!*

—From *The Little Book of Fat-busters* by Mimi Morgan

It seemed impossible that the pilots could land the big chopper in the inclined, heavily wooded acreage near the drop zone. But in a feat that would have put the best parallel parker in the world to shame, they must have located an open spot. The Chinook settled to earth as delicately as a butterfly landing on a daisy.

Commander Flattop insisted on eyeballing the secured zone before he allowed Frank or me to step outside. He took off with a small detail, leaving us behind with four guardsmen who turned up from another chopper. While we waited for them to report back, I strained to hear any more sounds of gunfire. None came.

Finally, a walkie-talkie on the belt of one of our bodyguards crackled out an announcement: "Delta area successfully secured. Five prisoners taken. No casualties." I breathed a sigh of relief.

Our little group set off on a sticky, miserable trek to the drop zone. The rain had tapered off, but was still coming down. I wore Lieutenant Henderson's cape over an armored vest that had my chest squeezed in a vise-grip—the vest's designer obviously hadn't accounted for 38DD soldiers. While my breasts sweated and swelled against their retaining wall, the ankle I'd injured the previous week kept turning under me in the mushy soil. It made me think that short hauling down a rope wouldn't have been so bad.

After seeing me stumble a couple of times, our burliest guardsman appointed himself as my personal Sherpa. Using his heavily muscled arms, he levitated me over the most difficult spots. It was like a mud stage version of a pas de deux.

I sent silent blessings my partner's way for not grunting each time he hoisted his zaftig ballerina.

The first thing I noticed about the drug farm was the trash. Huge plastic jugs (that contained pesticide, I later learned), beer cans, food wrappers, and other wastage were heaped in piles next to a row of field tents—aka hooches—that had been created by stretching earth-colored tarpaulins across wires suspended between trees.

Carved into the side of the mountain and artfully hidden among the sheltering evergreens, terraced layers of earth stretched out in all directions. Marijuana plants were growing in neat farmer's rows down each layer. They looked healthy and well tended.

Groups of uniformed officers were tromping about the scene, each group wearing vinyl jackets with the colors and back labels of their respective law enforcement agencies: SBI, DEA, and the North Carolina Highway Patrol Aviation Unit were all represented, in addition to my National Guard buddies. In the distance, I saw guardsmen loading marijuana plants into huge nets. I assumed that the Chinooks would later attach those nets to hooks and carry them away for disposal elsewhere. A couple of police photographers were hovering at the edges of the nets, angling for some close-up shots of the haul.

A short distance away, Lieutenant Henderson and Crash stood watch over a group of five glowering men who were seated on the ground with their hands cuffed behind their backs.

Lieutenant Henderson's face cracked into a smile when he saw Frank and me approach.

"Welcome to Cannabis Green Acres, ma'am," he said, while Frank taped Crash standing guard.

DEA Agent Garcia, who was standing a few feet away from the group and making some notes on a metal-backed notepad, looked up at me and grunted out a greeting. "You came along on a lucky ride, Kate. We hit the jackpot today—landed ourselves a big fish."

"What big fish?"

Garcia pointed to the prisoners. "See that guy in the middle? He's a cartel runner the Feds have been looking for. Connected to several gangland murders." He raised his voice to be overheard by the group. "Say a polite *'Buenos tardes'* to the lady, *maricón*."

The *maricón* he was addressing looked up and locked eyes with me. I recognized him immediately.

"I know that guy," I said. "It's Antonio Torres."

Agent Garcia's brows shot up. "Antonio Torres de la Cruz," he said. "You *know* him?"

"Not the de la Cruz part. He was the boyfriend of a girl I knew—Marnie Taylor—who *supposedly* died in an accidental fall." I stared at Antonio, who glared back at me.

Antonio spat on the ground. "You brought these

cops up here with you," he said. "I should have nailed your fucking *boca* shut when I had the chance."

Lieutenant Henderson shifted his M60 in Antonio's direction. "Watch your mouth, hairball."

"You're the one creating headlines today, Antonio. I'm just reporting them," I said to him.

Agent Garcia pulled me aside to ask me about Marnie Taylor.

In response to his questions, I said, "The SBI—Investigator Powell—is in charge of the investigation into her death, and they're also looking into the murder of a woman named Libby Fowler last fall. And from what I've heard, they think Libby was killed by someone connected to one of these types of drug operations. She was attacked at Pittman's Bluff—that's not far from here, is it?"

"Not far at all." Agent Garcia scribbled furiously on his pad. "As a matter of fact, Investigator Powell is on-site today. Right over there." He nodded toward a heavyset, fiftyish man who stood about twenty yards away, conferring with a couple of other men.

"Oh, good! I've been wanting to talk to him," I said. "Hang on a second, I'll be right back."

After giving Frank the "stay back" sign, I approached the group where Powell was talking.

"Inspector Powell?" I stuck my hand out toward him. "I'm Kate Gallagher. We spoke earlier about—"

Powell's face reddened. "I've got no comment for the media at this time. *No* comment. Nothing. Right. Now." He stomped away, elbows bent and waggling his hands in the air like a revival preacher on a Bible rage.

Frank came up behind me and leaned in conspiratorially. "You know, Kate, I really think that guy has the hots for you."

"Shut up, Frankenstein." I used his least favorite nickname while punching him lightly on the forearm.

Then I dragged tail back to Agent Garcia, who'd observed my exchange with Powell with an amused expression.

"I guess some arms of the law don't like to hug reporters," Garcia said. "So look—here's the bottom line. After we wrap things up here today, our operations reps will hold an assessment meeting. I'll mention everything you've told me, and we'll try to connect the dots. Would you be willing to share your notes with us if we need to get more info?"

"Certainly I will, on this story—I just hope you'll nail this guy Antonio for everything he's done." I handed Garcia my card with my cell number scribbled on back. "Here's another number if you need to reach me after hours."

"Good deal. Thanks."

I hoped the task force would connect the dots in a pattern like the one that was forming in *my* head: I thought it likely that someone from Antonio's drug operation had killed Libby Fowler; and then, months later, perhaps, Marnie had discovered something about Antonio's real profession as a drug dealer. I knew Antonio was dangerous. Perhaps he had nailed her *boca* shut to keep her quiet. Permanently.

Our chopper escort couldn't spare time to make a detour to Pittman's Bluff so that Frank and I could grab our footage; we'd have to hike back up to the spot the next day on our own.

We rode to Ashland in the smaller attack chopper instead of the Chinook, because the big craft had heavy hauling duties to complete. The last time I saw it, the giant hauler and its crew of National Guardsmen was lifting into the skies trailing a net filled with marijuana plants.

Once our escort chopper dropped us off at the Ashland airport, I used the portable satellite phone to call in my script of the day's events to Channel Twelve. Then Frank and I collected the rental SUV that the weekend producer had reserved for us.

My next call was to my friend Riley, to see if Frank and I could spend the night at Body Blast.

When I told him what I wanted to do, Riley said in a flat, lifeless tone, "Sure, Kate. Whatever you want."

My friend sounded despondent.

"What's going on, Riley?"

He let out a chest-rattling sigh. "I checked Khan into rehab last night," he said. "That's why I didn't get your message earlier. Our friends and I did an intervention with him. Even his gambling buddies got in on the act. We insisted that he get help, or we'd cut off all our ties to him."

"Wow. I'm so sorry, Riley. But it's for the best. I know you did the right thing."

"You do? *I* don't." I heard something swell in his throat. "What if rehab doesn't work? Khan seemed so completely . . . broken. He was sobbing like a little boy."

"Well—"

"Right now I feel like running away from everything and starting over somewhere else, where no one knows me. The camp, my life here . . . I just want to throw it all away."

"You're not throwing *anything* away right now, Riley," I told him in a firm tone. "At least, not in the middle of an emotional crisis. I won't let you."

"Thanks, Kate." I heard him swallow hard. "Of course—you and your friend can stay here, no problem."

"Well, certainly he's my friend, but he's also a colleague. Frank's my cameraman."

"Oh?" Riley's voice went up an octave. "What exactly do you have in mind? You're not planning to do a story from here, I hope?"

"Oh, no, don't worry. The cops just busted a drug dealer who they think may have had some connection with Libby Fowler's death. They're looking into it."

"Oh, God, really?"

"Yep. And get this—this same guy was Marnie Taylor's boyfriend. So there may be a connection between the two deaths. I was at the operation in the mountains where they arrested him today, and we want to get some more footage tomorrow. But our coming here tonight is just a friendship call."

"Okay." The tension in Riley's voice eased. "We've got some empty rooms—you and your cameraman can come on by tonight. Since you won't be on the program this time, you'll get to hang out with the *real* Body Blast scene—my staff. It'll be much more fun for you that way, anyway."

"Sounds great, thanks."

By the time Frank and I reached Body Blast in our rental car, it was nearly six p.m. My stomach was doing hungry backflips because I'd missed lunch, but Riley had promised me we could grab dinner in the staff's dining room.

The prospect of dining at Body Blast was a bit dismal—protein shakes, raw veggies, and a yam weren't exactly what my taste buds were yearning for at that particular moment. But at least it would be fuel. I was starting to feel faint.

When Frank and I entered the lobby, Erica and Hillary were manning the front desk.

"Hi, Kate—are you checking into the program again?" With a puzzled look, Hillary glanced down at her guest roster, while Erica—who was wearing a sleek business suit for some reason—avoided noticing my nod of greeting.

"No, not this time. Riley's just letting us stay over tonight," I said, after introducing Frank. "He said we could grab some chow in the staff dining room. I'm totally famished right now—is it okay if we head there first?"

"Oh, sure thing," Hillary replied. "I'm going on break right now, in fact. I'll show you where it is."

Leaving Erica behind the desk, Hillary led us down a long hallway. Frank, I noticed, was silently checking out Hillary's flawlessly toned ass. I mimed someone peering at her butt through a pair of binoculars, which made him retaliate with a silent bout of air boxing. When Hillary turned around to see what was going on, I covered our tracks by extending a foot that sent Frank stumbling against the wall.

"Erica looks really dressed up tonight," I said to Hillary, who shook her head and rolled her eyes.

"Riley just promoted her to Darwin's old job as program director," she said, opening a door to a small cafeteria. "I think it's really gone to her head. I just hope she doesn't plan to turn this place into something way out. Like *Survivor: The Great Smokies.*"

If Erica had accepted a promotion, I had to assume that meant she wasn't planning to run off to open her own gym anytime soon.

The instant we stepped through the door into the cafeteria, my olfactory senses were hit by a wall of warm, familiar fragrance: cheese, oregano, and tomato sauce.

"Lasagna?" My spirits lifted. "Is that what you guys eat, for real?"

Hillary nodded. "The trainers are so active that we'd all be anorexic if we ate the food they give the weekend campers. Besides, that low carb diet really sucks."

We grabbed plates and moved down a buffet line that ran along the far wall. I loaded up with the sumptuous fare, which included—bless the gods that ruled the day—hot garlic toast. Then we sat down at one of two long tables, where people were chatting and eating.

To my right was Gordon, the masseur with gigantic forearms. I'd seen him before only in passing. As we ate, he and I chatted a bit about his bodybuilding aspirations. I took an instant liking to Gordon—he had a polite, country-boy manner that reminded me a bit of Lieutenant Henderson.

After I inhaled about half my lasagna, Riley entered the dining room. He gave me a little half salute. After loading up a plate on the line, he dropped into a seat I'd saved for him to my left.

"Have you heard anything more about how Khan's doing in rehab?" I asked him.

Riley shook his head. "They don't let the patients communicate with anyone—not even family—for six weeks." He paused. "Let's change the subject, okay? What's been up with you?"

Keeping my voice low, I filled Riley in on what had happened to my apartment the previous day, and about my suspicions that Yves Laplante was behind the break-in.

Riley's face drained. "I'm so sorry that I dragged you into this whole thing, Kate. I should have been a big boy and handled my problems myself."

I shrugged. "Don't worry about it. I have a cop friend who thinks they're going to nail Laplante pretty soon."

Then I added, "So, like I said on the phone, Frank and I want to go to Pittman's Bluff tomorrow, to get some footage of the spot where Libby died. Is there any chance you could take us up there?"

Riley's fork froze halfway to his lips. "You want me to take you to Pittman's Bluff? Um, I don't know, Kate. I—"

"Oh, don't worry about it if you can't," I said hastily. "We have GPS. Frank and I can find it ourselves."

"No way!" Riley looked appalled. "The terrain is

really rough. You'll get lost. It's just that right now, I don't . . . I don't really feel up to it."

Gordon, who'd been grilling Frank about the mechanics of videography while Riley and I were talking, interjected, "I can take them tomorrow, Riley. I know right where Pittman's Bluff is. Maybe me and Hillary could take both of them."

"What? You want *me* to go?" Hillary, who was sorting through a stack of neon pink flyers across the table, looked up with a startled expression.

Then she added in an unenthusiastic voice, "That would be okay, I guess. If someone can take my morning appointment."

"I'll get someone to take it for you, Hill," Riley said. "Thanks."

The sight of Hillary shuffling through the flyers jarred a fuzzy memory in my brain. "What are those?" I reached across the table for a sheet.

"These just describe the one-on-one work I do," she said, sliding it toward me. "Some people are totally unprepared for real workouts when they get here."

Riley scraped his chair back from the table and stood up. "I'm totally beat to hell tonight. I'm packing it in early." He looked at me. "We're putting you guys up in rooms 3A and B tonight, Kate. You know the way, right?"

"We'll find it, thanks. Don't worry about us."

"See you tomorrow, maybe."

Riley hurried away from the dining room without looking back.

When he left, I focused my attention on Hillary's flyer. It started off with an upbeat, Oprah-style description about how women could transform their lives through exercise. Private appointments with Hillary, it continued, could be arranged for mornings at five a.m.

As I stared at the flyer, the memory I'd been trying to retrieve finally bobbed to the surface.

Early on the morning that Marnie's body had turned up dead on the obstacle course, I'd discovered a pink flyer—just like this one—stuck between the sheets of her bed.

Chapter 24

A Call to Arms

Why, oh, why do female celebrities in fashion magazines insist on wearing sleeveless evening dresses, even during the dead of winter? Are they trying to make the rest of us feel bad by showing off their freakishly toned arms?

If you have arms that keep on waving, you can take a cue from Rocky Balboa. Grab a pair of free weights and do some shadowboxing. Crosscuts, uppercuts, left hooks (it'll put you in the right spirit if you imagine that you're punching out your news director) . . .

C'mon, girls, punch 'im out!

—From *The Little Book of Fat-busters* by Mimi Morgan

The hot pink flyer was still on my mind the next morning when our hiking group—Hillary, Gordon, Frank, and I—parked our SUV in a small dirt lot near the beginning of the Dragon's Tail. From there, a two-hour hike would bring us to the top of Pittman's Bluff.

I'd spent a restless night, thinking about the flyer I'd found in Marnie's bed the morning her body was discovered. The flyer advertised five a.m. workout appointments with Hillary—was it possible that Marnie had scheduled an early-morning appointment that day? Had something terrible happened to her, like an accident? If so, why hadn't Hillary reported it?

I tossed around possible approaches to the question as Hillary led the way up an incredibly steep trail—"trail" seemed a grossly inappropriate noun for what turned out to be a zigzagging goat path up Mount Pittman. I trudged behind Hillary, followed by Frank and Gordon, who had divided the load of camera equipment between them.

Thirty minutes into the hike, I was huffing and blowing enough steam to rival Snuffleupagus, and my calves felt as though they'd turned into cement blocks.

"This feels more like climbing, than hiking," I called up to Hillary, while grabbing an exposed root to pull myself up a steep slope. "Not that I'm *complaining* or anything."

She turned around and said, "This is a Level Three hike—it's probably a bit more than you were expecting today. Let's take a break."

The word "break" never sounded so good. There wasn't any ground level enough to lie down on, so I collapsed on top of a whale-backed boulder that provided a welcome, if somewhat rocky, respite.

When I looked around, I saw that Frank and Gordon weren't breathing hard, despite carrying all the equipment. The bastards weren't even sitting *down*.

"It totally sucks to be the wuss of the group." I reached into my backpack for my water bottle.

Hillary shrugged. "Don't worry about it," she said. "We're all on a fitness journey in life, just at different points."

"Well, right now, my journey seems to have stalled in Fat City."

"Here, let me show you something." Kneeling down, Hillary pressed her fingers into the back of my calves. Her hands were so strong that the pressure felt almost painful. "This'll help you loosen up those muscles."

"Ah-h-h," I said, enjoying the sensation of cement draining from my lower extremities.

Now seemed like a good moment to settle some niggling questions I'd had all along about Hillary. "I heard that you're originally from New York," I said, as she continued to massage my legs. "What brought you this far south?"

Her fingers stopped. "Who told you I'm from New York?"

"I guess it was Riley."

Hillary's smile tightened. "Oh, right. I keep forgetting you two are so close." She got to her feet. "I mean, *I* think that's fine, but Erica thinks you're Riley's little spy or something."

Erica was right, I thought with a twinge. But it struck me that Hillary hadn't answered my question, so I added, "So what *did* bring you south, originally?"

"I have family down here—my aunt Debbie lives in Durham. I stayed with her for a while when I was a kid. Then I moved back down here after college."

"Oh? Where were you at school in Durham?"

"Oh, a cute little school called Longleaf Day School. But I was only there a year."

Libby's friend Irene had told me that Longleaf was where she and *Libby* had gone to school.

"Did you know Libby Fowler when you went there?" The question bolted from my lips before I even had time to consider it.

Hillary stared at me. "*Libby?* N-no. I didn't." She paused. "Well, I may have *seen* her."

Before I could say anything else, she quickly added, "But Libby and I were in totally different crowds. I was mostly involved with the chess club, so I really didn't get to know her at all. Then I moved back up to New York."

Hillary did *not* strike me as a chess-club type. Chess clubs were often a refuge for shy, brainy kids, the ones who were often labeled—wrongly—"losers" by their peers.

"Well, when you ran into Libby again after all those years, did you—"

"Uh-oh. Looks like the rain's heading back this way." Hillary glanced up at the sky, which was beginning to shroud over. "I'm sorry to cut you off, but we should really get going—we don't want to get caught in a downpour."

I wanted to ask her more questions about Libby—and Marnie—as we hiked. But once we hit the trail, Hillary stayed too far ahead for conversation. I sensed that she was setting a Bionic Woman pace to avoid answering further questions. Plus, she'd whipped out a nifty tool—a telescoping trekking pole—that she was using to hook into the earth as she climbed. The only tool I had was my Swiss Army knife, which with its corkscrew attachment was better suited for hooking into bottles of Chardonnay.

God, that woman was in great shape. There was no way I could catch up; it was like climbing the stairs of the Empire State Building. As I pulled and clawed my way up the mountain in Hillary's wake, I made a silent vow that, boot camp or no, this hike spelled the end of the couch potato life for me. I was determined to get myself in top physical shape, and I would do it within six months.

I glanced back at Gordon and Frank, who were bringing up the rear. I thought I caught a flash of movement—something large and dark—moving farther down the switchback trail behind them. "Are there any bears up here?" I called down to Gordon.

"There are lots of black bears," he replied. "But they usually don't bother anyone."

Usually. That was comforting. I tried to recall whether my dad had ever sent me an advisory on how to escape from a bear. Actually, I think he *had* sent me one, once, back when I went to Girl Scout camp. But what had it said, exactly?

Frank, who had caught up with me, said, "How ya doin', Kate? You've kinda downshifted to turtle speed."

"Bite my rosy Irish ass, Frankenstein," I gasped. "I've got plenty to spare."

Gordon chimed in, "Hey, I could tie you to me with a rope and pull you up the rest of the way," he said. "You know, the way those Sherpas do with tourists on Mount Everest."

"I'm *fine*."

But in fact, I was verging on breakdown. The muscle-fire in my calves had spread to my thighs, and I was afraid both my legs would go into lockdown mode from all the stress I was putting on them. Despite those woes, I kept glancing back. There was a weird vibe in the air, as if we were being watched. But I seemed to be the only one who was picking up on it. Hillary was marching smoothly up the incline in the lead, and behind me, Frank and Gordon were trading stories about various assholes they'd worked with in the past. Maybe my brain was getting paranoid from exhaustion.

If a bear wasn't following us, what was it? Maybe something human. I thought about the drug operation the cops had busted the day before, and about how heavily armed—and dangerous—its operatives had been. There could be tons of them, hidden away up here in the mountains.

If we were being tracked by a drug-criminal type, that spelled trouble.

We'd stand a much better chance against a bear.

"This is where Libby died."

Hillary made that solemn pronouncement the moment our group straggled to the top of the promontory known as Pittman's Bluff.

The bluff was exactly the kind of place you'd expect to be murdered. Edged by scraggly evergreens, the rocky outcropping formed the leading edge of a precipice that overlooked a deep, boulder-strewn gorge. It wasn't a sheer drop, but still, a steep incline. Far below us, the walls and floor of the gorge were lined with scrub pine and jagged rocks.

Now that we'd reached the summit, I longed to sprawl on the ground and take a long rest. But I shook off the impulse.

"On the morning that Libby died, how did you all locate her body?" I asked Hillary. "Could you see it from up here?"

"Actually, Riley found her. When she turned up missing, he sent the rest of us scrambling off in all directions to look for her. For some reason he seemed to have a hunch she'd be down there, so he roped down into the gorge by himself."

Frank, who'd finished taking some initial shots, said to me, "Gordon and I are going to circle around the edge of the gorge and see if we can get a little farther down, Kate. I want to get some good tight-ins. We'll be back in a half hour."

"Okay, I'll call the newsroom on the sat phone and give them an update. We're running late."

"And whose fault is *that*?" He grinned at me.

I slapped my buttocks. "A big chomp right outa here, Frankenzoid. Anytime."

When the two men disappeared from sight, Hillary looked at me. "Actually I think I'll head out after them—I can show them exactly where to go."

"Hey, wait a second, Hillary. I—"

I wanted to follow up with a couple more questions about Libby. But Hillary was pulling away at a warp speed that would have left even the Bionic Woman in her dust. And I didn't have time to try to chase her down, because my bout of mountain turtle-crawl disorder had left us running dangerously behind schedule for that night's broadcast.

I extracted the satellite phone from the carrying pouch attached to my belt, then rotated out the antennae and punched in the numbers to connect to the newsroom. The LED display read SEARCHING . . . That meant the phone was searching for an LEO—a Low Earth Orbit satellite—to make the connection. But the connection wasn't happening.

I glared up at the clouds. "Come on, come *on*, asshole." I directed the challenge to any Globalstar that happened to be orbiting over the neighborhood. "I have zero time right now, and I *have* that friggin' 'clear view of the southern sky.' "

Sometimes, moving to a new position helped. Abruptly, I spun right and took a step in the direction of the bluff.

At that moment, I felt a searing explosion of pain in my left shoulder. I screamed and swung about.

I found myself standing face-to-face with Hillary. She stood inches away from my nose, holding her trekking pole in her right hand. She had it cocked back in the air as she zeroed in for the next strike. My last-second turn to get a better signal had saved me from getting KO'd with her first swing.

When I saw the shaft arcing through the air my way, I couldn't pause to consider why Hillary had suddenly gone postal on me. There was only enough time for a raw survival instinct to kick in.

Running away seemed the logical option, but Hillary was in far too good shape for that. I was going to have to stand and fight.

My father's advisory, "How to Survive an Assailant's Attack," came flooding back into my brain, almost word for word.

Control your assailant's weapon. Every move I made had to be focused on getting control of Hillary's pole.

Hillary was right-handed, so as the shaft swung through the air, I circled to her right so that she had to reach across her body to go for me.

Make sure you have your own *weapon.* My Swiss Army knife, to quote my beloved father, would be a "Tinkertoy" in a real fight. But hey, at least it was a *knife.* As I circled, I plunged my hand into my pocket and closed it around the folded-up knife. Then, with a sharp uppercut, I snapped it out and popped her in the nose with it.

The effect couldn't have been more gratifying if I'd hit her with a pair of brass knuckles. Hillary made a guttural noise and staggered back, her nose spurting blood.

I took advantage of the brief reprieve to open the Swiss Army knife's largest blade with both hands. Then, to keep her distracted, I tried insulting her.

"You fucking Luddite!" I screamed at Hillary as loudly as I could. I have no clue why that geeky Bronx cheer was uppermost in my jibe drawer. It probably had something to do with my earlier frustration with the satellite phone.

My nerdish taunt didn't slow her down by so much as a single nanosecond. Hillary hauled back to aim another ax-murderer swing at my throat.

"I guess you never developed the muscles in your *brain*, you moron," I continued, pivoting again and gasping for air. "Because you're gonna spend the rest of your life doing your workouts in *jail.*"

Despite the blood streaming from her nose, Hillary kept coming on strong. She flashed forward again with the pole. It was time to escalate to the advisory's equivalent of Defcon One—let the missiles fly.

The next time she swung at me, instead of pivoting, I ducked; as she thrust forward, I came up and speared the back of her arm that was holding the pole. I must have hit a sweet spot, because a mini-geyser of blood starting spurting from her triceps.

Squealing with pain, Hillary folded over and grabbed the back of her arm. Using my free hand, I knocked the pole out of her hand.

And that's when I should have stopped. I'd won the battle, but failed to pay sufficient heed to where our war was being fought. We'd brawled our way to the edge of Pittman's Bluff.

My finale was a bit of vengeful overkill—I delivered a sharp, vicious kick to her face.

When my foot connected with Hillary's face, she latched on to my ankle with an iron grip. I lost my balance and pitched forward. She hung on, apparently unaware of our mutual peril.

Next, I became aware of a sense of space opening up all around us.

We were toppling over the edge of Pittman's Bluff.

Chapter 25

Who Made These Stupid Rules, Anyway?

Our bodies are governed by some bizarre laws of nature, including the following:

- *You can gain weight faster than you can lose it*
- *Alcohol calories are much more dangerous than regular calories, because they sneak in snack buddies*
- *Fat is quick to promote you to a bigger belt size, but slow to promote you to a bigger bra size*
- *In the face of determined opposition, fat retreats from all the places you don't care about, then clings like holy hell everyplace else*

—From *The Little Book of Fat-busters* by Mimi Morgan

Nothing focuses your mind like falling over a cliff.

They should add that adage to the laws of infernal dynamics, right below the one that says, "An object in motion will be moving in the wrong direction."

The gorge below Pittman's Bluff angled down at a treacherously steep incline, like a silo chute. Only this chute was lined with killer-looking rocks that jagged out from the sides of the walls at all kinds of crazy angles. One wrong angle of impact on any of these rocks and you would be seriously busted up, if not dead.

The moment I knew we were rolling over the edge, I turned into a wildcat on a hissy-fit bender—clawing, grabbing, scratching, trying to snag anything—anything at all—that would break my fall.

Hillary screamed and let go of my foot. I couldn't see where she tumbled off to—and frankly, I didn't give a Rhett's damn—because I was too busy trying to save myself. I was tumbling helplessly toward two craggy boulders that were set closely together.

I tried to break my forward tumble by grabbing hold of a thick root that was protruding from the side of the ravine. I got a desperate grip around it, but my would-be root rescuer betrayed me by extracting from the loose soil wall like a rotten tooth.

But I'd given myself just enough time to swivel my body so that my butt was pressed against the side of the steep, earthen slope. Now as I went down, rather than tumbling, it was more like a surfing slide—I rode my butt down the rocky ravine, keeping my hands out for balance. I could feel the skin on my hands—and my ass—getting ripped up. But then I took a wrong bounce, and my head whiplashed against something solid.

I shot into the gap between the two boulders. And that's where I stopped. My legs were dangling, swinging wildly in the space that opened up beneath the rocks, but my butt was tightly wedged between them. And those buttocks weren't going *anywhere*. Bottom line: saved by the butt.

I was stuck, dazed and bleeding, but alive.

I had no idea if Hillary was.

The blow to my head on the way down had taken a temporary toll on my vision. Groggily, I tried to take stock of my surroundings. In the far distance, I heard Frank screaming my name. Then, from below, there was a crashing sound. Two tall, brownish creatures came into view at the bottom of the gorge. They started climbing toward me.

To my rock-slammed brain, they looked like a pair of bears—one tall, one shorter. The dog-shaped carnipeds clambered over the rocks, headed straight toward me.

This is all *I need right now,* I thought with a groan. A grizzly bear attack. But wait—they didn't have grizzlies in North Carolina. Only black bears. Someone should tell these Yogis they were out of their bear jurisdiction.

Miraculously, my dad's instructions about how to escape a bear attack came flooding back and took a front-row seat in my brain. The advice had something to do with clanging bells to scare them away.

Well, obviously it was too late for *that.* The final, last-ditch action to take—just before you got eaten—was to play dead.

That would be easy. I closed my eyes and tried hard not to breathe.

I was expecting the next sensation to be from a razor-sharp claw, ripping out my throat.

There was a series of dull thuds as the creatures approached. Then silence.

I cracked open an eyelid.

The taller bear spoke. "Jesus F. Christ, I hope we're not too late. Check her vitals."

These were *talking* bears? They must have been trained someplace. Perhaps even socialized.

I opened my eyes wider. "You bears on the lam from a circus someplace?"

The tall one said, "She's delirious—I'll go check the other woman."

I felt my clothes being loosened, then something

soft being placed gently under my head. I looked up. My brain fog cleared and I saw, not a bear's gaping fangs, but a face—human—wearing a Smokey Bear hat. I recognized the face immediately. It was the Amazingly Cute Ranger I met back when I was doing the Earthfest story.

"Hey, you're the cute ranger guy," I said in a weak voice. "But I forgot your name."

"It's Russell, Ms. Gallagher. Ranger Pike and I are going to get you out of here."

"Ranger *Pike*?" He must be the tall bear. "How—?"

"We were following your hiking party. But we lost sight of you just before you fell."

"We didn't *just* fall. Hillary attacked me. I was fighting back."

"We'll get all that sorted out once we get you both out of here. Ranger Pike is looking after Hillary. She's pretty busted up."

So someone *had* been trailing us all day—the rangers. At least that explained my earlier feeling that we were being watched. "Why were you following us?"

"A detective from Durham—Jonathan Reed—asked us to keep tabs on your hike this afternoon. I guess he was worried about you. You have an amazing friend there."

"You know what? I believe I do."

Imagine the most embarrassing moment that you've ever had from being overweight, and then quadruple it. That's what it felt like to have Ranger Russell extricate my ass from between the two boulders. It took much painful squishing, squeezing, and pulling before I finally popped out from the boulder vise like a human champagne cork.

But even more embarrassing than that was having said ass bandaged by the ranger. This was a hideous process that involved my completely removing my pants and underwear. And I was already sans T-shirt due to my brawl with Hillary, so I was basically down to my birthday suit.

The entire time I was enduring this humiliation, I could hear Hillary bitching and moaning in the distance about how I'd stabbed her. She'd survived the fall, but had evidently broken her leg.

So there I was, lying facedown on the ground at the bottom of the gorge with my head resting on a pillow fashioned from Ranger Russell's jacket, my butt exposed to the air in all its scraped-up glory, when Frank and Gordon reappeared. Without the shortcut that Hillary and I had made, it had taken them that long to work their way to the bottom of the gorge.

I ordered them to cover their eyes, and then was relieved to learn that there would be no need for a drawn-out discussion about who had attacked whom up on Pittman's Bluff.

"I got it all on tape," were the first words out of Frank's mouth as he covered his eyes with one hand. "Her taking the first swing at you with that pole—I got it all. Thank goodness I just happened to be taking a wide shot at that moment. I almost missed the whole thing."

"You never miss the good shots," I told him.

And then, as he reached stealthily for his camera, I added, "But if you take so much as a single frame of my bongoed-up butt, you're a dead man, Frankenstein."

Chapter 26

Women and Aggression

Women can be provoked to aggression, same as men. But they tend to be provoked in different ways. Studies indicate that men are most often provoked into aggression when their sexual vitality is questioned (natch). Women, by contrast, are much more likely to become aggressive in the face of condescension and insensitivity.

—From *The Little Book of Fat-busters* by Mimi Morgan

Two days later, I was lying in a similar position on my couch at home, with my bandaged butt angled at the ceiling. Jonathan was sprawled next to me on the floor, riding shotgun on my behind's behalf against Elfie, who like all cats had an unerring instinct for perching where you least want them to go. Which in my case, was at the summit of Mount Miserable Derriere.

Ever since Hillary's attack on me, my mind had been dieseling day and night about her motives, her possible connection to Marnie's death, and my conviction that she'd murdered Libby Fowler the same way she attacked me.

The moment I'd gotten litter-carried down the mountain (another humiliating experience that I won't describe), a couple of paramedics loaded me into an ambulance to get checked over. I used the ambulance ride to make some calls on the satellite phone.

My second call was to Libby's friend, Irene. She sounded confused when I named Hillary as Libby's possible attacker.

"Hillary Evans—she went to your school, Longleaf Day, for a couple of years back in middle school," I said, propping up on one arm on the ambulance gurney and raising my voice to be heard over the siren. I wished they'd shut that damned thing off. It only drew more attention to my embarrassing plight. "But now she's—"

"Hillary *Evans*?" Irene sounded confused. "No, I don't think so. There was a Hillary Holden back then—we all kind of tortured her, I'm afraid. She was a real tubbo."

"It's the same Hillary, except she's certainly not a 'tubbo' anymore," I told her. "I just talked to her aunt—she told me that Hillary went by her mom's maiden name—Holden—during the two years she was living down here in Durham. Her aunt told me she was mad at her dad for taking the family to Europe without her, so she temporarily switched her last name. Now she's back to Hillary Evans."

"I never knew that. I don't think anybody got to know Hillary back then—I'm afraid we just poked fun at her." Her voice had changed. "Oh, my God, *that's* why she did it? That's why she killed Libby?"

"That's what I'm trying to find out."

Now I looked at Jonathan, who was shooing Elfie off my butt again. "I simply don't believe that Hillary's a murderous sociopath—she really seemed to care about the women on the program," I said to him. "But I'm sure she killed Libby. And why go after me? Maybe my questions were threatening her. And I still can't shake the feeling that she was with Marnie Taylor when she died. There was this pink flyer that made me think—"

"You're right on track, actually." Jonathan, who'd had a light in his eye ever since he'd arrived at my house an hour earlier, lifted a laptop that he'd brought with him off the floor. He set it on the coffee table in front of me. "What you're about to see comes compliments of our friend Carla at the SBI. It's Hillary's official interrogation."

Then he went on to say, "But mind, you cannot use *one word* of this on your news show. Carla would cut off my balls. And she knows just how to do it."

"I won't use anything. Scout's word of honor." I made a facsimile of the Girl Scout finger sign. Or maybe it was Mr. Spock's Vulcan sign. Whichever. I meant it.

Jonathan reached across to the laptop and pressed a button.

The screen glowed with a close-in shot of Hillary.

She was seated on a stool behind a metal table, one leg encased in a white cast that splayed out at an awkward angle from the rest of her body. Her short-cropped head was hanging low, her hands drawn behind her back. Evidently, she was handcuffed.

Offscreen, I heard a male voice say, "So, Hillary, I want you to understand that we're being recorded now. Repeat for me why you attacked Libby Fowler on October second, 2007?"

In a lifeless voice, Hillary responded, "Libby and I knew each other back in the eighth grade."

"What happened between the two of you back then?"

With more energy, she responded, "You can't *imagine* what she did to me. How mean she was—her and her friends. They called me a pig. And that wasn't the worst thing. They . . ." She closed her eyes.

The offscreen voice asked, "What else did they do?"

"One time, I came into the shower room right after intramural volleyball. Libby had swiped my shirt out of my locker. She was prancing around in it, making fun because it was so big. She'd stuffed clothes underneath it to make herself look fat. She was chasing her friends around, shouting 'Watch out! Watch out! Here comes Hillary the Hippo!'"

Hillary lowered her chin to her chest.

The voice asked, "So when you met up with Libby again, ten years later, you decided that you would kill her? As payback?"

"Not at first." She paused. "Libby didn't even *recognize* me. Can you believe that?" She raised her head to face her questioner. "All the shit she and those girls gave me, she didn't even *know who I was*. And it's just because I look good now." Her head drooped back down. "And when I introduced myself to her, do you know what she said to me?"

"You tell me."

"Libby said, 'Oh, my *God*. You're Hillary the Hippo from the eighth *grade*?' And then she giggled and said, '*Whoops*, sorry about using your old nickname.' And then she said, 'It's so amazing that you managed to get all that weight off. How long do you think you'll be able to stay down? Don't most of you people gain it back?' "

"What happened after that?"

"Well, she kept *pretending* to apologize for the stuff she and her friends had done to me back in the eighth grade. But her 'apologies' were incredibly insulting and patronizing, like, 'Wow, you've really transformed yourself from Rosie O'Donnell into Rosie the Riveter, haven't you? But haven't you gone from one extreme to the other? Isn't that just as bad?' "

"You felt angry about what she said? About her laughing at you?"

"Did I feel *angry*?" Hillary squeezed her eyes shut.

"I thought I'd put all that stuff behind me," she continued in a wracked-sounding voice. "The horrible humiliation I felt as a child, the rage. And then, what happens? Along comes this strutting little B-Ho from my past. She brought it all back."

When she received no reply from her interrogator, Hillary's eyes popped open. "*Yeah,* I felt angry. I felt angry enough to strangle her, right then and there. But I waited until the next day. I wanted to make it look like an accident."

"Well, you didn't do a very good job of that, Hillary. We knew that Libby was struck on her head before she fell."

The rage drained from Hillary's face, and her neck drooped again.

"And what about Marnie Taylor?" the questioning voice continued. "You said earlier that you were with her on the morning that she died."

Staring down at the table, Hillary said, "I met with Marnie one-on-one, for a private session, early that morning. I pushed her into meeting me that morning. I really wanted to *help* her. I was trying to get her over the obstacle course wall. But then something happened."

She ground to a halt, then continued, "Marnie fell backwards off the wall. I couldn't break her fall. There should have been two of us spotting her that morning, because she was so heavy. Somehow her neck twisted back when she landed. It was really bad. She was gasping; she couldn't breathe. I . . ." Hillary looked up with a pleading expression in her eyes. "About Marnie . . . *please* understand, I couldn't help her. She fell off that wall. It was a freak accident. And then she just . . . went. She died."

"Why didn't you try to get help for her? Report what happened?"

"*Report* it?" Hillary shook her head. "Look. Marnie

was already dead, and you people were giving us all the third degree about Libby. You think I would tie myself to *another* suspicious death? I had to stay quiet. I had no other choice."

"And the attack on the television reporter, Kate Gallagher? Why her?"

"Kate." She directed her gaze at the ceiling. "You know, I actually *liked* Kate, at first. But she just wouldn't stop asking questions." Hillary raised her shoulders as if she were trying to bring her hands forward, but they were restrained by the cuffs. "I mean, you people—the cops—you seemed to give up on Libby's investigation, after a while. I knew from the news that you were blaming it on drug dealers. But Kate—she kept coming back and back, always with more questions. And each time, she got closer to me. She just doesn't stop coming. She's like the Terminator with a microphone."

"So . . ."

"So when I got a shot at her, I took it. I figured you'd blame it on the drug criminals again."

"Are you feeling any remorse today?"

"About who? About Marnie? Yes. I couldn't help her. I—I failed her. She trusted me, and I let her down."

"What about Libby? Do you feel sorry for killing her?"

No response. Hillary stared stonily ahead.

"And Kate? Any second thoughts about the attack on her?"

"Kate wouldn't let up. It was her or me."

"It's going to be *you*, Hillary—you're going to be in jail for a good long while."

That's where the tape ended.

Jonathan clicked off the laptop and said, "It's amazing what people will confess when the DA threatens them with the death penalty."

"Wow," I said. " 'The Terminator with a microphone.' I guess that's flattering, in a backhanded way."

Jonathan shook his head. "So Hillary killed a girl who called her Fattie back in the eighth grade. Even after ten years in Homicide, I never stop being amazed at how little it takes for some people to commit murder."

Then it was *my* turn to shake my head. "I don't think you can possibly understand how vicious girls can be to each other at that age. And it sounds like even as an adult, Libby liked to twist the knife." Then I added, "With one exception, I'd never commit murder, but sometimes I can understand why people do it."

Jonathan stared at me. "Who would be your one exception?"

After a pause, I said, "The man who killed my mother."

He flinched. "I'm so sorry. I never knew your mother was murdered. I assumed she died of cancer or something."

I shook my head, and the room went silent. Finally I said, "It was the morning of my thirteenth birthday. Mom left our house to pick up my birthday cake. I'd made a special request for my favorite kind, a Black Forest cake. They only carried it at this one German bakery across town. When she got there, she walked in on an armed robbery. The guy got spooked—or maybe he was just a psycho—and shot up the place. I never saw her again."

Jonathan stroked my hair. "That's horrible. I'm so sorry, love."

I didn't cry—not right then. Jonathan circled his arms awkwardly about my shoulders, and I pressed my face into the sofa cushions. My shoulders shook with a breaker of tearless sobs.

Finally, Jonathan said, "Your mother's murderer. If

you ever do find this bloke, are you sure you'd actually want to kill him?"

"I won't know until the day I find him, but I think I'd have zero qualms. My dad's been working my mom's case all these years. When he retires, if they still don't have her shooter, I'm going after him."

"I'll help you. But please don't force me to arrest you for homicide, however justified it might seem."

Before I could answer, a sharp knock rattled the front door.

"Bother it to hell. What now?" Jonathan got to his feet and opened the door.

Standing in the threshold was my friend Riley. His arms were wrapped around a basket of goodies that included . . .

"Whoopie Pies!" I surfaced a grin to my face and tried to throw off the excruciating pain—the emotional kind—that had engulfed me. "And they're the real ones—from Maine. Riley, you still know how to get a girl excited."

"Well, darling, this is no time to be worried about dieting." He crossed the living room, set the basket on the coffee table, and knelt down. "When the rangers phoned to tell me what happened—I thought I was going to have a heart attack." He rested his forehead against the edge of the couch. "I'll never forgive myself for not going with you yesterday. I'm just so glad you're alive. Are you okay?"

"I'm fine. As you can probably see, all I have is a banged-up butt."

"That's from the fall yesterday? I was just wondering whether I needed to have a word with your boyfriend." Riley got to his feet and gave Jonathan an impish, sidelong glance.

"What's the latest with *your* boyfriend, Khan?" I asked him. "How's he doing in rehab?"

Riley shrugged. "Okay, I guess. I already got 'the

letter' where he confessed to all his transgressions—he admitted that he swiped that cash from my drawer—remember my telling you about that a while back?"

When I nodded, he continued, "In the letter, he also told me he set those fires. He didn't say this part, but my guess is that he was trying to score some insurance money, which he then planned to rip off to pay Yves Laplante."

"*Khan* set those fires? That's unforgivable. What are you going to do about him now?"

Riley grimaced. "Our relationship is officially O-V-E-R. I just wish I'd done it a whole lot sooner. My New Year's resolution is going to be to stop falling for bad boys."

Jonathan, who'd been quietly observing the two of us, spoke up. "Speaking of bad boys, FYI to you both, Yves Laplante is also in a world of hurt, legally. The SBI is moving against him on tax evasion charges. And I'm not going to let Durham PD forget about the break-in here the other day. I'm still convinced Laplante was behind it. We'll find something that sticks."

Riley looked at him, then smiled down at me. "Hey, this is a good guy to have on your side, Kate."

"I know," I replied. "Have there been any Darwin sightings since I ran that story about him, and you fired him? I heard from Marnie's parents that they've got a lawyer and they're going to press charges against him."

"They'll have to find him first," Riley said. "Darwin seems to have cleared out of town. He didn't even stop by to pick up his last paycheck."

Then he looked from me to Jonathan, who was staring at me again with an intense expression. "Well, as the fabulous Ms. Holm said in *All About Eve*, I guess at this point I'm what the French call de trop . . ." Riley said to me. "I'm going to head off."

"Oh, no. You don't have to go so soon, do you?"

With another glance at Jonathan, Riley said, "No, really—I've got to run to an appointment, anyway. We'll do our catching up later, sweetie. And thanks for everything." He leaned down and bussed me on the cheek, while whispering into my ear, "I think this guy's a keeper, Kate."

I smiled up at him as he straightened. "That's good advice, Riley."

When the front door closed and we were alone again, Jonathan reached toward my hand. He rested his fingertips lightly on top of mine.

"I never knew the emotional load you were carrying, Kate," he said. "There's a determination in you—a fierceness, I'd call it—that shines from you like a laser beam. I see it in your eyes. Others see it in the way you smite the targets of your stories. I didn't understand what drove you before. I think I'm beginning to."

I gazed at him. " 'Smite.' That's such a biblical-sounding word," I said. "Is smiting currently considered a crime punishable by law?"

"As long as you don't escalate your smiting to Murder One, this cop will let you plea-bargain with a kiss."

I volunteered to serve my sentence immediately.

Read on for an excerpt from the next Fat City Mystery,

MAKEOVERS CAN BE MURDER

Coming October 2009 from Obsidian

"Murder's never perfect."

—Billy Wilder

Everyone wants a body to die for.

Especially me. My name is Kate Gallagher, and I'm a perfect size sixteen, which is an *un*perfect size for someone in my line of work. I'm a reporter in TV news—a field where any female over a size four is practically an endangered species. Zaftig gals like me are vulnerable members of the newsroom herd, so I have to spend much of my time fending off News Barbies, who are constantly on the prowl for my job. In broadcasting, the law of the jungle is up or out, but for mostly cosmetic reasons (174 of them, last time I checked in with the scale), my career has stalled in my adopted hometown of Durham, North Carolina. For me, it might as well be called Fat City.

My body-slash-career problems came to a head last

summer, when I was summoned to the news director's office. My boss—Beatty the Beast—eyed me across his desk and announced that he had a brilliant idea for an investigative series.

"Quick weight-loss scams—they're a billion-dollar business." Beatty paused for dramatic effect. "What are they? Who suffers? Who's ripping off Thunder Thighs?"

He lobbed a glance at my hip zone, then added, "I want *you* on the fat-scam story, Gallagher. You know the territory."

I shifted in my too-tight wiggle skirt, which I really should have stopped wearing fifteen pounds ago. After too many fast-food dinners and no-show sessions at the gym, by now it was a waddle skirt.

"Well, I've heard of a place where they *claim* to melt off cellulite," I said. "First they slather you all over with some kind of cream, then they wrap you up in plastic and stick you in a sauna. It's just water loss, though—totally bogus."

"Fantabulous. That's a dynamite visual." Beatty raised his fingers in the air and twisted a pair of phantom knobs. "I see you doing the story in a bikini. You're being frosted with fat cream and shrink wrapped."

I blanched. "A *bikini*?" I said. "No way. I don't even own a bikini."

"You can expense it. We need reporter involvement on this one. I want a five-part series on diet scams for Sweeps Week."

When I didn't reply, his pale eyebrows shot up behind his glasses, which always represented the leading edge of an ass-kicking storm.

"Investigative stories are *your* beat, Gallagher," he said. "But if you can't handle this story, I'll put Lainey on it. She's itching to do a series. And I'm sure she'd have no problem wearing a swimsuit."

"Lainey would prance naked on a catwalk if it meant promoting herself," I said.

Beatty yanked off his glasses and tossed them on the desk between us. "In case you forgot, Gallagher, this station's ratings pay your salary, so spare me any yada-yada about how you won the Dupont Award and you only do *serious* news. We could use more people with Lainey's attitude around this newsroom."

Ouch. Lainey Lanston was my newsroom rival and personal nemesis. Formerly a print reporter at the *Durham Ledger*, she had always dismissed TV news as lame-brain puffery—until the morning she showed up for her first day of work at my employer, Channel Twelve. Ever since then she'd been breathing down my neck, trying to outscore me on getting lead stories. The fact that Beatty was calling Lainey by her first name meant she'd already oozed her way into his good graces. A bad omen for me.

I gritted my teeth and said, "Lainey's completely wrong for this story—I already have some sources. I'll do it."

When his eyebrows remained aloft, I added grudgingly, "Okay, including the damned bikini."

"Attagirl." Beatty flashed his teeth in a smile that might have been meant to be conciliatory. "And give me your usual hard-hitting stuff," he said. "Not like that piece of crap we ran yesterday about the escaped zoo tiger. We promote it as a killer, and then we show it having kittens."

"Cubs. Tigers don't have kittens."

Another air gesture dismissed me. "Whatever they are, they don't look like man eaters," he said.

I escaped from Beatty's office and cut a path through the crowded newsroom, avoiding the curious stares of my colleagues. I knew they were dying to pump me for information about my closed-door session with the news director, so I took refuge in an editing booth. Then I opened my cell phone and called Evelyn, a former desperate housewife turned delighted divorcee. Evelyn was my friend and go-to gal for the latest scoop on fighting flab. We'd met a couple years back when we were both on a wacky fruit diet at one of Durham's residential diet clinics (aka fat farms). But unlike me, Evelyn had kept off her weight. On the second ring, she picked up.

"*Oh* my God, I can barely talk." Evelyn's voice sounded agonized. "I'm dying my pubie hairs sunset blond. This stuff stings like a holy mother."

"I think you're supposed to use a special dye for that," I said. "Why are you going blond down south?"

"To make the carpet match the drapes, silly," she replied. "Tonight's the big night with Liam—everything's got to be perfect." Perfection was Evelyn's Holy Grail when it came to her body; she had her plastic surgeon on speed dial.

Over the sound of water being turned on, she continued, "Liam's helping me road test my brand-new breasts. With these D-cup babies and a hot blond Betty, he'll think he died and woke up to a centerfold. Are you at work?"

"Yes, and I have a huge problem," I replied. "I have to wear a bikini for a story. Can you imagine me shaking this jelly belly on TV? Right now I can't even *find* my abs underneath all this flab."

"Hon, no one will notice anything but those gorgeous blue eyes and cheekbones of yours," Evelyn said in an effort to console me. "But if you're worried, go see Dr. Medina. He's one of the top guys in the Southeast. Seriously; he did an awesome job on my breasts."

"Plastic surgery?" My throat released a little quack. "Yikes. Too drastic."

"But this isn't surgery. Doctor Medina has a new

thermo laser thingee that melts away the fat. It tightens your skin, too. And it only takes an hour—you can do it over lunch."

"I don't know, it sounds—"

Before I say that Doctor Medina's "thermo laser thingee" sounded like one of the weight-loss scams I was supposed to be reporting about, Evelyn steamrollered ahead. "I belong to a support group where we talk about body image," she said. "Everyone there is *raving* about Doctor M's lunchtime lifts. Come to our meeting tomorrow night."

When I hesitated, she added in a firm tone, "No thinking! Anyone who has to wear a bikini on-camera needs all the support she can get."

I couldn't argue her point. And besides, what did I have to lose by going to the meeting? And at the very least, I might be able to develop some information out of it.

"Support group" didn't come close to describing the Wednesday night meeting of the Newbodies; the weekly get-together was more like a tribal gathering, a ritual that involved much venting around the fire pit and the imbibing of copious amounts of spirit juice. It was fabulous.

"All of the women here are going through one of the four cycles of love," Evelyn whispered in my ear. "Breaking up, losing weight, having plastic surgery, or starting a new relationship."

Thank goodness, at least I didn't have to worry about the breakup part of the love cycle. I had an adorable boyfriend, Jonathan. Okay, maybe he *was* missing in action at the moment, but that was only because he was in the UK visiting his sick Mum. He'd be back in a couple days.

Evelyn adjusted the neckline of her plunging SkyTop. The four of us—Evelyn and I, and Evelyn's new boobs—were perched on a settee in Trish Putnam's living room. The women of the Newbodies were arranged in a semicircle at our feet, sprawled on scattered stacks of fringed floor pillows. Trish—a high-voltage blonde whose expression seemed permanently shocked into wide-eyed surprise—claimed that pillows were more "emo" than chairs. But they looked lumpy rather than edgy to me, so I was grateful that Evelyn had staked out the settee.

"Kate, I'm *so* glad you came tonight," Trish said to me. "Evelyn told me you're having a bikini crisis."

She thrust a platter of hairy-looking blobs under my nose and added in a whisper, "Don't worry about these oat drops—they have negative points on Weight Watchers. The more you eat, the more you lose."

"Good to know." I bit into an oat drop, which tasted like it had dropped from the end of a horse.

We went around the room to introduce ourselves and describe our body challenges. When it was my turn, I said, "I have to wear a bikini for a story. The Triangle viewing area is about to get a close-up view of my stretch marks on the six o'clock news."

My announcement caused everyone to shift back on their pasha pillows in horrified silence.

Trish recovered first. "Things could be worse!" she exclaimed. "If you were on network, you might wind up on the front page of the *National Enquirer*. Did you *see* what they did to Kirstie?"

This set off a round of nods, which quickly volleyed into spirited endorsements of Dr. Medina's cellulite remedies, including his lunchtime lifts.

"Dr. Medina's a miracle worker," Evelyn proclaimed. "If you don't believe me, just look at *these*!"

With a dramatic flourish, she ripped off her SkyTop, something she'd obviously been itching to do ever since we'd arrived. There was no bra underneath.

Freed of their netting, her breasts buoyed upward,

revealing a pair of perfectly round areolas and nipples the size and color of toasted mini-marshmallows. Evelyn's chest was living proof that the laws of gravity had been defeated by the Age of Plastic.

Evelyn's big reveal was met by squeals and enthusiastic clapping. When Trish jumped to her feet and joined her in a bump and grind, the room exploded with a cacophony of jungle calls and hooting. Trish must have been right about the pillows turning the emo on. We were chimp chicks gone wild.

My attention to the floor show was interrupted by a slap on my right shoulder.

"Where've you been, stranger?"

Jana Miller had commandeered Evelyn's spot next to me on the settee. She must have snuck in during the striptease.

I gave Jana a huge hug. "*You're* the one who abandoned ship, you rat!" I said, raising my voice to be heard over the commotion.

I hadn't seen Jana in almost two years. In her mid-forties, Jana was a fellow veteran of the fruit diet clinic, where she'd shed an incredible amount of weight—more than a hundred pounds. The instant she reached her goal, she got a quickie divorce and an even quicker remarriage. Then she and her new husband moved to Florida. Jana radiated with a Miami glow, from her metallic strappy sandals to her pageboy cut, which was shot through with streaks of gold.

"I'm in town for a consult with Dr. Medina," she said. "He took off some excess skin after I lost all that weight, but I think I might need a body lift."

I didn't know what a body lift was, and was afraid to ask. "Well, you look ten years younger," I told her. "Do we credit Dr. Medina for that, or is it married love?"

Jana's glow lost some wattage. "It's just Dr. Medina's magic, I'm afraid."

"Oh," was all I could think of to croak in response. Things must not be working out with her new husband. I wanted to kick myself for bringing up the topic.

Before I could dig myself any deeper, Jana said, "I'm actually on my way to have dinner with my daughter, Shaina," she said. "It's our first reunion in two years. She was so upset when I married Tom that she boycotted the ceremony and took off to do volunteer work in Belize. Now she's back."

Jana's daughter wasn't the only one who hadn't liked her mother's choice of a second husband. Tom was a self-proclaimed investor of "independent means," which was rumored to be no means at all. Jana, on the other hand, came from a Louisiana oil family. Most of her friends—me included—suspected that Tom married Jana for her money.

Jana leaned in. "Listen, Kate, I stopped by tonight only because Evelyn told me you'd be here," she said. "Can we have lunch tomorrow? There's something I need to talk to you about. It's kind of urgent."

"Of course." Her use of the word "urgent" made me add, "Are you sure you don't want to talk right now? We could find a quiet room."

But Jana was already reaching for her purse. "No, I've got to go meet Shaina or I'll be late," she said. "Tomorrow at noon? Brina's Bistro?"

"That'd be great." I tried to cheer her up with a grin. "I used to fantasize about their desserts all the time when we were on the fruit diet."

"Me too." Jana's lips responded with a smile, but not her eyes. "Thank you so much, Kate. See you tomorrow at twelve."

Without saying a word to anyone else, she headed for the door.

About the Author

Kathryn Lilley is a former television journalist and a lifelong dieter. She lives in Southern California. Visit her on the Web at www.kathrynlilley.com.